PRAISE FOR MAILBOAT III
THE CAPTAIN'S TALE

"The suspense is phenomenal."
~ Lt. Ed Gritzner, City of Lake Geneva Police Department

"Danielle Lincoln Hanna's Mailboat III, The Captain's Tale *has... [a] special magic completely different from the ordinary landscape of other mystery novels. I believe that's because of the author's sophisticated understanding of the nuances of human emotion, particularly the complex interplay between those who have been traumatized and the people with whom they interact in the aftermath of that trauma."*
~ David Congdon, Threat Assessment and Countermeasures Specialist

"For a new author, Danielle Lincoln Hanna has done a great job with the Mailboat series. Each book... keeps me guessing about what's going to happen next. Well done!"
~ Sam Petitto, ret. police officer

"Mailboat III *is back with all the action, suspense, and intrigue of the previous two books. It is an engaging and exciting page-turner that's difficult to put down.*"

~ Susan Beatty, reader

"*I had to chart a new course for my couch as Danielle Lincoln Hanna hooked me in to* Mailboat III: The Captain's Tale! *I love the first two books in her suspense series, and in this latest book, she continues to weave her thrilling tale tighter than a sailor's knot, keeping fans like me sailing through the book as quickly as possible.*"

~ JoAnn Schwartz Schutte, reader

"*The complexity of narrative, mystery and characters builds in the third novel of the Mailboat series. Readers learn new clues and history, and are left with more new questions at the end, leading them to await book four eagerly.*"

~ Stephanie Brancati, reader

"Mailboat III *is everything I hoped for, and more. I was excited to see that some important storylines were tied up, while other pieces of the story were developed in ways in which I did not expect... I have recommended this series to many, many people, and not one of them has been disappointed.*"

~ Nancy Diestler, reader

Danielle Lincoln Hanna

MAILBOAT

The Captain's Tale

HHP

HEARTH & HOMICIDE PRESS, LLC
MISSOULA, MT
2019

Cover photography by Matt Mason Photography
www.MattMasonPhotography.com

Cover design by MaryDes
MaryDes.eu

ISBN 978-1-7330813-4-4

BOOKS BY DANIELLE LINCOLN HANNA

The Mailboat Suspense Series

Mailboat I: The End of the Pier
Mailboat II: The Silver Helm
Mailboat III: The Captain's Tale
Mailboat IV - *coming summer 2020*

DanielleLincolnHanna.com/shopnow

JOIN THE CREW

———— ⚓ ————

Ahoy, Shipmate!

If you feel like you're perched on a lighthouse, scanning the horizon for Danielle Lincoln Hanna's next book—good news! You can subscribe to her email newsletter and read a regular ship's log of her writing progress. Better yet, dive deep into the life of the author, hear the scuttlebutt from her personal adventures, spy on her writing process, and catch a rare glimpse of dangerous sea monsters—better known as her pets, Fergus the cat and Angel the German Shepherd.

It's like a message in a bottle washed ashore. All you have to do is open it...

DanielleLincolnHanna.com/newsletter

MAILBOAT

THURSDAY
JUNE 26, 2014

CHAPTER ONE
RYAN

———— ⚓ ————

I stopped at Starbucks that morning.

"Blonde roast grande," I said to the girl behind the counter. One of the most caffeinated beverages on the menu. "I'm not used to working mornings."

It's funny the things you remember about those days you can't forget. That day turned out to be one of them. I remember I ordered a blonde roast coffee—and never drank it.

I carried my energy bomb to my patrol car, still wondering if the odd hours were worth not sitting on a bike seat all day. *It's a horse apiece,* I concluded—then laughed at the expression, as thoroughly Wisconsin as a cheesehead hat and as hard to understand by anyone not born in the Badger State. I got into my car, radioed that I was back in service, and rolled out of the parking lot.

I had just put my lips to the slot in the plastic lid when my radio made a screech, something akin to a seagull learning to yodel. It was the emergency tone, signaling all units to pay attention and stay off the air; we were about to receive emergency radio traffic. I sighed and raised my eyebrows. Already? We were hitting the ground running today. I tried to blink the sand out of my eyes.

The dispatcher's voice filled my cab. "Caller reports injured male. Eight twelve Wrigley Drive. Caller advises they are at the Riviera docks, on the Mailboat."

The Mailboat? Bailey sprang to mind—the foster girl whose abusive home I was trying to prove. A spike of adrenaline rushed through my system. I nearly crushed the coffee in my hand. It would have been no loss if I had. I was fully awake now.

I was mere blocks away. I set the coffee in a holder then brought the radio mic to my mouth. "Forty-four thirty-seven, I'm on it." I hit the lights and siren. I knew Steph could see my location from one of her monitors in the dispatch room at the station. My own mobile data computer—laptop, in English—showed I was closer than both the ambulance and the other units on patrol. "Any information on the nature of the injuries?"

Static. "Sorry," Steph said. "She isn't very coherent. All I can get is that a male subject is bleeding."

I didn't like the sound of that. I doubted the schedule or the routine at the cruise line had changed since the days when I was a teenage mail jumper. The only people at the Riviera docks this time of morning would be the Mailboat captain and his crew. Captain Tommy's son Jason, a long-lost fugitive, had been gunned down in the street only a few nights ago. This wasn't what life was supposed to be like in the quiet, lakeside resort of Lake Geneva.

I simply ground my teeth and depressed the button on my mic again. "Ten-four."

With little traffic in the tourist section this early in the morning, I had the streets to myself. I rounded the bend in Wrigley Drive, the lake sparkling to my right in the sunrise, and made for the Riviera, a Depression-Era brick building that was the heart and hub of the town.

There was a restricted parking area right beside the Riv, big enough for four or five cars. I pulled into a stall, reported my arrival on scene to dispatch, and jumped out of the patrol car. I could see the Mailboat from there. It sat placidly in the water, moored to the pier, along with the rest of the tour boats in the fleet—the sleek steam yachts and the majestic stern-wheeled paddle boats and the rest. I could hear a female crying.

I popped my trunk lid and retrieved my go bag. Inside was emergency medical equipment as well as extra rifle magazines and other gear. I was about to slam the lid shut when my eye fell on my tactical vest. Made of thicker stuff than my everyday vest, it was good against higher impact rifle rounds. Something told me to put it on. One of Jason's murderers had been killed in the shootout. But the murderer's accomplice was still at large.

I threw the vest on, then slung the strap of the go bag over my shoulder and grabbed my rifle from its mount beside the front seat. After checking the magazine, I made for the pier, moving under the archways that supported the square corner towers of the Riviera. Just as I emerged onto the quay, something grabbed my eye.

A bullet hole in the windshield of the Mailboat.

I leaned against the brick pillar and keyed the mic clipped to my shoulder. "Forty-four thirty-seven, requesting backup. Possible shooting incident at the Riviera."

Static was followed by the sign, "Ten-four," and a request for all units to respond.

I studied the pier and the boats quickly and systematically, left to right, top to bottom. Everything looked and sounded peaceful, except for the voice of the female crying. It was clearly coming from the Mailboat, the first on my right. Rifle to my shoulder, I moved in, praying the voice wasn't Bailey's.

Twenty-five years ago, my athletic experience as a wide receiver on the high school football team had earned me a hotly-contested job as a mail jumper. I guess they figured if I could chase a pigskin, I could leap off and on the tour boat to deliver the mail to the piers. During those long-lost summers, I had walked this pier every morning. I could almost see the ghost of my younger self wiping down windows. Stocking the snack bar. Sorting envelopes. Pulling pranks on my co-workers. I wondered how the younger me had never seen the ghost of my older self creeping down this same pier in full tactical gear.

The crying grew more distinct. I moved to the large, open window towards the bow of the Mailboat and peered inside.

It was Bailey. She knelt over the captain, crying hysterically, her hands stained with blood.

My stomach lurched. God, no.

For all those summer mornings I'd spent with Captain Tommy, the teenage Ryan had never foreseen this either. If I had carried over so much as a vial-full of childhood innocence into my adulthood, it shattered completely in that moment.

It had been decades since the last time I'd swung a leg through the mail jumper's window. No longer a lithe teenager, and encased to the gills as I was in gear, my entry wasn't as effortless as I remembered. I contorted my way through the window, then dropped down next to Bailey. I scanned the captain's body. He was lying on his side. A red stain over his abdomen leapt out at me, the fabric of his shirt soaked through and plastered down around a small, round hole. I put it at a .22, no bigger than a 9 mil. Besides that, I could see no other injuries.

"Bailey, where's the shooter?" I asked as I let the go bag slide from my shoulder.

Bailey didn't answer. She was crying so hard, I wasn't sure how she was breathing.

I slung the rifle over my shoulder then unzipped the medical kit and pulled out a pair of nitrile gloves. As soon as I'd snapped them on, I shook Tommy by the shoulder.

"Tommy, can you hear me?" I asked loudly. He was unresponsive.

I leaned down and put my ear close to Tommy's nose and mouth. His breaths were shallow and far between. But he was breathing. I could work with that. The killer hadn't succeeded this time. Not yet. I didn't mean to let him, either.

I clicked the transmit key on my mic. "Forty-four thirty-seven. We need Flight for Life. Elderly male has GSW to the abdomen. He's unresponsive. Whereabouts of the shooter unknown. The scene is not secured."

The radio clicked. "Ten-four."

I paused then activated the radio again. "Steph..." How could I say this without using Tommy's name over the air? Anyone could be listening over a police scanner or even a phone app. But Steph was smart. Hopefully she could read between the lines. "Tell the chief immediately."

There was a delay on the other end, then Steph replied, "Copy that."

I hoped the pause meant she'd grasped the full meaning. The Mailboat captain was Chief Wade Erickson's best friend. Wade needed to know.

I swept my hand over the captain's back but found no blood, no exit wound. So I grabbed him by the shoulder and hip and gently rolled him onto his spine, then tilted his head back to ease his breathing. I glanced at Bailey. "Are you okay?"

She tried to wipe tears out of her eyes with the backs of her hands so as not to smear blood across her face. She failed. "He—he—he's bleeding," she gasped between sobs.

Yeah, I could see that. The bloodstain was small, but they usually were with abdominal wounds. The worst damage would be invisible to the naked eye. I grabbed a pair of scissors from the go bag and cut open his shirt. There it was. An ugly little wound in his left flank. My own blood boiled. Who would dare? Who would *dare?*

I heard sirens wailing towards us as I ripped open a package of QuikClot gauze. Backup was finally here.

I glanced at the mail girl. "Bailey—?"

She sat on her heels, tears streaking down both cheeks. She had pressed the back of her hand to her mouth and was biting the skin. Hard. Her breath was interrupted by sobs.

For the first time since I'd met her, she was not *good, okay, fine.* She hadn't acted this way after witnessing the shooting between Jason Thomlin and Charles Hart. In the face of incredible violence to two men she hadn't known, she'd been stoic. Emotionless.

But it wasn't the same with Tommy.

In a blink, I finally understood her whole world. Or a huge chunk of it. Here was one person she hadn't shut out of her bruised heart—the only person, so far as I knew. I remembered how Tommy had been like another father to me when I was her age. He was just the kind of guy you could talk to about anything, from being left out of the party at the popular kid's house to your anxieties over being accepted into the college you'd set your heart on. It was no miracle he had found the hidden inlet to Bailey's soul.

But now his life—Bailey's life—depended on seconds. *You're not leaving us, Tommy,* I thought. *Not today.*

Starting with one end of the gauze, I carefully packed it deep into the wound. The hemostatic agent with which it was infused would accelerate his blood clotting. He didn't so much as flinch or show any sign of waking. QuikClot was an insanely invasive technique but got the job done fast. There was a reason the military swore by this stuff.

"Bailey, did you see who did this?" I asked.

She didn't reply. Didn't move. Stared at the captain as if watching the curtains close on the world itself. She was still biting the back of her hand.

"Bailey? Where is the shooter? Did you see him?"

Slowly she shook her head.

"You just found Tommy lying here?"

She finally lowered her hand into her lap and nodded.

The sound of the sirens intensified until they were just on the other side of the Riv, where they wound down to silence. Voices shouted. Car doors and trunk lids slammed. My radio sputtered.

"Forty-four thirty-seven, where are you?"

Mike Schultz. I took one hand off the wound long enough to press the button on my mic. "We're on the Mailboat. No sign of the shooter. PR indicates he likely left the scene already. Administering first aid now."

"Ten-four. We're headed your way."

I cringed as I thought about what came next. Bailey needed to be cleared. Just for protocol, just for our own safety. But she hated being touched. Every time I tried, she flinched as if it burned.

"Bailey, do you remember last time?" I asked as I continued to pack the wound. In hindsight, it was the stupidest question ever. For one, of course she remembered. Jason and Charles' deaths had only been a few days ago. For another, why would I remind her? The words were out now, though, so I rolled with it. "It's going to be like that. They need to know you're not a threat. Just do what we ask, okay?" I said. "Everything's going to be fine. We want to keep you safe."

She sat in silence, hands in her lap, eyes on the captain.

"Can you lie face-down on the floor, honey?" I said. "Arms above your head?" She may as well be comfortable while we cleared her.

For a moment, she didn't move. But finally she slid down to her stomach and rested her arms on the floor over

8

her head. But she kept her face turned so that she never took her eyes off Tommy.

"That's perfect, Bailey. Just relax. We're going to take care of you."

Footsteps pounded down the quay. I twisted my neck to look out the window. Mike Schultz and three others approached, encased as I was in tac vests.

"Which one's the Mailboat?" Ted Franklin asked.

Schultz frowned. "Seriously? Where did you grow up, man?"

Franklin, a thirty-five-year veteran of the LGPD, popped his eyebrows, making his narrow face appear even longer. "Here," he replied. He shrugged. "I've never taken one of these tours. You know how it is when you live in a place..."

"Whoa, man, you need to show a little more love to your hometown."

I rolled my eyes. This was not the time to pick up tickets for a Mailboat tour. "Over here!" I shouted. "Get this place cleared so we can bring in the medics."

Schultz made eye contact with me and nodded, then issued directions for conducting the search. Franklin was his senior in years but not in ambition; everyone knew Schultz was next in line for a sergeant's rank. He and Franklin entered the Mailboat while the other two stepped onto the open deck of the steam yacht moored on the opposite side of the pier.

Schultz nodded at Bailey. "Is she the PR?" he asked.

"Yeah," I replied. Person reporting.

"Has she been cleared?"

"No."

Schultz leaned over Bailey. "Miss, I'm Officer Schultz. We just need to search you for everyone's safety."

She made no reply.

Schultz leaned closer. "Miss?"

I sighed. "She's okay. She doesn't talk much." That may have been an understatement.

Schultz quirked his head then ran his hands over Bailey's body—her shoulders, her waist, her ankles where they were covered by her shoes and socks. Her jaw tightened and her nostrils flared. That was all. She never moved her eyes from Tommy.

"Clear," Schultz reported. He patted Bailey on the shoulder. "All done. You can sit up if you want."

She didn't move.

Schultz tipped his head, trying to catch her eye. "Are you hurt, miss?"

Bailey didn't answer.

I groaned inside. I wished she would talk—just talk someday. "I don't think she's hurt," I said. "Go ahead and clear the rest of the boat. I'll keep an eye on her."

Schultz gave a little shrug then stood up and nodded Franklin to lead the way toward the stairs in the aft.

I listened to the team's progress over the radio while I applied direct pressure to Tommy's wound and counted three minutes to let the QuikClot do its thing. Boat by boat, the team announced "clear." Finally, Schultz gave the green light to the medics to enter the scene.

Paul Garner and David Myers rushed down the pier with a cot and a medical bag.

"The bird's on its way," Paul said, referring to the helicopter. He lowered slowly to his knees beside me. Decades as an EMT hadn't been kind to his joints. "What have we got, Brandt?"

I reported on the patient's stats and the procedures I'd performed so far.

"Nice job," he said as he checked the wound packing. He leaned his ear close to Tommy's nose and mouth to check his breathing, laid his fingers over the carotid artery for a pulse. "Responsiveness?"

"Unconscious since I got here," I replied.

"Breaths are only eight per minute. We gotta get a tube in him." Paul unzipped his medical bag.

David Myers nodded to Bailey as Paul handed him a mask with a bag attached. "The girl okay?" David asked.

"Yes," I said. She still hadn't moved. I glanced up at Schultz as he entered the boat again. "Schultz, can you take over with this? I want to get Bailey out of here." The medics would appreciate the space to work in the already-confined boat. Besides, I didn't know how Bailey would react to watching the procedure. She'd seen enough terrors already. In fact, she'd seen more terrors in sixteen years than anyone should see in a lifetime.

Schultz took over my job of applying pressure to the wound. I got up from my knees, peeled off my gloves, and turned to Bailey. Gently, I slipped a hand through her arm. "Bailey?" I said softly. "C'mon. Let's go."

Bailey's eyes, glassy, were transfixed on Tommy as David fitted the mask over his face and began sqeezing air. Paul unfurled a roll containing an array of tubes, a laryngoscope, a litany of beak-shaped blades, all in different sizes...

I lifted Bailey by her arms and tried to set her on her feet. "C'mon, let's get you out of here."

Her body went rigid. *"Nooo!"*

Her scream raised the hair on the back of my neck. She tried to wrench away. I held her more tightly, hoping to break through her panic, wanting to hug her close, wanting to latch onto her brain and suck away all the bad memories, all the pain. She only fought harder. Kicked. Flailed. Her shrieks nearly shattered glass.

"Bailey, honey, it's okay," I tried to tell her. "Everything's going to be okay."

Her shoe crashed into my shin. I bit back a swear as the pain stabbed into my bone. But I held her tighter. I held onto her as I had eleven years ago, when I'd taken her away from her mother. When I'd handed her over to foster care. When I'd thought I was doing the right thing for her.

She'd been silent then. Blank. Uncaring.

11

Not anymore.

Tommy mattered too much to her.

My throat tightening with emotion, I wrapped her in a bear hug, pinning her arms to her chest, and carried her off the boat kicking and screaming.

You can't leave us, Tommy, I brainwaved to the captain. *I can't help her on my own. Bailey needs you.*

CHAPTER TWO
BUD

Bud snuck into his bar through the back and slammed the door behind him. As soon as he was inside the kitchen, he yanked off his leather vest. He needed to get it in its hidey-hole. He wasn't such an idiot as to run around wearing his signature outfit in broad daylight—his kill clothes, he liked to call them. Like them heroes who duck into phone booths to put on a cape and tights. Only he weren't no hero. And he knew better than to dress in tights.

Rita, the head waitress, leaned against a steel countertop opposite the grills and the deep fryer. As usual, she'd tried to plaster over her wrinkles with a thick layer of makeup. Her black mini skirt was barely longer than the apron strung around her curvy hips. Bud didn't have no dress code around here, and this was why.

She glanced up from her magazine, the kind full of celebrity gossip about who had cheated on who. Snapping a wad of pink bubble gum, she eyed Bud up and down. "Your butt's hanging out."

"Huh?" He hitched up his pants, but they felt fine.

She nodded. "Your butt. What's that, a Colt?"

Bud glanced down at his waistband. The butt of the gun was hanging out. "Ruger," he corrected, wondering how she could confuse the two.

"Oh." She snapped another bubble and turned back to her magazine. "The ex had something like that."

Bud dug in his jeans pocket and crossed the kitchen. He shoved a crumpled mess of twenties into Rita's hand. "If anyone asks, I was with you all night."

She eyed the cash, then shrugged. "Okay." She folded it and tucked it down her blouse, into her bra. As Bud headed for his office, she called after him, "Better get them ribs started. You promised everybody barbecue today."

"In a minute. Let me put this stuff away."

She buried her nose in her magazine again. "Why d'you even bother with this place?" she went on. "You clearly make more money at your night job."

Ignoring her, Bud went into his office. He kicked the door shut behind him and knelt down next to the safe, sitting on the floor under a mess of unopened letters. He spun the dial until the safe clicked open. Then he rolled the vest up into a ball and threw it inside next to the cash drawer and piles of twenties and fifties. Next he pulled out a gun cleaning kit, sat down at his desk chair, and proceeded to erase any evidence that the weapon had been recently fired.

Bud felt eyes watching him. Thanks to the many sordid details of his life, he'd developed one of them sixth senses people talked about. He looked up.

His door hadn't latched. A pair of eyes, bulging behind thick glasses, peered through the narrow opening. A thin body was draped in a white tee shirt as big as a tablecloth. It was Jimmy Beacon, the dishwasher.

"The hell you want?" Bud growled.

The kid jumped. He pushed the door open a little further and held up two fists full of beer steins. They were Bud's personal collection, stuff he'd picked up at various breweries around Chicago, a few online buys, a couple of imports from Germany. He kept them all in his office where no one else could put their dirty lips on them.

"I finished washing these, sir," the boy said.

Bud had forgotten he'd asked the kid to clean them. But he liked the way Jimmy called him "sir." The boy was intimidated by him. Bud liked the feel of that. The same way he'd intimidated the old man, just before he shot him in the gut.

"Oh, shit," Bud said, appeased. "Put 'em on the desk." He motioned casually with his gun.

The boy's eyes dropped to the firearm and the blood drained out of his face. He sidled into the room, set the steins on the drift of paperwork on the desk, and scuttled out again.

Bud watched him go and shook his head. He was a funny one, that kid. More fish than human and a pretty sorry hand at dish washing, to boot. Bud glanced over his steins but couldn't pick out any obvious smudges this time. Still, he didn't mind keeping the kid around.

Bud settled back and contemplated intriguing possibilities about Jimmy Beacon. Like Bailey, Bud's foster kid, Jimmy was the pliable kind Bud could shape to his liking. Invite into his office. Pay him compliments. Form dependencies. Talk him into things the kid would be ashamed to tell a living soul about.

But Bud had never tried. Not with Jimmy. Idiot that the little dishwasher was, Bud also sensed the kid had a built-in creep sensor. God only knew where he'd picked up that shred of common sense.

Eh, Jimmy wasn't worth the trouble. He was too scrawny and greasy anyway—not good looking by anybody's imagination. He'd probably never had a girlfriend. Never been on a date. Maybe the kid would be grateful for Bud's attentions someday. He snorted with laughter.

15

As he polished the Ruger, he set thoughts of Jimmy aside and contemplated his morning's work on the Mailboat. Whether the captain lived or died, Bud felt pretty confident he'd taught the old man a lesson. Bailey belonged to *him*—Bud. He dared Tommy Thomlin to interfere again—siccing the police on him. Trying to pry Bailey away from him.

Bud grinned to himself. The whole thing had gone damn well, he thought. Damn well, indeed.

So long as The Man didn't find out.

CHAPTER THREE
RYAN

———— ❄ ————

Standing by the open doors of an ambulance, I fumbled through nitrile gloves to secure a small yellow envelope. Inside was a muslin swab with a blood sample that I'd just collected from Bailey's clothes. The camera slung over my arm was now full of photos of the bloodstains on her person. If we were lucky, Tommy wouldn't have been the only one who lost blood today. Perhaps the perpetrator had left us something with which to identify him. I liked to think that Tommy had fought back.

Amy Miller, an EMT, sat inside the ambulance on the bench opposite Bailey and tapped the ends of a stethoscope together. She nodded her chin at me. "You done yet?"

I nodded. "All yours."

She slapped a pressure cuff over Bailey's arm.

As she did, the distant whirl of chopper blades drew my attention. I looked skyward. Flight for Life was here, heading east toward Veteran's Park. Below on *terra firma*, Paul, David, Mike, and Ted jogged a cot through the arches of the Riviera toward another ambulance. The ground crew would meet the helicopter at the park, a wide-open space free of trees and power lines where they could safely land.

Then Flight for Life would airlift Tommy straight to the trauma center in Milwaukee.

I watched the EMTs from across the street. Paul squeezed a BVM every five seconds, an air bladder that forced air into Tommy's lungs. Meanwhile, Ted Franklin peeled off his tac vest and dug in his shirt pocket, producing a pen and notepad. If Tommy came to and was able to communicate anything, Franklin would be there to record it. If the worst happened, maybe we'd at least be lucky enough for a statement.

They loaded Tommy's cot into the ambulance. Latched the doors. The siren wound up toward its full pitch and the ambulance pulled away, hurrying toward its rendezvous with the helicopter. As it disappeared down Wrigley Drive, I wished Tommy whatever luck was mine to give.

Mike Schultz crossed the street toward me and the incident command area. A flurry of patrol cars, Bailey's ambulance, and the Mobile Command Unit had organized further up Wrigley Drive, far enough away from the crime scene to ensure the heavy traffic we created wouldn't compromise evidence. Mike released the straps on his helmet and cocked it on the back of his head, the chin straps dangling loose on either side of his jaw.

"Got everything?" he asked, motioning to the little pile of paper envelopes I'd created on the floor of the ambulance.

"Yeah," I said and finished notating the last one: Who I'd collected the sample from, where on her body I'd found it, et cetera, et cetera.

He hooked his thumbs in the arm holes of his tac vest. If he was trying to look like a World War I doughboy, he was doing a great job. His open face and light blue eyes had the youthful look of an optimistic new recruit—never mind his ten years' experience. "What did the girl have to say?" he asked in a voice low enough that Bailey wouldn't hear.

I glanced at her. Wrapped in a blanket that Amy had thrown around her shoulders, she stared out the back of the ambulance. At first I thought her gaze was fixed on me, until I realized it went further. She was watching the ambulance as it sped away. She was watching Tommy.

"Nothing," I said. "She hasn't talked yet."

"Need a hand?" he offered.

"No, I've got it," I replied—though I wasn't convinced myself. Bailey didn't like to talk any more than she liked to be touched. I held up the camera and the envelopes. "Mind putting these in evidence?"

"Sure thing, man." He took the materials and moved toward the Mobile Command Unit. As he walked, he clicked a pen and began scribbling his name on the evidence log attached to each packet. Even this small passing between hands had to be recorded.

Loosening the straps on my tac vest, I enjoyed a deep, less-restricted breath and leaned against the door of the ambulance. Bailey's knee caps peeked out from between the folds of the blanket, still smeared with blood except where I'd wiped little bits away. She stared out the open doors and down the street, ignoring the technician pointing an infrared ray into her ear from a tympanic thermometer. By now the ambulance was long gone, and yet Bailey wouldn't turn away.

"You okay, Bailey?" I asked.

Nothing. Her face was vacant. Featureless. As if her soul had been sucked out. An unsettling feeling nagged at me, insisting I'd seen a look like this before. I was even more disturbed when I remembered where. Cadavers.

The thermometer beeped. Amy studied the digital screen and jotted a note. "Stats are fine but..." She quirked her head, widening her eyes as if to signify something that was too obvious to be said. And it was. Bailey wasn't good. "We'll take her to Lakeland in a minute. My partner's just checking there are no other reported injuries."

19

I nodded. Lakeland Medical Center in Elkhorn was only a fifteen-minute drive. I decided I'd be bringing Bailey home afterwards. I certainly wouldn't depend on her foster dad Bud Weber to do it. It sickened me I'd have to call and let him know what had happened. Like he cared.

I lifted a foot onto the bumper of the ambulance and leaned on my knee, shifting the tac vest in search of a comfortable way to distribute the weight. I studied Bailey's face, hoping some gentle, direct eye contact might bring her back to the surface.

"They're taking him to Froedtert," I said. Froedtert Hospital in Milwaukee was a Level I trauma center. They had the equipment and the staff for literally everything. If the President of the United States himself suffered a medical emergency anywhere in the state of Wisconsin, that was the hospital they'd take him to. I felt those odds offered a strong dose of comfort. But much as I wanted to assure Bailey that Tommy would be all right, I couldn't make promises. All I could do was believe with every fiber of my being that he would fight to live.

I wished Bailey would fight to live, too. Everything about her said she didn't care anymore.

I sighed. "You're going to be okay. We're here for you. All right? We've always been here for you."

Her body couldn't have been more immobile if it had been carved in granite. I had a feeling my attempt at interviewing her was going to be an abysmal failure. It probably didn't matter. As far as I could tell, she hadn't seen anything.

At the sound of approaching footsteps, I looked behind me, then smiled with relief at the sight of Bill Gallagher, the police chaplain.

He clapped the shoulder of my armor and rested a hand on his belt, his motions casual, but his face and tone somber. "Heard there was a hubbub and thought I'd drop by. Schultz said you might want me over here."

"Bailey, this is Bill Gallagher," I said. "He's our chaplain I told you about."

No response. I wasn't sure she'd blinked the whole time I'd been standing here.

Bill exchanged a glance with me, then flashed a grin, as if to say nothing about the current situation intimidated him. He turned to the EMT. "Mornin', Amy. Mind if I join you in there?"

She patted the bench. "Hop on in. You coming with us?" She stowed supplies back in a carefully organized go bag.

Bill hauled himself up into the ambulance. "Well," he grunted, "if present company doesn't object." He settled down on the bench opposite Bailey. Resting his elbows on his knees, he studied her face a moment. "How you feelin', Bailey?"

She didn't acknowledge him. Instead, her eyes shifted upward. I glanced over my shoulder and saw a black silhouette rise in the distance, while the sound of chopper blades drifted to our ears. Flight for Life was taking off and Tommy with it.

Bill watched the helicopter for a second, then spoke to Bailey again. "I understand you put in the call for 911." Impossibly, his mountainous voice had settled into a smooth, low register, rumbling like a sleeping bear. "I don't know if anyone mentioned this, but you did good. Brought all these people here." He glanced around at the swarm of flashing emergency vehicles and chuckled. "I know it looks like a three-ring circus and sideshow but..." He searched Bailey's eyes. "We're here to help. We're here to help Tommy. And you. We're gonna take care of you both."

At her continued silence, anxiety built in my chest. I dropped my gaze and rocked as I leaned on my knee. I couldn't stand to see her like this. I wanted her to talk or cry or even try to beat the hell out of me again. My shins were still throbbing, but I would have gladly volunteered as her punching bag.

Bill kept talking, as if convinced she actually heard everything he said. "I s'pose you're feeling pretty stunned right now. Well, that's nothing strange. The body and the brain, they've got these self-defense mechanisms. Somethin' bad happens, sometimes you just pull inside yourself—kinda like runnin' away, but without goin' anywhere. So, you just run away for a little while, if you need to. You're safe right here." He jerked his head toward me. "These big lugs won't let anything happen."

If I'd been running video, the camera never would have picked up the subtle shift in her expression. The way her face softened by the tiniest degree. The way her eyes felt a little less distant. In that moment, she took a step from something dead and cold to something living. I counted it as nothing less than a miracle and decided on the spot to nominate Bill for the department's Citizen Gallantry Award. Technically, it was for saving a life. But Bailey had been dead from the day I'd met her, and this was the first I had detected a vital sign.

Bill had seen it, too. He nodded gently. "That's right, Bailey, you're safe here. It's over now."

She still didn't speak. Didn't move. But she was listening.

The chaplain planted a hand on his thigh and twisted in his seat to follow her gaze into the blue. "What do you see, Bailey?" he asked softly.

Current progress aside, I didn't believe Bill would ever get the response he'd asked for. She had an almost unbroken track record of never answering questions.

I was stunned when her lips actually parted. Her voice was a mere breath.

"Black," she said.

Black? I glanced at the sky to see if the helicopter was still in view. But it was gone. Nothing but a brilliant, cloudless blue. Golden sun poured through a canopy of leaves and sparkled off the surface of the lake. But it dawned on me that Bill could have posed the same question at any time, in any place, no matter what Bailey was doing, and would have gotten the same answer.

Bill nodded. "What else do you see out there?"

She whispered. "Nothing."

Nothing but black. I wasn't so sure anymore I wanted to know what was inside Bailey's mind. Every time I caught a glimpse, it broke my heart. Before long, the remaining pieces would be too small to break down any further, unless they were ground with a hammer.

"What do you feel?" Bill asked.

She whispered again, even quieter. "Nothing."

Bill nodded. "Hurts to feel nothing, doesn't it?"

A muscle in her jaw flexed, and for the briefest moment, I thought she was going to cry. She didn't.

Just let it out, Bailey, I brainwaved to her. *Please, still be alive in there.*

Amy whispered to Bill. "We're ready to go." The ambulance bobbed as her partner climbed into the cab and slid behind the wheel.

Bill nodded without taking his eyes off Bailey. "Do you want me to come along?" he asked her.

These were always the stickiest questions for her—the kind that required her to have an opinion. I expected we would all be long dead before she opened her lips again.

Bill wasn't intimidated. "Twitch your pointy finger if you want me to come."

My eyes dropped immediately to Bailey's hand, clinging to the edge of her blanket. Seconds dragged by, and she didn't move—until finally her index finger curled a little tighter.

I am not ashamed to say I nearly cried.

Bill smiled. "Sounds good to me, Bailey." He glanced at me. "Ryan?"

I had to take a bracing breath. "Keep in touch with me," I said. "I'll be over as soon as I can." I was qualified for evidence collection and would be needed here at the Riv.

He nodded.

I helped Amy secure the doors then stepped onto the curb to make room for their exit. The ambulance pulled out into the street and turned north, toward Highway 12 and the hospital in Elkhorn.

Feeling a little shaky, I rubbed a hand down my face then turned to scan the scene. The street. The park. The Riviera. The Mailboat. Our silent witnesses. It was time to make them talk. To make them tell us what the hell had happened here. And it was time to turn this town upside-down and find a man with a gun.

My eyes lingered on the fountain in front of the Riviera. Streams of water arched around the basin toward a central pedestal. On top of it stood a stone angel, wings spread, eyes staring down tenderly at all who passed by, one palm extended as if in blessing. The Angel of the Waters, she was called. Her older sister lived in Central Park, New York. For a decade, this beloved replica had kept watch over the courtyard, the Riviera, the heart of the town. I couldn't help wondering where she had been this morning, when this had all gone down. How could she have dropped her guard when it was Tommy who needed her? He'd walked beneath her shadow every day since she'd taken up office. It wasn't like she never noticed him.

Stiffening my jaw, I strode toward the Mobile Command Unit, the black truck that served as on-the-go meeting room, evidence collection room, and whatever-we-needed room. I fixed my mind on the idea that Tommy was going to pull through. I forcibly rejected all thoughts to the contrary.

I'd finally found the portal into Bailey's heart—a tiny one, big enough for just one person. And if Tommy died, that portal would close, I feared, forever. The last flicker of light in her life would snuff out. And I would never find her in the darkness.

CHAPTER FOUR
MONICA

Breathe in. Breathe out. One foot after another. Don't rush it. Find the cadence.

As usual, I was starting my day with a morning jog along the lake, the shadows of maples and oaks still long across vibrant green yards. Far less usual, I was working out the details of three violent deaths in a single week and what they all had to do with a high-end burglary ring that had gone bust in the nineties. The last two members of the ring were dead now—apparently at the hands of an old man with a warped idea of how to win love. And what had that broken devotion gotten Charles Hart in the end? A bullet to his brain.

A simple though tragic case, the chief and my partner Detective Lehman both insisted. Once we found the killer's missing accomplice, we'd have the answers to any lingering questions.

But the missing accomplice *was* my lingering question. How had Hart convinced anyone to become involved in his personal vendetta? I couldn't shake the sense that we hadn't uncovered half the facts yet. That it was all smoke and mirrors up until this point. In short, that Charles Hart wasn't the man behind the curtain.

But who was? And what was he after?

The rock music streaming through my earbuds was cut off by an appropriately ridiculous rendition of "Hail to the Chief." Without breaking my stride, I tapped a button on my wireless earbuds.

"Finally miss me, Chief? Christ, I'll be there in an hour." I was still seething that he'd made me take time off in the middle of the investigation.

A hum in the background suggested he was driving. "Monica, they need you at the Riv." The tone of his voice left no room for merriment.

I slowed to a stop. "What's going on?"

"There's been another shooting."

Anger surged through my veins like black poison. I bit back the urge to yell at him that I'd been right and he'd been wrong. Instead, I forced air through flared nostrils. "Do we have an ID on the victim?"

"It's Tommy."

Fury was replaced with shock. My muscles went slack, my knees watery. "What?"

"Flight for Life is taking him to Froedtert. I'm headed there now."

I ran my hand over my hair, pushing the loose strands back into my ponytail. "Oh my God." Of course. Tommy had been warned. A message written on his window in blood. *Cleaning House.* I dug my fingertips into my skull. Who was cleaning house? Who? The ring was dead now. All three of them—Bobby, Fritz, Jason...

Unless there was a fourth member we'd never known about?

"How fast can you get to the Riv?" Wade asked.

I turned back toward my house and pushed my pace. "Thirty minutes." I had to change out of my running gear. Drive all the way to Lake Geneva. For the first time in my life, I was sorry for the twenty-minute drive from Fontana to the other side of the lake. "What's the status on the perp?"

"At large. Neumiller and Lehman are on their way to the scene, too. Just get there as soon as you can."

"Right." I choked back a lump in my throat. "What's Tommy's condition?"

"Serious. That's all I know."

At least he was alive. I closed my eyes briefly, even as my feet pounded over the trail I knew well. "Keep me posted."

"I will."

I hung up and kicked my pace to the highest gear. I wanted to scream. I wanted to tear someone's lawn up. I wanted to beat the crap out of the trees. For the love of God, why Tommy?

Why hadn't I tried harder to convince Wade that this case wasn't over yet? But I hadn't. And now Tommy had paid the price for our blindness. I couldn't stomach this happening on my watch.

I'd worked with Tommy as a mail jumper when I was in high school and college. He'd been a mentor to me. To all of us kids. Part of me envied Wade's drive to Milwaukee. But there was nothing I could do for Tommy there.

My job was here at the lake, tracking down the sick son of a bitch who had dared raise a hand against the Mailboat captain. My job was a game of wits, and I was *not* going to lose this round.

That unknown accomplice was going to rue the day he had crossed me.

CHAPTER FIVE
WADE

Wade heard a click through his Bluetooth earpiece as Monica hung up. She had been right. He'd let down his guard. And now this had happened. But decades as a cop, and now his position as chief of police, had trained him to focus on the road ahead, not the rearview mirror. He glued his eyes to the highway, mentally cataloging everything that needed to get done. Top of that list was getting to Froedtert. Making sure Tommy was okay.

His wife Nancy reached over from the passenger seat and slid a hand through his arm. It was only then that he realized how tight his grip was on the steering wheel. He forced himself to relax. Nancy didn't talk. They'd been married long enough that they both knew when to speak and when to let the other think. And Wade had plenty of thinking to do.

Wade and Tommy had known each other since they were school boys. From the day they'd met, Tommy had been like a big brother watching over him. Wade secretly felt the roles had reversed over the years, but he would never dare say so to Tommy. Whoever was the eagle now and who the vulnerable fledgling, there was no denying that everything Wade was today, he owed to his oldest friend.

Wade breathed deeply and consciously pumped his grip on the steering wheel to relieve tension. Tommy would be fine. He was a tough old curmudgeon and tough old curmudgeons didn't give up easily.

Nancy broke the silence with an audible parting of her lips, a tiny intake of air. "Roland," she said.

It took Wade a moment to follow her line of thought. "You're right." He reached to his phone in its holder and woke it up again with a touch of a button. Nancy may have been a museum tour guide, but she was also a cop's wife and could process the available facts just as well as he could—often faster. It had only taken Wade a beat longer to realize what she was implying. Roland had been warned, too. The same cryptic but deadly message: *Cleaning House.*

"Monica can call him," Nancy suggested.

Wade shook his head. "She's got enough to do." He activated the voice assist and spoke the number into his device. Hopefully, Roland hadn't changed his land line. Wade had fallen out of his good graces long before cell phones had come into use.

The line rang.

Wade whispered to Nancy, "Why is it I forget to take out the trash every Monday, but I can remember Roland's number?"

She smiled. "Because you're old."

The line clicked to life. "Markham residence, this is Roland."

Wade's mouth went dry, all the words tumbling out of his brain like brittle bones. At the sound of Roland's voice—and the same telephone greeting Roland had learned by rote as a boy—Wade suddenly wasn't sure what year it was, or even what decade.

His jaw stiffened. This was strictly a business call. But a long trail of bad blood was not easily ignored. In hindsight, it was fair to say the two of them never would have been boyhood friends without Tommy as the glue that held them together. But all of that had dissolved when they'd grown up and Wade had taken the badge. Meanwhile, Roland's son Bobby had taken to flirting with the wrong side of the law. Roland had assumed old ties might buy his son some leniency. It hadn't.

Seventeen years ago, with his partner dying on the pavement, Wade had gunned Bobby down in an alley after the boy's last bank heist. The tang of blood was as sharp in Wade's nostrils today as it had been that night.

"Roland, this is Wade," he scratched out.

"Oh." Silence. Intense. "Good morning, Wade. What can I do for you?" His tone was suddenly firm and professional, as if he were speaking with a client at his bank. A client who was *not* about to get a loan.

"I don't want you to waste any time, Roland. You need to get out of town for a while."

"I'm sorry. What is this about?" The confusion in his voice carried over the line.

"It's Tommy. There was an incident this morning. He's been shot, Roland. He's being airlifted to Froedtert. I'm on my way there now."

The other end of the line went quiet again. "Tommy?" Roland finally murmured. "How...?"

"I don't know any details yet. My team's working the crime scene right now. Roland, I don't think you should be on your own. You and Tommy were both warned."

"Yes, I suppose we were." He was quiet for another moment. When he spoke, his tone was once again professional. "Thank you for telling me, Wade. Perhaps I'll spend the day at the country club. I'll work the rest out from there. And I'd appreciate it if you kept me posted on Tommy's condition. Perhaps you might have Monica update me," he added with tact.

The country club. As if a killer couldn't find Roland at one of his favorite haunts. Wade tried not to sigh audibly. He pictured Roland sitting at a linen-draped table overlooking the lake, sipping a cocktail and shooting the breeze with other members of the lakeside gentry. Then Wade pictured a masked gunman waltzing in and mowing down the lot of them in cold blood.

At least asking Monica to update Roland later would provide an excuse to verify the old fool was still alive. Maybe she'd have more clout with him, too. Convince him to take his own life a little more seriously.

"I'll do that," he said, and bit back the rest.

"Very good," Roland replied. "Thank you for calling." And he hung up. A tone beeped in Wade's ear.

Wade growled under his breath and kneaded the steering wheel.

Nancy touched his arm. "Do you think he'll do it?"

Wade shook his head. "Roland is used to the world waiting on him hand and foot. I can't see him letting anyone oust him from his own home. Especially me." He drummed the steering wheel. "You're right, I should have had Monica call him."

"I'm sure she'll check in on him when she has time."

Wade impulsively tapped his phone awake again. "I'll have them send extra patrols past his house." He shifted an eyebrow. "And the country club, apparently."

He asked voice assist to dial his lieutenant. While the line rang, he watched the wooded scenery flash by, a mesmerizing cacophony of color. He called himself a veteran law enforcement officer. A chief of police. It was his job to keep his town safe.

He hadn't even kept his best friend from harm.

CHAPTER SIX
LAKE GENEVA, SUMMER 1951

———— ✤ ————

Wade Erickson, eight years old, sat on the edge of the playground with his back to the brick wall of the school building. It was summer, but the recess yard was abuzz. He hugged his knees and watched the other kids play. He never joined them. He was too small and the bigger boys teased him. But he liked to watch. Sometimes he even brought a sandwich, like today. But it was still in the tin. He was watching the game.

White sandbags were scattered across the yard in the shape of a diamond with a pitcher's mound in the middle. Wade watched the kids pitch and bat and fill the bases. One of them, a short, skinny, but gutsy-looking boy with sandy hair and freckles, was playing the position of both catcher and umpire. Wade knew the kid could bat, too. And pitch. But somehow, whatever role he played, he always doubled as umpire. The other kids rarely argued with him. He was much older than Wade, a sixth grader, and his name was Sebastian Thomlin—but for some reason, everybody called him Tommy.

A loud clang snatched Wade's attention away from the game and he turned to see his lunch box tumble across the ground as if launched with rockets. It spit out his peanut butter and jelly sandwich so that the jelly stuck to the grass.

Wade looked up. A boy leered over him, wearing pleated tan shorts and a sky blue sweater vest and a tie. His black hair was perfectly combed, his shoes shined. Two other boys laughed from behind their leader.

"Peanut butter and jelly?" the boy said. "Is that all your mom can afford to put in your tin?" He put his hands on his knees and leaned over Wade. "Mine is full of things like mutton and steak and chocolate mousse. Have you ever even had steak, Shorty?"

Wade was still trying to imagine what chocolate mousse might be. He dropped his eyes from the tall boy and crawled forward on his hands and knees toward his sandwich. He peeled it off the lawn and tried to put it back in the lunch box. But the tin now had a dent in the lid the shape of the other boy's shoe and it wouldn't close right anymore. Wade tried to pop the tin back out but it wouldn't go.

"Aww," the boy in the sky blue sweater mocked, "what's the matter? Is it broken, Shorty?"

His face warmed. Wade's mother said his small size wasn't his fault and any time he brought it up she would turn right around and try to whip up a feast out of the meager supplies in the fridge. The next day, Wade would find her crying over a grocery list and an empty pocket book. After that happened a few times, Wade quit complaining that the other kids called him Shorty.

"I've got an idea," the boy said. "Ask your dad to get you a new tin."

His two buddies snickered. Wade felt his face redden even more.

The boy in the sky-blue sweater leaned in closer. "Where's your dad, Erickson?" he taunted.

Wade didn't answer. No one was supposed to know... His mom made him promise...

"How come you won't tell me where your dad is?"

Wade scrounged up a tiny bit of courage and gave the boys his most ferocious scowl. "It's none of your business!"

"None of my business? Why not? I don't mind telling you where *my* dad is. He's a banker. And he works in a big, white marble building. And we have a big house in town and another big house on the lake. Now tell me where *your* dad is."

Wade didn't have a big house on the lake. And he wasn't sure what his dad did—back when he did things for a living. But he was pretty sure it had nothing to do with marble buildings. Unless it was breaking into them.

"It's none of your business!" he repeated. It was his only line, and he was sticking to it.

"Aww, c'mon, Shorty, tell me." A wicked smile creased the boy's mouth. He gave Wade's shoe a playful kick. "Tell me why you're cryin' all the time, huh?" He kicked again, this time on the shin and a little harder.

"Ow!"

The boy pulled a pout. "Did that hurt, Shorty?"

His two cronies closed in, their eyes glowing like hyenas. Wade glanced between them, his back to the wall, the possibility of escape slowly disappearing. Finally, the two boys dove at him, grabbed him by the arms, and pinned him in place. Wade tried to squirm and kick. They only laughed.

"You're too soft, Wade Erickson," the bully said, pulling back his sleeves. "Wanna find out how hard I can punch you?"

"Leave me alone!"

The boy cracked his knuckles. Made a show of loosening up his hand. Finally balled it into a fist and drew back.

Wade closed his eyes and turned away. He didn't want to see this part.

But instead of taking a punch to the face, Wade heard a soft thud and the bully crying out, "Ow! Hey!"

Wade peeked. The bigger boy had whirled to face the diamond. His hands were clapped over his rear end and a baseball bounced away from him through the grass.

"Who hit me?" the bully demanded.

The entire game had stopped. Everyone was pointing at the bully, laughing.

The sandy-haired kid, who had left his post at home plate, calmly scooped up the ball in his glove as it rolled back to him.

"What do you think you're doing, Thomlin?" the bully yelled.

"Personal foul! On the bench, Markham!" Sebastian Thomlin shouted back, socking the ball in his glove as he chewed a wad of gum.

"I'm not playing your stupid game," Roland Markham replied.

The boy strolled across the grass toward Roland and his cronies. "Very well, then. No disorderly conduct in the grandstands. I reserve the right to refuse admission to any spectator."

"Shut up, Thomlin!" Roland shoved the sandy-haired kid in the chest with both palms.

Sebastian stumbled backward but kept his feet. Without a flinch, he shook his head. "I'm warning you, Markham, a personal attack on a game official is a serious offense."

Roland grabbed him by the front of the shirt and rattled him, his nose mere inches from the would-be umpire's. "You keep going on like some kind of madman, and I'll—"

Smack.

Sebastian clocked him square in the nose.

Roland staggered backward, clutching his face. "Owww!" he screamed. Flecks of red spattered his sky blue sweater vest. He took his hands from his nose, looked at them, and screamed again. Tears ran down his face. "I'm telling my dad!"

"Fine," Sebastian said. "Tell your dad. But I've got something to tell *you*." He poked a finger into Roland's chest for emphasis and chewed some more on his gum. "If you ever wanna make trouble for Wade again, you're gonna have to get past *me*." He pointed his thumb at himself.

Wade gazed in wide-eyed wonder. This kid he hardly knew was offering to be his bodyguard?

Roland scampered off with his buddies in tow. "You'll be sorry for this, Thomlin!"

Sebastian's friends swarmed in to pat him on the back, congratulations ringing through the air.

"What a punch!"

"Did you see him cry?"

"You sure put him in his place!"

Wade smiled right along with them at first, but the euphoria soon faded into confusion. No one seemed to notice he was there. Left outside of the celebratory circle, he felt invisible—never mind the whole fight had been about him.

"Say, you better watch your back," a girl in braids advised Sebastian. The sandy-haired kid never seemed to mind having girls on his team. They said he'd let just about anybody join. "Roland's gonna have it out for you now," she said.

He waved her off. "Ahhh, I'm not worried. C'mon, let's finish our game."

The kids hollered as they ran back to the baseball diamond. But Sebastian lingered. He looked back at Wade. He socked the ball in his glove again and snapped his wad of gum.

"Wanna play ball?"

Wade's eyes popped. "Me?" Despite the rumors, Wade still couldn't believe Sebastian was inviting him.

"Yeah, you. You know how to play ball, don't you?"

Wade sat up straighter and tried to frown as if offended. "Sure, I do."

"You're small, but I'll bet you're fast."

"I'm real fast."

Sebastian smiled. "Prove it to me. You can be on my team."

Wade scrambled to his feet. He fell into step beside the boy, who tossed and caught the baseball as they headed toward the diamond.

"By the way," Wade said, his cheeks warming again, "thanks, Sebastian."

The boy grimaced and caught the ball again. "Nobody calls me 'Sebastian.' It's Tommy. Tommy Thomlin."

"Oh." He couldn't help thinking it was a funny name. Like John Johnson or Donald MacDonald. "I'm Wade Erickson."

Tommy shook his hand. "Pleasure to have you on my team, Wade. Strictly a rookie position, you understand."

"Oh, I understand." Wade almost added "sir."

Tommy tossed the ball again. "So where *is* your dad?"

Wade hung his head. Yet somehow he felt okay telling Tommy. Hopefully his mom wouldn't mind. But it was really hard keeping it all inside. "He's in jail."

"Oh. You see him much?"

"Not much." Not at all, actually.

"When's he coming back?"

"I don't know. Soon." That was a lie. Wade didn't have a clue when he'd see his dad again. But he lived on the idea that it could be any day.

"Yeah, it won't be long," Tommy agreed. "By the way, I hope you don't hold it against Roland." He caught the ball again. "He only bullies everyone else 'cause he doesn't know how to make friends."

Wade didn't answer. It seemed like a poor excuse for ruining a sandwich and a lunch box. But he wasn't about to argue with Tommy.

Still, he liked to believe that if he ever got big enough, he'd put Roland Markham in his place. Yeah, he'd put him in his place real good.

They got to home base and Tommy shouted to a stocky boy, "Hey, Billy! Hand Wade a bat. Let's see what he can do!"

CHAPTER SEVEN
BUD

Bud Weber's phone rang as he dumped bottles of ketchup into a kettle for his celebrated barbecue sauce. You could always guarantee a rush-hour slam the day he whipped up his special ribs. It was his mom's recipe. She had been a hell of a cook. She would have been pretty damned proud to see him now—owner of his own bar and grill, feeding the masses on recipes she'd taught him. He couldn't have turned out much better than that.

He reached for his phone as it rang the second time, tucked it between his ear and his shoulder, and spanked the ketchup bottle. "Yo?"

"Where are you?" It was The Man.

"Mornin', sunshine. I'm at work. Where are you?"

"Never mind where I am," The Man snapped. "Tommy Thomlin's been shot."

"Really?" Bud gasped. "Why, that's terrible. My God, what's this town coming to?"

"Bud Weber, did you shoot him?" The Man's tone left no room for jokes.

Bud scowled and tossed the empty ketchup bottle into a garbage bin. It made a ring around the rim before crashing into other glass bottles and tin cans inside. "Of course I shot him. What do you think, there's some other serial killer running around besides you and me?"

"You didn't kill him. He's still alive."

"You don't say?" Bud scooped brown sugar into a measuring cup, packing it down like his mom had taught him. "So, my foster kid found him, huh? I thought he woulda bled out before she got there. Oh, well. I thought about killin' him outright, but what's the fun in that? Killing 'em all gets so boring. Ain't how cats do it—did you know that? They like to play with their catch for a while. I once saw one eat the legs off a spider, one-by-one." He dumped the sugar into the kettle.

There was no answer on the other end of the line.

Bud frowned. "Hey, pal, you still there?"

"I'm trying to process your stupidity."

Bud laughed.

"He'll *remember* you, Weber. He'll talk."

"Nah. He knows I'll kill him if he does. Bailey knows I ain't no saint, and she's never talked." He stirred the barbecue sauce and tried a taste. Not enough spice. He liked his dishes to deliver a kick. Just like his punches and his .22. Haha.

"You've put me at risk."

"How ya figure? Just 'cause you pay me doesn't mean I can't work my own gigs on the side." He dashed a canister of his secret spice blend over the kettle and gave it a stir. "I had some personal business to settle with the old man, and I settled it. If the cops *do* come for me, there's no reason to tell them I got anything to do with you." He lifted the spoon to his mouth for another taste when a thought hit him and he paused. "I don't suppose you're gonna dock me some pay for this?"

"All of it."

He dropped the spoon into the kettle. Barbecue sauce splattered the wall. "Now, wait a second. Just 'cause you're sore—"

"We're severing all ties, as of this conversation."

Bud stared at the spatters, which looked for all the world like dried blood. Nah, nah, this couldn't be happening. The Man would never fire him. He chuckled. "Hell, that's a funny one. You had me going for a minute. You ain't got anybody but me to do your dirty work for you."

"Wrong. I've found a replacement."

"What the—?"

"I can't have a rogue agent in my employ. I'll settle what I owe you, and that will be the end of it. From this moment forward, I never knew you."

The line went dead.

Bud stared down into his barbecue sauce, the phone still between his shoulder and his ear. "Well, shit."

CHAPTER EIGHT
MONICA

I paced the interview room while Bailey slouched in her chair, picking at a thread in the seam of the gray sweat pants I'd given her. This was the second time in a week that I'd taken her clothes as evidence. She seemed indifferent about it. As if she'd accepted evidence collection and police interviews as her new normal. I glanced at the floor and noted that she'd slid her feet out of the flip-flops I'd provided—a size too big, but it was all we had in stock. She swung her bare feet back and forth, bumping the chair legs with her heels.

Brandt sat in the corner, drumming his fingers on a battered, ring-bound notebook. I didn't need him here. But he hovered over Bailey like a hawk, as if she would break into pieces the minute he looked away. Near as I could figure, she had no fondness for him. Huh. Something we could agree on.

"Did Tommy say anything?" I asked. "A name? A description? Words they exchanged?"

She shook her head. Swung her feet.

When Ryan brought her back from Lakeland Hospital, he'd suggested I wouldn't get anything useful out of her. Of course, I hadn't listened. I meant to leave no stone unturned. But only five minutes into the interview, I hated to admit Ryan was right. She had seen nothing, heard nothing, arrived only after the incident had happened. And apparently Tommy had told her nothing.

I massaged my brows. It had been another too-clean crime scene, though not as devoid of clues as Fritz Geissler's murder, the first case in the killing streak. I had ballistic evidence this time. Two bullets. I'd found one lodged in the Mailboat's sound system, the other in the cabinetry above it. We never did find the one that had gone through the windshield, but we did pick up four cartridges. Rimfires, so we were looking for some kind of .22.

We had found .22 rimfires from Jason Thomlin's shooting as well, but neither of the two guns recovered from that scene had been a .22. The crime lab should be able to tell us whether the casings from Tommy's shooting and the ones from Jason's had come from the same weapon. Professionally, I was supposed to hold off an opinion until the results were back. But seriously, it wasn't like shootings happened in Lake Geneva every day. At least, they never used to. Whoever had killed Tommy's son had tried to kill Tommy, too.

Everything hinged on the missing accomplice. But I needed some shard of evidence to lead me to him. All I knew so far was that he carried a .22 and was able to move through the world while barely disrupting anything in it.

I eyed the girl in the interview chair again. We'd found no gun at the scene. Nothing resembling gunshot residue on Bailey's hands. Once again, she was only a witness. But God damn, how had she just *happened* to show up at two separate shooting incidents in one week? What did she have to do with any of this?

I stopped pacing and planted my hands on the back of my chair. "Bailey, do *you* know who the shooter is?"

Without looking up, she shook her head. Just continued to twist the loose thread around her pointy finger. Wind it on. Wind it off. Wind it on…

"Bailey…" I let my tone turn a little sharper.

She looked up. Met my eye. But her expression was dead. She didn't care about me or my questions. But neither did she fear meeting my glance. Letting me know she didn't care.

"How are you tied up with all of this? You're just a kid. A mail jumper. A waitress at a dive diner. These people— they're all tied to a burglary ring that fell apart before you were even born. How do you keep popping up in my investigation?"

"I don't know," she said blandly.

"You don't know?"

"Bad luck."

"Yeah?"

"Yeah. It's like my parasitic twin."

Parasitic twin. A rare medical condition in which one twin grew within the other rather than beside it. Her disturbing analogy was no understatement. Brandt had filled me in on some of the details of her life. Her mother was a druggie who'd OD'd. Her father had been MIA. Her life was a string of placements and re-placements in the foster care system, with barely a moment to catch her breath in between. It was safe to say this kid had never really had a break.

"Let's go back to last week," I said. "The kidnapping and shooting you witnessed on South Lake Shore Drive. Jason Thomlin's death."

Ryan shifted in his chair and drummed the notebook harder. He avoided looking at me but sighed and shot daggers into the corner of the room with his eye. I knew that look. He was annoyed with me. Doubtless he thought it out-of-bounds for me to bring up a previous traumatic incident while Bailey was still in such a fragile state.

Well, too bad. I was wearing the detective's badge, not him. And I meant to find the man who had tried to kill Tommy. These incidents were all part of some plot that was only growing, not shrinking. The chief finally seemed to realize it. Apparently, it had taken an attack on his best friend before he figured that shit out.

"I don't know who the guy was," Bailey said. Her voice was flat. Emotionless.

"I know. But I want you to think for just a minute. Have you remembered anything about him? His body type? What his face looked like? Something he might have said? A mannerism? Something he was wearing?"

Bailey opened her mouth then closed it again. She swung her foot, bumping the chair leg with each pass. "He was big. And he was wearing a leather jacket. You know, with a bunch of silver knobby-things. Like what bikers wear."

I reached for my notebook, barely daring to believe my luck. "Good, Bailey, good." I jotted a note, even though the camera in the corner of the room was recording everything. Notes were easier to review than reams of footage. And I never trusted technology to work as advertised. Just like I never trusted anything. "How big was he?"

She bumped the chair leg and shrugged. "I don't know. Big. And tall. Like a bouncer, you know?"

"Six foot?" I prodded. "Six foot six? Seven foot? How big are we talking?"

She looked up and scowled, her nose wrinkling in a manner that was both ferocious and impossibly adorable. "I don't know. I wasn't measuring him for a suit."

I couldn't help smiling. The kid had a little fire. Didn't help my investigation any, but I admired it in her. Especially after all she'd been through. "Anything else?" I asked.

She shook her head.

"Have you ever seen that leather jacket before?"

Again, she shook her head.

"'Kay. I want you to keep thinking about him. If you remember anything, let me know right away. Understood?"

Bailey nodded.

I eyed the broken girl seated in front of me. I'd be lying if I said I hadn't been nervous about meeting her again. Something about her made me frighteningly vulnerable. I couldn't risk letting her through my Wall a second time. I had too much work on my plate to worry about breaches of my personal bubble. But she hadn't tried to storm the gates this time. If I didn't miss my guess, she was too busy shoring up her own defenses. Witnessing the deaths of Jason Thomlin and Charles Hart had been traumatic for her. Finding Tommy had been nothing short of devastating. I didn't need to be a mind reader to see that. Or to understand it. The mail jumper was never born who didn't look up to Tommy and love him. So had I.

Sighing, I straightened my back and tried to catch Bailey's eye. "I'm going to do my best, Bailey. We all care about Tommy. I promise I won't rest until I have some answers."

Bailey didn't respond. Ryan did. His gaze left the corner and met mine, an eyebrow lifted. My Wall had come down and he had noticed. I said nothing. Merely cocked an eyebrow to match his and turned away.

Bailey did strange things to me. She wasn't even trying to assault the Wall today; instead, I had opened the door voluntarily. It was unprecedented. And more than a little frightening. That door was made of rust.

I leaned forward, resting my arms on the chair back. "I have one more question for you," I said softly. It was a tone of voice I don't think I'd ever had the chance to use before. Maybe like a mother to a child. "I'd like to see your arms."

She didn't move, other than to continue worrying the loose thread in the seam of her pants.

"I already know what's there," I said. A week ago, Tommy had reported the appearance of new bruises, beyond the black eye he had reported initially. The bruising around her eye had now faded to yellow. As for her arms, the emergency room staff at Elkhorn had alerted us to the fact that a handful of marks were still barely visible.

Bailey finally lifted her arms. Her eyes still dead, detached, she rested her elbows on the table, hands in the air, the outer bones of her forearms facing me. Five red bruises marred her skin, two on her left arm, three on her right. They were about two inches wide and tapered off with the curvature of her arms. They hadn't been as deep as the trauma to her eye; they were almost faded. Still, my blood seethed. By the way Ryan flexed his jaw and wiggled his foot, he was none too happy himself.

"How did you get these?" I asked.

Bailey didn't answer. But she looked me in the eye, daring me to try to make her talk. Her Wall was up again, fully manned for battle—a wall no sixteen-year-old should ever have had to build.

"Did somebody hit you?"

Still nothing but the hollow stare.

I wouldn't let her win this time. "Bailey, I can read what happened like a book. Those were made by a belt. I can tell from the series of dots running down the length of each mark. Based on the location on your arms, these are self-defense wounds. Someone tried to hit you in the face or on the head and you raised your arms to protect yourself."

Bailey's expression didn't so much as flinch. It amazed me that she could be so utterly devastated by the violence acted upon Tommy but so stoic about that which was directed at her.

"Did they say they'd hurt you again if you told?"

Nothing.

"Was it your foster dad?"

Still nothing.

I sighed and straightened. "I think you have your own reasons for keeping your cards close to your vest." I reached into a pocket in my portfolio and withdrew a business card. "Here." I tossed it on the table in front of Bailey. "When you change your mind, give me a call."

Bailey studied the card without touching it. "Are we done?" she asked.

"You tell me."

Bailey sat quietly for a moment, then scraped her chair back and stood beside it. She resumed her stare at me. The card remained on the table.

Ryan sighed and rose. "C'mon, Bailey. I'll take you home." He held out his hand to guide her toward the door.

I was relieved this interview was over. As I organized my notes, my cell rang on the table. "Hail to the Chief" teased the tension in the room.

"Hang on, Ryan, it's Wade."

Ryan stopped in the doorway.

I picked up my phone. "What's happening?"

"He just got out of surgery," Wade replied through the line. "They're getting him settled in a room. If he comes out of anesthesia okay and can come off the breathing tube, we may be able to talk to him. I don't have a recorder or anything. Can you head up here?"

"I'll be on the road in five," I said. "What's the prognosis?"

"Surgery was successful, but he's not out of the woods. I'll fill in the details when you get here."

I nodded, even though Wade couldn't see the gesture. Perhaps it was only an attempt to loosen the lump in my throat. "I'll be there in an hour."

"Thanks, Monica."

I hung up and hurried to organize my papers. "He's out of surgery," I told Ryan. "I'm headed up there now."

"How is he?" a tiny voice inquired.

I turned to the petite girl. Her eyes were suddenly alive. Bright with worry, yet veiled as if ashamed that she had asked. I didn't have the heart to threaten her frail thread of hope, even though I barely knew anything myself. "He's tough, Bailey," I said. "Just keep reminding yourself of that."

Ryan tilted his head to look her in the eye. "Do you want to go see him?"

She didn't answer, but a muscle twitched in her jaw. Something deep in the recesses of her eyes looked both hopeful and desperately conflicted. Her reaction confused me. This was the Mailboat captain, for God's sake. Why *wouldn't* she want to see him? Maybe I was just projecting my own feelings. I didn't know what her relationship with Tommy was like.

"I'll take you, if you want," Ryan offered. He glanced at the clock on the wall. "My shift ended forty minutes ago. I can change and give you a ride. We'll swing by your house and you can put on some street clothes."

She pondered the question for a long moment. Finally, she gave a tiny nod.

I tucked my portfolio under my arm. Even if I hadn't had a professional reason to be at Tommy's bedside, I didn't need dramatic pauses to figure this shit out. Not when it came to Tommy. True, he and I had barely spoken in years. But the shadow he'd cast over my life as a teenager wasn't easily forgotten.

Bailey's attitude was impossible to read. Whatever. I had miles to cover. A case to solve. "I've gotta hit the road," I said, passing them.

"We'll see you there," Ryan replied.

I paused in the doorway long enough to exchange glances with him. Mine was full of snark, just to remind him: Any interactions between the two of us, outside of business, were strictly prohibited. I couldn't care less whether I saw him at Froedtert. I couldn't care less whether I saw him in hell.

I still couldn't forget the night I'd seen him with another woman in our bed.

CHAPTER NINE
BAILEY

Riding in Ryan's personal car was even weirder than riding in his patrol car.

For one, I guess I'd just assumed that any Audi in Lake Geneva probably belonged to a lakeside well-to-do, not a bicycle cop. But the four interlaced circles glittered at me from right in the middle of the steering wheel. Maybe he liked movies. After all, no self-respecting silver-screen cop would dare be caught in anything less than a pair of blue-tinted sunglasses and a jet-black Audi.

His ratty jeans and tee shirt formed a sharp contrast, though, to his leather-seated ride. So did the sandwich wrapper he'd grabbed off the passenger seat before I'd slid into the car. In every way, this was a different side of Ryan Brandt than the one I was used to seeing, the uniformed cop bristling with weapons and electronics like some sort of crime-fighting cyborg.

I kept asking myself why he was showing so much interest in me, and I kept hating the thought that came back. Bud always showed a lot of interest in me, too. Always told me I was pretty. Always told me I was a good girl. And then he'd tell me to take my clothes off.

As I watched the trees flash by on either side of Interstate 43, I couldn't stop shaking. I didn't want to take my clothes off.

Ryan frowned at me, his mouth downturned under the blue sunglasses. "Are you cold?"

I didn't answer. I was trying too hard to keep my teeth from chattering.

He reached to the dash and flipped the switch under the icon that looked like a chair floating on wavy arrows to heaven. Moments later, warmth radiated through the gray leather upholstery into my bum. It was June, for God's sake. This was so dumb. But the warmth did help my shivers.

Why had I said yes to this? Even if I survived these fifty minutes of terror, arriving at the hospital in Milwaukee would be worse. I pictured a waiting room full of Tommy's friends and family. They would all be there. And they'd pretty much look at me and be like, "So-o-o... *who* are you?" I didn't have any right to show my face there. It would be like barging in on people when they were at their lowest, when they needed private time. Together time. I should never have agreed to this.

But going home would have meant burying my face in a pillow and crying for the rest of the day, dying to know if Tommy was all right, but accepting that in reality I would be the last to hear anything, good or bad, because no one would think to tell Bailey Johnson. I was just his mail jumper, for goodness sake. I had no right to love him the way I did.

I'd sworn I wouldn't.

As he'd lain on the deck bleeding, I'd realized it was my fault. Because everyone I care about, I lose. That's the rule. So I'd promised the universe I'd quit loving him, and maybe then he'd be spared.

But I was failing so bad at that. So bad, I hadn't told the police detective everything I knew.

Like who the man in the black leather vest was.

I argued with myself that I didn't know for sure. I didn't know at all. It had been dark. Everything had happened so fast. But I'd lived with Bud Weber for two years now—a mind-blowingly long time to be in a single placement. You'd think I'd recognize him in the street if I saw him.

If I told the cops and I was wrong, there would be hell to pay. Bud wouldn't appreciate me getting him in trouble.

If I told the cops and I was right, I'd be making a deal with the devil. I'd finally lose Bud, but in doing so, I would lose Tommy. I'd be sent to a new foster home. A foster home anywhere in the county. Anywhere in the state. Homes were hard to find. But if I really cared about Tommy, I would take the devil's deal and banish myself from his life. That way, he would live.

I let my forehead hit the window and tried not to let the tears fall. Why did loving someone have to be so hard?

Please don't die, Tommy...

"Did you have a good talk with Bill?" Ryan asked, plunging into the morass of my thoughts like a sewer worker in hip waders.

I closed my eyes and sighed. Why did Ryan keep trying to make conversation? He was ridiculously persistent and clearly just deceiving himself by now. He knew I didn't want to talk.

He tried again, as if he'd gotten used to serving balls to an empty court; as if he were lobbing them over the net just for the fun of watching them bounce aimlessly. "He's a great chaplain, that guy. We're lucky to have him. He told me he'd be sure to keep in touch with you."

I watched that ball fly out of bounds, too. Yes, the chaplain had said he would keep in touch with me. And yes... I'd had a good talk with him. If you could call it that. He had done most of the talking, just as Ryan was doing now. The chaplain had seemed nice. Worked really hard to make me feel better. But it was his job to act like he cared.

People literally paid him to do it. It wasn't the same as having people in your life who actually loved you.

On the side of the Interstate, woodlands and cornfields gave way to criss-crossing suburban streets and bright little businesses, their storefronts red and yellow and blue as if someone had spilled little cans of paint all over the green landscape. The neighborhoods looked so small and quiet, as if they weren't the forerunners of the sprawling city beyond; as if they had nothing to do with the explosion of paint and color splattered all over the shores of Lake Michigan.

The lanes thickened one-by-one, cars merging from the on-ramps and joining the flow of traffic like the teeth of a zipper. Just when it looked like things couldn't get any more crowded, the Interstates stacked three high, one overpass on top of another. Everything moved hypnotically fast. I studied the doors of the cars beside us, expecting to glimpse our names scratched into the paint just before the ear-splitting screech of metal-on-metal.

I was going to Froedtert. I was going to Froedtert to see Tommy. Maybe it was better if we both died in the middle of a five-car pile-up. That would solve my dilemma for me. No offense to Ryan.

I broke my gaze away from the swirling trance long enough to peek at him. One hand rested on the wheel; the other was crooked in an L shape across his jaw while his elbow rested on the window ledge. He glided through the urban rat's nest as if touring a country lane. He was clearly a practiced hand at navigating chaos. Which meant I probably wasn't going to be lucky enough to die on the Interstate.

I sighed and looked out the window again. The heated leather was now roasting my backside, but I didn't care. We were almost there. The one place I shouldn't be.

Moments later, Ryan pulled off the Interstate and merged into one of the major arteries of the city. Froedtert

Hospital suddenly loomed ahead, its buildings white and glittering like a range of blocky mountains covered in snow and ice—a sprawling land of healing and terror that made my heart freeze and thaw by turns. Somewhere in that endless world of glass and concrete was Tommy.

At the thought, my brain zapped alive like a blast of arctic air—then crashed into frigid blackness. Too much to think about. Too many emotions. I embraced the darkness like the depths of a frozen sea and let my brain go fuzzy. I let myself check out the way I did anytime I couldn't figure out the mess in my head. I wasn't here. None of this was real. To be involved in my own life right now was too much work.

The Audi's blinker clicked and Ryan turned off the busy street toward the main entrance. I eyed the doorway and my fate. In the midst of a circular lawn, a silvery sculpture rose from a bed of flowers, looking like four abstract hands holding up an empty ball. The sculpture glittered in the sun, all safe and dreamlike and inviting. I wanted to climb the hands and curl up in the ball and watch the hundreds of people go by with their hundreds of problems and feel like I was floating somewhere between worlds, non-existent. And all the windows in the hospital would burst and rain down on me like rivers of ice and I could squeeze out all my pain at once.

A cool shadow passed over us as Ryan turned into the parking garage. He perched the sunglasses on top of his head so they seemed to balance on the points of his spiked hair. He found a parking space, shut down the engine, and turned to look at me.

He cracked a little smile. "Let's go find Tommy."

The words sent a shot of terror through my core.

But my head nodded. As Ryan got out of his side of the car, my hand opened my own door and my feet stepped onto the pavement. My brain thought about blackness and darkness and how safe it was to be lost and alone, where no one could chase you, corner you, take everything from you—right down to the people you loved and your desire to live.

Ryan swung his keys around his finger before tucking them into his pocket. He led us out of the parking garage, past the silver sculpture, and toward the hospital doors. Like with the rat's nest, he seemed to know where he was going. I floated behind him through the darkness.

We passed under a glass awning where cars dropped people off and picked them up. Valets grinned and nodded and waited to take people's keys. Out of the blackness in my mind, a fantasy world materialized. A world far safer if only because it wasn't real. I pretended I was walking into a five-star hotel instead of a hospital. I was wearing a slinky golden gown like in the '30s and my hair was bobbed, framing my face in luscious waves. A golden headband shimmered with diamonds and held aloft a pale white peacock feather over my ear.

We stepped into a huge, rotating glass door. The trim was black and the door hummed as a motor turned it round and round. In my mind, it became an Art Deco masterpiece with handles made of brass pipes you pushed yourself. We emerged into a lobby with a two-story ceiling and little trees in pots. The plants could stay. I covered the floors in luxurious red and gold rugs, shipped from the East via the Orient Express. The celebrated Inspector Poirot stepped up to the front desk...

Better known as Ryan Brandt. Actually, he didn't look anything like Inspector Poirot.

A black woman with hair in crazy-tight cornrows smiled up at him. "Can I help you?" she asked.

I concentrated on the pen holder beside her and turned it into a pedestal-style telephone, like a golden daffodil in a black and gold vase...

"Thanks, yes," Ryan replied. "We're looking for a patient who arrived this morning, Tommy Thomlin." He pulled a face and looked at me. "Crap. What's his real name, Bailey?"

The pedestal telephone disappeared. The oriental rugs. The blast of the distant train whistle. I turned to give Ryan a brilliant blank stare. Tommy wasn't his real name?

Ryan looked back at the receptionist. "Anyway. Thomlin." He spelled it. "He arrived by Flight for Life."

Her long fingernails, painted candy-apple red, tapped across her keyboard. "Sebastian Thomlin?"

Sebastian? I darted my gaze to a fake potted tree so no one could see my bug-eyed expression. The luxurious hotel finally melted wholly and completely and dumped me out in the real world. Men and women breezed by in blue and white scrubs, ID tags twirling on lanyards around their necks. Old people in wheelchairs stared hollowly out the front windows. People with appointments studied directories posted on the walls, listing thirty departments on every floor.

My heart beat out of my chest. What was I doing here? I had no right. I didn't even know Tommy's first name. Nerves ran up and down my spine in such a brilliant display of fireworks, I thought I was going to throw up.

"Sebastian," Ryan repeated. He grinned. "Sure, we'll go with that."

"He's in Surgical ICU." She pointed down the hall. "If you proceed to our Family Center, they'll be able to give you more information on his condition. It's just down the hall and on your left."

"Got it. Thanks." Ryan patted the counter top and turned away, apparently assuming I would be right behind him. He made it three whole paces before he realized he was alone. Stopping, he turned and found me rooted to my spot. He gave me a little smile, then jerked his head, inviting me to follow.

I thought longingly about brass doors and daffodil telephones. But maybe it would have been weird of me to hang out in the lobby pretending to be a young debutante when I'd come this far to see Tommy. Ryan had driven all this way. I pulled my feet off the floor and fell in step beside him.

"'Sebastian,'" Ryan muttered as we walked the corridor. He laughed to himself. "I knew it wasn't 'Tommy.'"

I hadn't.

Down the hall, we found a sign hanging from the ceiling, informing us that we'd arrived at the Family Center. I stared up at it as we passed underneath. Even the sign screamed that I wasn't supposed to be here. This place was for "family." Tommy's family.

Ryan turned into the waiting room and walked up to the desk. He was just saying hello to the receptionist and spelling Tommy's name when a voice sounded from somewhere deeper in the Family Center.

"Ryan!" A tall man with a white buzz cut and a policeman's uniform appeared around a corner. He beckoned to us.

Ryan smiled to the receptionist. "I think we found our party. Thanks." He walked up to the tall man and clasped his hand. "Hey, we made it."

Was that supposed to be a big deal?

The man looked down at me. It was a long drop. I had to crane my neck just to see his face. "You must be Bailey Johnson," he said.

I nodded.

Ryan motioned to the man. "Bailey, this is my boss, Chief Wade Erickson."

I noticed the trim on his uniform was all gold. Ryan's was silver.

"We finally meet," the chief said. He offered his hand. His shake was strong yet tinged with sadness. I wasn't sure how I could sense something like that through a

58

handshake, but I could. I knew instantly this policeman wasn't just here on business. His next words confirmed it. "I'm a good friend of Tommy's," he said. His eyes seemed to warm over as he looked at me. "We're glad you came."

Really? Why? I was literally barging in where I had no business to be.

He waved for us to follow. "We're in here."

He led us past the general waiting area and opened a door to a private room. It was lined with chairs and sofas and a table. Canvas blinds shaded the windows that opened to the rest of the waiting room so that we could see nothing but shadows moving around on the other side.

I was surprised to see Robb Landis there, my boss and Tommy's boss. His family had owned the cruise line company on Geneva Lake for three generations. He always wore an impish grin and brightly colored chino shorts that crossed oddly with his age—forty-something—and his position in the lakeside community. Dressed in peach today, he sat near Monica Steele and another woman I'd never met. I imagined this woman's friends would say, admiration in their tones, that she'd "aged gracefully." She could have been anywhere from her late fifties to her early seventies, and I didn't think makeup or a facelift had anything to do with it. Her blond hair was done up in artful whisps and gold bangles glittered from her wrists. Introductions went around, apparently for both my benefit and Ryan's, and I learned the woman was Nancy Erickson, Wade's wife.

I counted noses again. Three cops, a cop's wife, and my boss. Where was Tommy's family? Maybe they lived out of state and hadn't arrived yet.

"How's Tommy?" Ryan asked as he and the chief settled into chairs.

I stayed on my feet, leaning against the closed door. I didn't feel I had any right to make claim on a chair.

Chief Erickson sighed and leaned back, crossing his long legs. He stretched one arm along the back of the duvet, around his wife's shoulders, and massaged his brow. He looked tired. "Surgery went well and his condition is stable. They're taking him off the ventilator now. Hopefully he'll be able to breathe on his own."

Detective Steele sat in a hard chair at a table in the corner, chewing a hangnail. Her ever-present black leather portfolio sat in front of her. "When can we interview him?" she asked, taking her thumb out of her mouth only long enough to pose the question.

"We're just waiting for the green light from the SICU staff," the chief replied. "You brought an audio recorder?"

She tapped her pocket. "Right here."

I frowned, my insides twisting in all kinds of unhappy feelings. She was going to question Tommy—just like she had questioned me. Did she have no idea how bad it sucked, being forced to relive every second of the worst moments of your life? I wanted to stop her from doing it, but didn't know how. I wanted to protect Tommy, which felt weird. It was enough to drive me back to the rotating door and my debutante ball…

The stylish woman, Nancy, smiled at me and leaned forward. "You can sit, dear. There's lots of chairs."

Merely being singled out bumped my heart rate into overdrive. "I'm fine," I said. "Thanks."

She tilted her head and smiled compassionately, accepting my refusal outwardly but not inwardly.

"Bailey's the one who called 911," the police chief said to Robb Landis. "Tommy might not be here if it wasn't for her."

Wow. He obviously hadn't seen what went down. I'd been barely functional.

Robb grinned. It was an expression he used freely and easily like summer sun and a cool lake breeze. But this time there was something deeper about it. Not so jocular, more serious and sincere. "Tommy always says you're early to work," he said. "Good thing you are."

My stomach churned and I thought I was going to be sick again. They were wrong. I was the reason Tommy had almost died. It was my fault. I'd allowed myself to love him. Bad things always happened to the people I loved.

Clearly, I was *still* loving him. I was here, when I should have been as far away from Tommy as possible. I needed to stop this. I needed Ryan to take me home. But I couldn't bring myself to ask him. It would be stupid, after he'd driven me all this way.

A phone rang from a table top in a corner.

Wade Erickson sprang to his feet. "That'll be the doctor."

I think that's when I realized just how big Froedtert Hospital really is. It was literally too time-consuming for a doctor to walk all the way from Surgical ICU to the waiting area to give friends and family the update.

Chief Erickson crossed the room in three lanky strides and picked up the receiver. "This is Wade."

My heart flopped around in my chest like an injured bird. I held my breath and strained my ears but couldn't hear a thing from the other end. The police chief's face was an unreadable blank. He said things like "okay" and "mmm-hmm" and that was all. At last, a tiny smile lifted one side of his mouth. That smile had to be a good thing. *Please, oh please, be a good thing.*

"Thank you very much," the chief said. "My detective and I will be right up to speak with him... Yes, I understand. But it's imperative we try... Thank you."

He laid the receiver down. Monica Steele was already on her feet, clicking a pen impatiently. "Ready when you are."

"He's off the ventilator?" the chief's wife asked. I mentally thanked her. I would have died if the chief and the detective had left before he could tell us what was going on.

Wade nodded. "Breathing on his own, and responsive to voice and touch."

61

Mrs. Police Chief closed her eyes and sighed. "Thank God."

I came as close as ever to crying but fought it back. It probably wasn't smart to let myself hope.

"They said we can go ahead and try to get his statement," Chief Erickson said. But he held up his hand to Detective Steele as she tried to breeze past him toward the door. "They said he's a little out of it. Hard to say what we'll get, if anything."

She shrugged. "We have to try."

The chief nodded. "Agreed." He turned to the rest. "We won't be long."

Robb nodded. "Take all the time you need, Chief."

I scooted away from the door to let the chief and Detective Steele through. Mrs. Police Chief tilted her head at me as the door clicked shut behind them.

"Come sit down, Bailey. You've had a long day." She tapped the space her husband had just abandoned.

My feet *were* getting a little sore. But instead of taking the seat next to her, I slid into the one closest to the door. It was a tall chair with a little footrest. The police chief's wife smiled. Apparently turning down the seat next to her was okay.

I reviewed the faces around me again. Mrs. Erickson, Robb, Ryan. I finally found the courage to ask, in a very small voice, "Where's Tommy's family?"

Mrs. Erickson made a sad smile. "Wade's as good as a brother to him. He's power of attorney, in fact. Tommy doesn't have anyone else."

My eyes bugged out again, but this time, there were no potted trees to stare at to hide my shock. Tommy didn't have a family? For real? How could I not know that? Come to think of it, I should have. The rest of the staff at the cruise line were always bringing family around to take a tour and watch them work. I'd thought I was the only one who never did. Now that I thought about it, neither did Tommy.

I hadn't known his real name. I hadn't known he didn't have a family. I mentally smacked myself. What business did I have loving someone I barely knew? Why was I always living in ridiculous fantasy worlds?

Maybe because fantasies were all I had.

A tiny voice piped in with a curious observation: Tommy was all alone in the world. Just like me.

My smarter half slapped me again. *Quit it. He's not yours. Stop play-acting like he is.*

Robb leaned forward in his chair, a big, comfy-looking recliner. His elbows were on the armrests and hands strung together. "FYI, Bailey, there won't be a Mailboat tour tomorrow. And probably not the next day, either." He shrugged with his hands. "On account of that I don't currently have a Mailboat." Robb had a funny way of making light of things—even this.

"Is the damage bad?" Ryan asked.

He shrugged. "Well, I can drive it. But I'd rather not do that with a bullet hole in the windshield. And the sound system is shot—literally." He laughed at his unintended pun. "She's up at the repair docks in Williams Bay right now. But I won't have some of the parts until tomorrow." He looked at me again. "Brian's going to deliver the mail with the cabin cruiser. So I guess you can have a couple days off."

I twisted the hem of my shorts around my finger. "The Mailboat's never missed a day."

Robb shook his head, for once a sad frown crossing his face. "Hardly ever." His family had been running the Mailboat for three generations. He would know better than anyone—except maybe Tommy.

Lame. The two things that never changed. The Mailboat. And Tommy. And in the course of a single morning—gone.

The Mailboat would be back.

Would Tommy?

I squeezed my eyes shut. *Quit it. Quit it. Quit it.* I tried to picture myself in a slinky, golden gown, whirling and twirling across a ballroom floor. One by one, dashing men in tailcoats and white ties swept me off my feet. But I remained aloof, dancing beautifully but looking the other way, the debutante who could not be bothered by the world or anything in it.

I didn't belong anyway.

CHAPTER TEN
TOMMY

———— ✲ ————

"Tommy?... Tommy?"

My eyes opened. I didn't ask them to. They just did. A reflex to someone calling my name. Nothing registered but a blur of dull light, yellow and gold, and the vague outline of a man, a shadowy brown.

My side ached. I felt dense and dead, like a stone. Something beeped beside me, over and over like an angry seagull. It was too loud. I blinked again but still couldn't focus. The effort hurt my eyes.

Forget this. I shut my eyes again. Tried to go back to sleep.

"Tommy? It's me. Wade."

Didn't care if it was the President himself. I mumbled something to the effect.

"What was that?" he asked.

I licked my lips. My tongue felt thick and dry like cotton. My throat ached as if someone had crammed a rod down it. I elaborated. "Ow."

Laughter. Two voices. There was a woman in the room, too.

What room? Where was I? I felt like someone had dredged my carcass from the bottom of the lake.

"Yeah, I suppose," the man said.

Suppose what? I'd lost the conversation. My brain staggered like a drunken sailor from one disjointed notion to the next: My next-door neighbor hadn't mowed his lawn in a week. The digital kiosk in front of the library was advertising a talk on the history of the Riviera Ballroom and the Big Band Era. I hadn't filled out the engine checklist on the Mailboat. No one had washed the windows or stocked the snack bar. We weren't gonna be ready in time for the tour. None of it mattered.

Through the morass, my mind struggled to grasp one elusive thought that seemed so much more important than the rest. But what was it? Fear of never finding it churned in my chest.

I blinked my eyes open again. The answer was somewhere in the blurry yellow light. Maybe. The thought had to do with something—no, someone very important to me...

The shadow of the man leaned closer. "Tommy, do you know who shot you?"

He was large. Lowering. A brown blur, he blocked out the golden light. I knew him. No, no I didn't. His voice shifted. Took on a thick Chicago accent. And now I heard it inside my head instead of in my ears, where it was more real, more intense than the voices around me a moment ago.

"Want any more, Tommy?" The liquor on his breath soured in my nose. He dragged the barrel of the gun across my cheek, scorching. A pool of warm blood was already soaking into the fabric of my shirt.

My heart began to pound. The seagull screeched faster. *"You'll bleed out before she gets here."*

Bailey. The thought I wasn't supposed to forget. Bailey-girl. I couldn't let the man with the gun find her. Hurt her. I tried to move—to warn her; to protect her—but my body was made of lead.

I squeezed my eyes shut. "No, don't hurt her."

The brown shadow spoke. This time, I heard it with my ears. "Say again, Tommy? I didn't catch that."

Ignoring him, I concentrated on the only thing that mattered: finding Bailey. Where was she? My vision cut in and out and I saw a pair of knees beside me, spattered with blood. I saw the tears in her eyes. I saw her father's silver helm dangling from her neck on a ball chain. How could I have abandoned her? The silver helm was supposed to bring her home...

She shook her head and whispered, "I'm sorry."

Sorry? Why? I was the one who needed to be sorry. I'd known for days that she was my granddaughter, and I hadn't told her. I reached for her hand but found only empty air. "Bailey..."

"What about Bailey?" The voice in my ear asked, humming like a nagging insect.

I scowled and shook my head to chase it away. Didn't he get it? Bailey had to leave. The gunman was still here. I could feel him. Hovering over me. His breath on my face. "He'll kill her."

"Say again, Tommy? I don't understand you."

"Bailey."

"I got that part. What about her?" The shadow leaned in closer.

Suddenly, I couldn't see her anymore, my Bailey. There was no one but the shooter, leering over me. *"I could put you out of your misery."*

"No," I groaned, panic rising. "I haven't told her."

Tears stung my eyes. I'd never told her that she was my granddaughter. That the father she'd never known was the son I'd rejected. And now I was gonna bleed out before I could tell her. Where was her hand? I'd had it only a minute ago...

"Tommy." It was the woman's voice. Fingers both delicate and firm closed around my shoulder. "It's me, Monica. Bailey's fine. She's here. We'll send her in to see you in a minute. But please, Tommy. Can you tell us who shot you?"

Bailey was all right? My brain latched onto that and nothing else. The lowering shadow hadn't gotten her. I sighed—aching in every rib—and relaxed back into what felt like a pillow under my head. Bailey was safe.

"Tommy?" the woman's voice prodded.

The yellow light faded toward the cool darkness of sleep. I craved it like a long drink of water.

The man's voice again. "Never mind, Monica."

The hovering figure withdrew. Cold relief flooded me. The shooter was gone. Bailey was safe. My Bailey-girl. I could still tell her.

But where was her hand?

CHAPTER ELEVEN
BAILEY

I jumped as the door beside my chair swung open. Detective Steele stepped into the room, glanced around, and looked down at me. I waited for the police chief to walk in behind her, but he didn't.

The detective's eyes seemed tired. Like she'd just had her ass kicked by something she couldn't kick back. Her portfolio hung by her side in a limp grip. She wasn't clicking pens anymore.

"He's asking for you, Bailey," she said.

My eyebrows popped up. I glanced around the room for another Bailey. There wasn't any. Why would Tommy want to see me? I could think of only one possibility. He was mad. He'd told me what to do back at the Mailboat—just stop the damn bleeding. How hard could that be? And I'd sat there frozen and let him bleed.

"Where's Wade?" the police chief's wife asked.

"Talking with the doctor," Monica replied. "He'll be back in a minute."

Ryan planted his hands on his knees and rose, then looked at me with a half-cocked smile. "Ready? I'll go with, if you like."

Or maybe Ryan could just go by himself and offer my regrets.

Detective Steele held up a hand, stopping him. "You should wait a minute. I think the interview tired him."

I didn't bother hiding my scowl. The anger burned. Her interviews were like eating your vomit again, chunk by chunk. I tried to tell myself she had reasons—catching bad guys and all—but how many criminals had she caught, anyway? None. It wasn't worth it.

The police chief's wife leaned forward. "Did Tommy tell you anything?"

Monica shook her head. "He's still very disoriented. All we got out of him was Bailey's name."

My chest tightened as if I'd breathed in an iceberg. This was worse than I thought. He was that eager to chew me out? Never mind the guy who shot him; he just wanted to get his hands on Bailey Johnson. *Just stop the damn bleeding.*

I told myself I was confusing him with Bud. Tommy would never be angry with me like that.

But why did he want to see *me?*

I pulled my feet right up into the chair and rested my chin on my knees, imagining I was inside the silver ball. I closed my eyes and felt the broken glass fall over me like raindrops. My blood dripped from the cuts, washing me in a pain that soothed.

CHAPTER TWELVE
RYAN

I stood awkwardly in the middle of the room, jangling keys in my pocket and rocking on the balls of my feet. I wanted action. I wanted to do something, even if it was just delivering Bailey to Tommy's bedside. Forced to stand here waiting and watching just about did me in. It was getting harder and harder not to just swoop her up in a hug, inserting myself between her and the repeating nightmare that was her life. But my gut told me hugging her wouldn't go over well. Maybe Tommy held those privileges—if anyone did.

A glance at Monica didn't make me feel much better. Something about seeing Tommy had rinsed the starch out of her spine. It wasn't like she'd never seen the effects of violence before. But her shoulders slumped unevenly. Her eyes glittered, damp. The sight took me aback. She never lost her professionalism. Ever. Besides, I'd assumed her tear ducts had closed up shop years ago.

She tapped her portfolio against her leg, then took a deep breath and straightened her back. "I need to stretch my legs." She tossed the leather binder down on a chair without so much as a look or a word to anyone and walked out the door.

I eyed that portfolio where it sat cock-eyed on the cushion. It held all her case notes. All her leads. A veritable phone book of contact information. She never just left it places. She'd sooner leave her pants behind. Something wasn't right.

While Nancy Erickson and Robb Landis resumed conversation in the background, I rubbed the knot forming in the back of my neck. I shouldn't worry. Monica was a big girl. But I tried to remember the last time I'd seen her cry.

It had been ten years ago. An accidental death investigation when we'd both been working in Madison. A teen girl had snuck her friends in for a party while the parents were away. They'd been hard at it all night and woken up the next morning with hangovers, only to discover the girl's two younger sisters floating face-down in the backyard pool.

As closely as we could piece it together, the five-year-old had fallen in and begun to drown. The eight-year-old must have jumped in to save her little sister and been pulled under. Several teens remembered hearing screaming but thought the younger girls were only playing. The oldest sister had even yelled at them to shut up.

Monica had vented for hours when she got home that night. The carelessness. The pointlessness. Then she'd simply broken down and cried. That one had hit her hard. Two little angels lost for no reason. I remembered wrapping her up in my arms and letting her work it all out of her system.

She didn't know I'd cradled another woman the night before. To this day, I didn't know why I'd done it. Or why I kept doing it. They say most spouses offer a second chance. Not Monica. I was lucky to grab an overnight bag on my way out the door.

I quit fidgeting with the keys in my pocket, telling myself to sit down and rejoin the conversation instead of standing in the middle of the floor like an idiot.

But all of a sudden, my arms felt profoundly empty, as they had many times over the past ten years. To alleviate it, I'd gotten into the habit of simply swinging by a bar, dressed in a sufficiently tight tee shirt to show off my eye candy. I'd wait maybe half an hour or more, looking the girls over before taking my pick. I'd buy her a drink. We'd dance. I'd suggest rounding our evening out at my place or hers. The guys always cursed my good luck. The next morning, I'd wake up with a woman in my embrace, but the ache still lodged in my chest like a spear.

I was sick of living with it. I wanted to wrench it out for good and forever, never mind the bleed-out that could follow.

Impulsively, I made for the door. "I'll be back," I told the room at large and didn't wait for an answer.

Passing through the Family Center, I emerged in the main corridor, where I scanned left and right over the heads of the foot traffic. Which way had she taken? The hospital extended almost indefinitely in either direction. I peeked into the chapel directly across the hall, but it was empty. Monica wasn't the church-going type.

I planted my hands on my hips and tuned out the swarms of pedestrians. If I were Monica, where would I go to be alone? Where in all of Froedtert Hospital...?

Oh. Of course.

I walked toward the main entrance. From there, I hung a left at an intersecting hallway. It was as long as a runway. I had to stretch my eyes, but far away I recognized the lithe form, the tan slacks, the black shirt, the cop's gait.

I hesitated. Technically, I was stalking her. She wanted to be alone, that was clear. I should leave her to her thoughts. But maybe I'd done far too much of that.

I followed her.

She was covering ground at a clip, her long dark hair swinging from shoulder blade to shoulder blade in its long, tight ponytail. I followed more slowly. There was no need to rush. She was free to disappear and I knew I wouldn't lose her. After crossing the entire hospital, she would turn right at the elevators and go down one floor to the emergency room entrance. I knew it as surely as I knew I had once loved her with every fiber of my being.

It was a long walk with far too much time to think. What would I do? What would I say? The smart thing would have been to strategize. But I didn't. Everything about this moment felt criminally wrong—and yet as natural and right, as simple and true as a clean spring rain. I didn't question a single step I took.

Monica eventually vanished in the crowd. I maintained my unhurried pace. Minutes later, I turned right into a little lobby with four elevators. I didn't press any of their buttons. Not yet. Curiosity drove me to see if I'd guessed correctly. If I still knew Monica Steele as well as I had when we were lovers. When we were man and wife. Maybe it would prove something to me. Maybe it would nudge me toward taking that last critical step—toward seeking her out and seeing if her presence in any way dislodged that spear in my chest.

Instead of boarding one of the elevators, I drifted towards the skywalk that opened just beyond them. It led to one of the many parking ramps that ringed the hospital. I stepped into the glass tunnel, feeling as if I were walking on air. A few steps in, I stopped and peered down into the cul-de-sac driveway and the emergency room entrance below. Froedtert Hospital spread out on either side like great white wings, sweeping the air, reaching out and up, welcoming the desperate and battered into its arms. In the middle of this rotunda, directly below my feet, was a tiny park, bathed in the sunshine that spilled over the crest of the hospital.

I hooked my thumbs in the belt loops of my jeans and studied the park below. It had changed since the last time Monica and I had been here. It used to be just a grassy space. But somewhere in the intervening years, they'd built a sidewalk that meandered through trees and shrubs. A circular trellis, growing with vines, shaded the walking path. They'd even put in a fountain on one end, a rectangular slab of rock with water spilling over its front face.

And there in front of the water feature stood Monica. Her hand clasped over her mouth. Her shoulders shaking.

I'd been right. She was exactly where I'd expected. More than that, I knew why she was here. Why she was crying. I knew every thought and every memory going through her head right that moment. But far from relieving the ache, all that knowledge was merely a pair of hands on the spear shaft, twisting it torturously. I'd never felt so empty and alone in my life.

She didn't want me here. I shouldn't go down.

So I did.

I retraced my steps to the elevators and took them one floor down to the emergency room lobby, then walked out a set of rotating doors into the sunlight. It was really white out here. I reached up to drop my shades over my eyes but stopped my hand before I could touch the frames. My sunglasses were more than smart protective eyewear while on the job; they were also one of the shields I wore. Anonymity was comforting in a stressful situation. But now was not the time to hide. She needed to see me, not her own tear-streaked reflection, tinted blue.

I followed the curve of the sidewalk and the sound of splashing water. The fountain appeared from behind short, decorative trees: a long slab of polished gray stone out of which a sheet of water poured into a bed of rocks and disappeared into the ground. Monica stood in front of it, biting her fist, eyes screwed shut, tears tracing down both cheeks.

I crept in as close as I dared and stopped. She looked up, eyes glittering. I waited for her to lash out at me. To dish up a cutting remark. To send me away with my head hanging and my tail between my legs. To my amazement, she didn't. Nor did she try to hide her tears. She just stood there, looking as hurt and empty as a woman could. For a moment I thought I was looking at Bailey, all grown up but no less lost.

"He'd be happy you came here," I said, daring to speak. "My dad always thought the world of you."

She breathed hard and stared up at the hospital windows. "Let's get real, Ryan. He thought I was a good kid, but he was too lost in a bottle to give a rip about you or me."

The spear twisted a little harder. She was right, of course. But somehow, that fact had never stopped either of us from loving him. Maybe even looking up to him, strange as that sounded. We had both turned out to be cops, just like him. Maybe at one time, the name "hero" could have been applied to my dad. But the repeating heartwreck that was our career had eventually eaten him alive. Left him desperate to escape. To forget. The hollow eyes. The broken lives. Unbridled hatred. But he'd been too loyal to the badge—to the people he'd sworn to serve—to go into any other profession. So a glass of hard liquor—or three or four—was the tonic with which he hoped to wash his soul.

I glanced around the park. "They've switched this place up a bit."

"Yeah," Monica said. "Good. Some things you just gotta bury."

I scratched behind my ear. Maybe she had a point. There really were no happy memories associated with this place, unless it were just a time when Monica and I had been able to turn to each other for comfort. To reach out in the dark and know without flinching that we'd find each other's hand in a heartbeat.

I eyed the red emergency sign over the door, vivid against the white of the hospital. My dad had hung on for a full day. But there was only so much medicine could do after you rolled your vehicle nine times. His blood alcohol content had been .210. We figured he'd simply blacked out behind the wheel. Thankfully, he hadn't taken anyone else with him.

Monica and I had come here a lot during those last twenty-four hours. Just to hang on. To hope. In the end, Dad must have decided he'd just had enough. Sometimes a sick heart only wants to let go.

I tried to tell myself that what we were going through now wasn't at all like then.

"I suppose I shouldn't have followed you," I said.

She simply looked into the sky and swallowed hard.

I wanted to offer her something more meaningful than empty words. An embrace would only win me a slap to the jaw—or more likely a knee to the nuts. Instead, I tentatively stepped forward, touched her elbow, and guided her onto a slatted wooden bench. She went placidly. I knelt beside her, one knee on the pavers inscribed with memorandums to loved ones. Again I was shocked she wasn't fighting me off.

"I was just remembering," she said, staring into the curtain of water, "how Tommy used to tease us when we were kids."

I grinned. That's right. He had. I'd almost forgotten. What I could never forget—what neither one of us could ever forget—was the fact that Tommy had been there for us when people like our own parents simply weren't.

She sniffled and shook her bangs out of her eyes. "He used to tell me if I walked around with my nose any higher, I'd get a nose bleed."

I laughed but didn't dare comment. There was still a chance she was simply setting me up for an argument.

Those waters could turn into an undertow. So I simply replied with one of my own anecdotes.

"Remember when I was named Most Valuable Player on the football team?" I asked. "I was being pretty grand about it. But Tommy pretended not to know what 'MVP' meant and kept substituting his own ideas. 'Mighty Vain and Pompous.'"

She laughed through her tears.

"'Master of Vicious Pranks.' 'Mostly Victorious Posthumously.'"

She choked, smiling, and wiped at her eyes.

I smiled, too. Tommy'd had a knack for putting us in our place with a wink and a smile. You could never make him mad. Yet you knew better than to cross him. Come to think of it, I had no idea how he'd kept so many teenagers in line for so many years. We must have tried his patience.

I'd forgotten how good it felt to make Monica laugh. It suddenly dawned on me that I'd forgotten a lot of things. Competitions to see who could insult the other worse—back when it had all been in fun. Movie nights that devolved into popcorn fights. Midnight runs to the station to drop off dinner for whoever was working late. Long kisses at the door when one was on day shift, the other graveyard. We had a sync. A vibe. We were partners in every sense of the word. We knew intrinsically that we had each other's six.

Well. One of us did.

I'd forgotten all these things on purpose. They only brought back the ache. The awareness that my arms were empty and always would be, because they had been made for one woman alone.

As she stared hollowly into the falling water, I wished I could see the light in her eyes again. It had been so beautiful, so full of life, so mesmerizing. Like a bonfire. Like something that ate up everything in its path and left it fundamentally changed, purified somehow, revitalized. But that fire had been snuffed out years ago. By me.

"You going to be okay?" I whispered.

She looked into her lap and nodded.

I found myself studying the curve of her cheek. The sweep of her dark lashes. Most spouses offer a second chance. Maybe Monica simply required a hiatus of ten years before extending that grace. Did I dare hope? My heart pounded with both terror and thrill at the possibility.

The ache screamed. Beat its fists against my chest. Hated on me for what I'd done to her. What I'd done to us. Begged me to fling wide the door, grab her hand, and pull her back into my arms.

I firmly pried the longing away, finger by clutching finger, and tucked it, wrestling and squirming, into a box. *Don't be hasty,* I warned. Losing patience and moving too fast would ruin everything. Monica's official status was that she hated Ryan Brandt. And for good reason.

In fact, I hated Ryan Brandt, too. What kind of idiot threw a woman like this away? The woman who had been your only soul mate? There would never be another. Trust me. I'd checked them all. If Monica ever chose to forgive me for the scar I'd left on her heart, I'd be the luckiest man in the world.

CHAPTER THIRTEEN
MONICA

———— ⚓ ————

Ryan and I walked back into the hospital together and down the long corridors. I didn't have the energy to hate being seen with him. I was wrung out—from the investigation, from worrying about Tommy, from the inexplicable thing that had happened between Ryan and me out in the park. I'd let him see me cry. I'd let him see me laugh. What was wrong with me? Where the hell was my Wall?

When we made it back to the Family Center, I stopped outside the door. Hallway foot traffic washed by, and I lowered my voice for only Ryan to hear. "I'm just getting my portfolio and going home," I said.

His eyes flickered with concern. "You're not staying?"

I shook my head. "We won't get anything out of Tommy today. He doesn't know where he is. And I have too much to do back at the office." I rolled my eyes and shrugged with a dramatic sigh. "I thought I was busy before."

He nodded. His face still held that gentle look, as if afraid of breaking something made of gossamer thread. "Well... just don't work yourself too hard."

Too hard? Thanks to Wade's naiveté, we were up to our necks in the worst murder investigation in our town's history. And now Tommy was the one to pay. My fists clenched. "I *told* Wade—" I bit my tongue before any more of my pent-up frustration could slither out. No need to vent my beef with Wade in front of Ryan.

But Ryan frowned. "Told him what?"

I groaned and tapped my foot, torn between elaborating and keeping my mouth shut. In those long-lost days of our past, Ryan and I would come home and debrief each other on everything—the good, the bad, the bizarre. There was nothing we wouldn't tell each other. It was frightening how naturally I felt myself slipping back into the habit.

I was too tired to fight the urge. I let go and went for the free-fall.

"That it isn't over," I said. "That there'll be more killings. Our man—whoever he is—isn't done. He has some sort of agenda." I pointed a finger, as if Ryan were somehow responsible. "Roland Markham needs to watch his back better. That *idiot*—" I grit my teeth "—needs to get his act together and take this whole thing more seriously. Instead, he's just... *sipping tea* on his pier—"

"Hey, hey," Ryan shushed, laying a hand on my arm. "You've warned him, right? You've told him what he can do to safeguard himself. I assume we're sending extra patrols past his house. Aside from tracking down the killer, your job with Roland ends there. Don't try to carry the world on your shoulders. We know where that leads."

I swallowed hard. Ryan's dad had cared so deeply, had tried so hard to fix everyone else's problems, he'd finally just cracked under the pressure. Still, the lesson was lost on me. I *needed* to fix this. This was *my* hometown. These were *my* people.

Maybe my inability to see past those warped needs was due to distraction. To the fact that Ryan's hand on my arm was warming my skin, sending electricity up and down my spine, giving me gooseflesh.

No, these little physical tells were merely signs of resentment. Anger. Of course they were. How dare he touch me? This sensation, like falling over a cascade, couldn't have been because Ryan Brandt still had an effect on me. I wouldn't let it be.

I wrenched my arm away and marched into the Family Center, ignoring the way Ryan's eyes fell, downcast, as I stormed past him. Well, he should know better than to try to be nice to me. He should remember he was an asshole.

Brandt following like a berated puppy, I breezed into the waiting room where the others were congregated. Wade had returned from his talk with the doctor. He sat on the sofa, legs stretched in front of him, an arm around his wife's shoulders. His eyes were as tired as if he'd run all the way to Milwaukee from Lake Geneva.

"I'm heading back, Chief," I said, grabbing my portfolio from the chair where I'd thrown it. "I've got a massive report to write."

He nodded. "I'll keep you posted."

I slid the audio recorder out of a pocket in the portfolio. "You need this?"

He held open his hand. "Just in case."

I tossed it to him across the room. "See you when I see you," I said and turned to leave. I pushed my way past Ryan without a goodbye. But I felt his eyes following me and it raised the hairs on my arms again. I needed to get out of here. To get away from him. Away from the sensations still vibrating all over my body. Away from dangerous memories...

I marched toward the main entrance, clutching my portfolio in a death grip. My stomach churned painfully and I rubbed my belly. Moments later, I realized what I was doing. Jumping, I forced my hand to my side. My heart pounded as fear rushed through my bloodstream. My God, I'd kicked that mannerism ages ago.

I broke into a run. This was getting to be too much.

I burst out of the rotating door and stormed down the sidewalk toward the garage where I'd parked the department car. Fresh tears squeezed out of my eyes. My hand sneaked across my belly again. To my horror, I didn't have the strength to fight the mannerism away. The pain was coming back. The Great Emptiness around which the Wall had been built. The hollow, gnawing ache for someone beautiful whose face I'd never known. Whose hand I'd never touched. Someone perfect and irreplaceable.

I thought I'd backfilled that hole ages ago. Ruthlessly. With leftover building materials from my Wall. I'd flung that shit in there and stomped it down. More than anything, more than Ryan, more than all the villains in the world, I feared this empty place in the middle of my belly.

The empty place of Ryan's child, long gone. The child we'd almost had. The child he'd never known about.

CHAPTER FOURTEEN
RYAN

The breeze Monica created as she left the waiting room slapped me in the face as firmly as any palm to the cheek. Once again, all my best intentions had gone awry—but how I'd managed it this time, I had no clue. Maybe I should have known better than to let myself hope like some lovesick but clueless teenager. Yet hope had felt so good.

For a moment.

I glanced at Wade, Nancy, and Robb Landis, hoping no one had noticed the awkward atmosphere Monica had left in her wake. But their attention was on Nancy as she asked Robb about the cruise line's annual Fourth of July fireworks tours. Still, I felt as if I were standing in the middle of the room in nothing but my underwear—a nightmare I used to have a lot when I was in high school. Feeling a need to cover my bum somehow and divert any lingering attention away from Monica's sudden exit, I turned to Bailey.

"You ready?" I asked, forcing a smile.

Bailey looked up with big eyes. The kind you see in commercials for adorable homeless animals. The kind that made me want to reach through the TV screen, scoop them up out of their dirty cement kennels, and take them all home.

I sighed. Everything about the world right now felt so fundamentally wrong. But one thing I knew: Bailey belonged with Tommy. Even if *she* didn't know that.

I tried again, touching her shoulder. "C'mon, Bailey. I'll go with you."

Her eyes, round and damp, quivered a moment in fear. Then she slid off her stool and fell into step beside me, head bowed so she could stare at the ground.

Okay. Relationship building, round two. I'd have to try really hard not to ruin this one as well.

CHAPTER FIFTEEN
BAILEY

———— ✦ ————

Ryan led the way down a hall and into an elevator. As the ground whooshed beneath us, my entire body quivered. Tommy wanted to see me. Tommy had asked for me. That was all they could get out of him. Like everyone else in my life, he wanted to yell at me for what a failure I was. *Give me your hand,* he'd said on the boat. *You have to stop the bleeding.* And I'd just sat there and stared at him, too afraid to move.

The elevator bell dinged. I'd forgotten I was in an elevator. The bell startled me so violently, I felt bile rush into my throat. I swallowed it back as Ryan and I stepped through the doors.

Like a piece of debris caught in a ship's wake, I followed Ryan down a hallway, tumbling and turning, merely along for the ride. He pushed open a swinging door into another part of the endless hospital and motioned me ahead. The flotsam that was me breezed through on sheer momentum, then settled back behind him as he led us down the hall to a nurse's station. He pulled out a thin leather wallet and showed it to the nurse on duty.

"I'm Officer Ryan Brandt with Bailey Johnson. Chief Erickson cleared us to see Sebastian Thomlin."

The nurse studied his ID—not a driver's license, but a plastic card with a logo of a sailboat in a circle. It was the same emblem as the patch Ryan wore on the shoulder of his uniform.

The nurse nodded and pointed to our left. "You can go in."

Ryan thanked her and guided me toward the room she'd indicated. Instead of a door, there was a curtain as wide as an entire wall. Ryan's hand on my shoulder moved me along, a scrap of driftwood now being pushed by the waves breaking off the ship's bow. Things like waterlogged bits of driftwood don't feel anything. You don't feel anything when you've switched everything off. It was my last defense. Whatever happened on the other side of that curtain, I didn't want to be there.

Ryan motioned me to go through first.

I didn't. When the ship stopped, I stopped. I stood there in the hall, staring at the course weave of the tan curtain, unable to move, as if I'd snagged on a long frond of seaweed and was now bobbing pointlessly in the water.

Ryan sighed and leaned down. Planting his hands on his knees, he put his eye level at mine. His eyes were brown. I'd never really looked before. I don't like looking people in the eye. I saw now that they were that really warm shade of brown, like wood stain when it's still wet and glittery and you can see all the layers of the grain for the first time, almost like you can see right through them like the faces of a diamond. I looked into all those layers and I just kept falling and falling and falling...

"Bailey," he said, and I fell a little slower. "There is no better place for Tommy in the world than right here. They're going to take good care of him. The best. But he needs us, too. He needs to know he's surrounded by the people who care about him."

Okay, but that was the problem. It would be fine if "the people who cared about him" meant, like, his wife and kids and grandkids and all. But this was *me.* I'd made the *mistake* of caring about him. Just like I'd made the mistake of caring about Jason Thomlin, even if it was only for an hour or so. And now there Jason was in a coffin and here Tommy was in a hospital. The cosmos couldn't be any clearer than that—except of course to let Tommy die, too. Whoever ran the universe was suspending Tommy by a thread over an abyss while staring me significantly in the eye, the way your foster parents do when you can make a good choice or a bad one and they don't feel the need to tell you which is which.

I was receiving a warning this time. A very lucky warning. I should be as far away as possible. It was probably the only way to save Tommy's life. Yet here I was. Because I couldn't quit caring about him.

Ryan laid a hand gently but firmly on my shoulder and reached for the curtain.

Oh God, this was it. I screwed my eyes shut and waited for the earth to explode. But it didn't.

Instead, curtain rings clinked together as they slid across a rod. Air swished across my face and heavy folds of fabric sighed as they piled together. Ryan squeezed my shoulder a little tighter and nudged me forward. I slid my feet across the tile floor. Sensed the door frame pass my left ear. Felt a tiny shift in the sound of our footsteps as we left the big, open hall and entered a small, enclosed room. The curtain rings clinked behind us again.

My whole body trembled. I told it to quit. Ryan would feel it. He'd know I was scared. But I didn't know how to make the shaking stop.

For a moment, I was too afraid to open my eyes. But Ryan would be mad if I didn't. So I did. I blinked and looked at Tommy.

I didn't realize I knew him. His face was gray and limp, as if the soul had gone out of him. Tubes and wires moored him to machines like a boat to a pier, as if to keep him from drifting out to open water because he was in no way seaworthy right now. Up at the repair docks. Only it was the captain this time and not the boat.

My throat tied into a knot. Not the kind you could slip loose with a flick of the wrist; the wrong kind, like the first time I'd tried to tie up the Mailboat and Tommy had to tell me I wasn't doing it right.

This couldn't be the Mailboat captain.

One of the machines chirped softly and regularly, like a weathered old pier that creaked and groaned with the washing of the waves while the boats bumped against it. In fact, I could see the waves, a long green line of peaks and troughs on a black screen. They were so tall, yet never broke into whitecaps. Just rocked the pier and the boats back and forth, eliciting a little squeak each time. The small sound washed over me again and again, until, to my surprise, I thought I could hear it talking to me. Not in words, but in feelings. Comfort. Security. And something I'd never felt before. I think people call it love.

It was the sound of Tommy's heart, filling the entire room. I closed my eyes. Pictured myself curled up on the bow of the Mailboat. Felt the glossy paint against my cheek and the warm sunshine as the boat rocked back and forth. I felt the wind on my face—a Geneva Lake wind, the purest air in the world, so clean it smelled like the dawn of life itself. As his heart beat, I felt Tommy's presence all around me. Warm. Safe. I wished I could stand here like this forever.

Only I couldn't. I'd never been able to stay anywhere forever. And it sucked. My moor lines slipped every damn time. They were never knotted at all, right or wrong.

"Go ahead," Ryan whispered. "Let him know you're here."

Didn't he know already? I wished Tommy could feel me cocooned inside his heart. I could feel it, and it was so real.

"What if I'm not supposed to wake him up?" I whispered.

"Just talk to him," Ryan replied. "He doesn't have to wake up to hear your voice."

What was I supposed to say? What *was* there to say? The things I felt—they didn't have words. Language fell to the side, as useless as a broken oar.

I crept forward. Touched the railing on the side of the bed. Looked into Tommy's face and waited for inspiration to strike, but it didn't. I couldn't talk out loud. But I had plenty to say in my head.

I'm sorry, Tommy. I'm so sorry I loved you. I'm trying to stop, but it's so hard. You have to come back to the Mailboat. You have to be there for always. I couldn't stand it if you weren't there anymore and it was all my fault.

My hand twisted around the railing. This was all wrong. I shouldn't be here. Maybe it wasn't a railing in my hand at all. Maybe it was a moor line. And maybe I should just let it go. Maybe I should just tell Ryan everything and move on to my next foster home.

Tommy's eyelids twitched. His chest rose in a deep breath. I glanced at Ryan, but for once, he was the one who watched and said nothing, like a seasoned mariner studying the weather.

Tommy's eyelids fluttered open, just barely. At first they stared blankly ahead. Then they shifted to me. They were hazy. Distant. As if they saw nothing. But a moment later they changed, came alive, like a shaft of light breaking through clouds, and I knew he saw me.

He tried to speak but his lips barely moved.

"What did you say?" I asked, my voice a little feather.

He didn't reply. Just breathed several times and stared at me down that single shaft of light. Slowly, he rolled his hand over, palm up, fingers open.

I looked at his hand. Then Ryan. But he was still the silent mariner, staring over the sea.

This was my call. Only I didn't want to make it. I wanted to comb the world over for some other Bailey. Because every time this Bailey fell for the idea that somebody cared, it all backfired. The last time I'd held somebody's hand, I was like six, and where was that family now? Oregon or something. And they hadn't taken me with. Where was anybody who had ever held me or given me a hug? Gone somewhere. Where was my mom? Dead. She'd left me nothing but the memory of her name, Kalli. Where was my dad? Never gave a damn about me in the first place.

If I took Tommy's hand now, they may as well order his headstone. 'Cause that's just what happened to people in my life. They either left or they died.

"Bailey?"

I almost hadn't heard Tommy over the thunderhead of my own thoughts. But when the sound of his voice finally sank in, the storm rumbled into a harmless, steady rain. "Yeah?" I asked.

"Give me your hand," he whispered. His palm was still upturned. Waiting.

Tears blurred my eyes. That's what he'd said on the boat. When I was too scared to help him. And now I was refusing again. I had to. I couldn't risk caring about him. He would die if I did.

I kept my hands firmly on the rail.

Ryan shifted from foot to foot, groaned a little as if making up his mind, then slid toward me. As gently as if he were picking up a fallen bird, he slipped his fingers under my wrist and placed my hand in Tommy's. With our three hands clasped together, he gave a squeeze.

Tommy's fingers curled around mine. His eyes closed and his head settled back into the pillow.

A tear ran down my cheek.

"It's okay, Bailey," Ryan said, letting go. My hand was now alone in Tommy's. "He wants to know you're here."

The tears fell faster. No, no, no. This was all wrong. It was too dangerous. The curse was lurking, waiting to take Tommy away. I knew it was, and yet I couldn't resist the temptation it offered. Like an angry, screaming siren, it shrieked at me, a hapless sailor too enamored by the siren's beauty to save myself. *Tommy cares about you, little love,* she crooned. *He asked for you. He wanted to hold your hand. Now come a little closer so I can drown you...*

I gave in to her threats and temptations. I squeezed Tommy's hand tight and let the tears stream down— knowing it meant he would leave me in the end.

They always did.

CHAPTER SIXTEEN
LAKE GENEVA, 1951

Hands stuffed in his pockets, Roland stormed down the sidewalk kicking a tin can. The label had fallen off several blocks ago—something about vegetable soup. He'd left the scrap of paper in the gutter to bleach. Bared now to the bright summer sun, the can clattered across the concrete as he kicked it and kicked it and kicked it again. He was supposed to be out on the lake right now, wind and sunshine and spray in his hair. His dad had promised to take him sailing this afternoon.

But he hadn't.

"I'm sorry," his mom had said, trying to shoo him out of the house before her ladies' club arrived for tea. "Dad had to stay at the office. He'll come to the lake tomorrow. Now go find something to do, will you?" And she slammed the big white door in his face with all its curlicue molding, leaving Roland alone under the soaring pillars that flanked the porch.

He'd wandered down the lake shore and all the way into town, finding no one but the tin can for company. Why did they even *have* such a big house? Two of them, to boot—one here and one in Chicago. Every corner echoed with loneliness.

So Dad had to stay in town. It wasn't the first time Roland had heard that excuse. *We'll go sailing together tomorrow. We'll go to the fair together tomorrow. We'll do everything together... tomorrow.*

Roland stood over his tin can and scowled, his face heating. He took his hands out of his pockets and clenched them into fists. "Why do I ever believe you!" he yelled.

He gave the can an almighty kick, sending it skittering over the sidewalk. It landed in the grass on the edge of the schoolyard. He stormed after it, hoping he'd put a big, fat dent in it.

He turned it in the grass with his foot. It was still perfectly round and shiny, though scratched. Rats. He lifted his foot and stomped on it, making it dance all over the sidewalk but failing to crumple it. Why did they have to make cans so strong?

The sound of kids drew his attention. He was at the baseball diamond. It was that lousy Tommy Thomlin and his crew. They were forming up their teams, Tommy and another boy calling out names one by one.

Roland wanted to punch them all.

"Wade's on my team!" Thomlin announced.

The kids cheered and slapped the little runt on the back as he ran through them to join Tommy. Tommy tousled the top of his head, tipping his cap sideways, and handed him a bat. Wade straightened his cap, then tapped the bat against his toes like he was a pro at the big leagues—even though he was only half as tall as the other boys. Why did Thomlin even hang out with that infant?

Roland's stomach roiled at the memory of Tommy punching him in the nose just last week. Thomlin had humiliated him. And when Roland had told his dad, the old man only scolded him for getting into fights and ruining a sweater.

He balled his fists again. He should march over there and punch Tommy back and throw sand in all their faces. But they might gang up on him. Maybe he'd wait. Find Tommy alone sometime. Roland would bring his cronies and teach that kid a lesson he'd never forget.

Tommy looked up and saw him standing at the edge of the park. The skinny young umpire seated the ball in his glove. "Hey! You wanna play ball?"

Roland gawked, questioning his hearing. "Huh?"

Tommy adjusted his stance and his cap, impatient. "I said, you wanna play ball?"

Roland squared up his shoulders and sneered. "Why would I want to play ball with *you?*"

"Cuz, Billy's team's short a player. Can you catch?"

"Sure I can catch." He wasn't about to let anyone call his ball playing skills into question.

"Can you run?"

"Better'n any of you."

"Think you can tag out this guy?" Tommy grinned mischievously and tousled Wade's hair again.

Roland took that as an insult. Baby-Face Shorty? He had to be joking. "Don't make me laugh, Thomlin."

"Then prove it to me. I dare ya to tag Wade out."

Tommy tossed the ball across the lawn. Roland was unprepared but managed to catch it before it bopped him in the chest. He looked down at the scuffed white ball and its red stitching. What should he do with it? Throw it in the dirt and march away? Steal it?

He eyed little Wade Erickson and another plan came to mind. Maybe he should join their stupid game. Maybe this would be a good way to get his revenge—without risking any of them beating the daylights out of him. He would simply embarrass their pet runt at baseball. He'd watched them before. They played like little kids. But he knew how to play for real—he was on the team at his private school back in the city—and he would show no mercy.

"You in?" Tommy prompted.

Roland eyed him confidently. "On one condition."

"Name it."

"I play shortstop."

An outburst of protest arose from both teams. Shortstop was no throw-away position. Most of the balls that collided with a bat would head his way. Clearly, they didn't trust an outsider with such an important role.

"Why should I let you?" Billy demanded, captain of the other team.

"'Cuz I'm the best darn shortstop you've ever seen, that's why," Roland shot back. "It's shortstop or nothing."

The kids continued to grumble. "Get our ball back! Get him out of here!"

Roland scowled, fury boiling up in his chest. "You want your ball back? Fine!"

He pitched it to Tommy. Hard. Tommy threw his glove up just in time. It sank into the leather with a smack. The kids stared at their leader, silent. Slowly, making sure all the kids were watching, Tommy peeled off the glove and shook the sting out of his hand. He was smiling.

"Let him play shortstop, Billy," he said, a twinkle in his eye.

Billy frowned. Roland had proved he could pitch, but clearly the kid still had reservations. Tommy winked and jerked his head toward Wade. A knowing grin spread across Billy's face. The rest of the players began to smile and nod, elbowing each other in the ribs.

Roland wondered if he'd made a mistake. What did they know that he didn't? Wade was on Tommy's team; how would that help Billy? But it was too late to change his mind. He'd made the challenge. He'd never back out now and give them fodder to torment him all summer long.

Billy stared at Roland. "All right, Markham. Shortstop it is."

He tossed him a glove. Roland caught it.

"But," Billy added, raising a finger, "you miss one ball and you're in right field. Understood?"

Roland sneered. "Right field is for pansies." He sank his hand into the glove. "I'm not a pansy."

Roland turned and took his position between second and third base. Billy stood on the pitcher's mound. The game began.

The first two balls that came Roland's way, he caught as easily as if he had a magnet in his glove. He scooped them off the ground and shot them to first base, kicking Tommy's runners off the diamond before they knew what happened. Roland's teammates cheered. He'd made good on his boast. He was greased lightning and precise as a Swiss watch. Well, he should be. Roland's school was known for its demanding standards, both in the classroom and on the sports field.

Two of his runners out, Tommy peeled off his cap and seated it over his blond hair again, frowning over his selection of batters on the bench. Then he turned and caught Roland's eye from across the field with a sly grin. He slapped Baby-Face Shorty's shoulder and motioned him toward the plate. Roland laughed as Wade trotted off with a bat that was too big for him. Tommy was trusting the inning to a baby? This was a joke.

"Hey, Shorty!" Roland yelled from across the diamond. "Do ya think you can hit the ball this far?"

Wade ignored him and stood over the plate. Hefting the bat over his shoulder, he gave it a couple of gangly swings, then tapped the plate as if he had a career with the pros. Roland snickered. Tommy was obviously too soft to kick a little kid off the team.

Billy stepped a little closer to home plate and threw the ball underhanded, letting it sail slowly like a baby robin. Roland nearly laughed his head off. Despite the easy "pitch," little Wade missed it by a mile.

"Strike one!" Tommy called from behind the catcher, playing umpire again. As always, no one questioned his bias, and so far he hadn't given Roland reason to, either. Only his sanity.

Billy tossed the second ball. The force of Wade's swing and the weight of the bat nearly spun him in a circle. But enthusiasm didn't make up for accuracy. The ball plopped into the catcher's glove.

"Strike two!" Tommy called.

"C'mon, Shorty!" Roland taunted, socking his fist in his glove. "He's giving them to you. Put it right in here. Give me a chance to put you out!"

"Just keep your eye on the ball, Wade," Tommy coached.

Wade let the bat dangle at his side and stomped his foot, staring tiny daggers at the pitcher. "I can't hit those, Billy! Give me a real ball!"

Billy laughed and shrugged. "Okay, Shorty."

He stood in the middle of his mound. Wade wiped his nose on his sleeve and lifted the bat over his shoulder. Billy coiled into a tight pose and watched the catcher's signals. He shook his head. Shook his head. Nodded. He slid his foot back. Threw out his arm. His fingers were positioned for a fast ball. It flew at Shorty Wade Erickson like lightning. Roland braced, hoping Wade would drop the bat and run. A ball like that would break his arm.

Crack.

Hide connected with wood and the ball shot into the air. Roland's jaw dropped. How could a scrawny kid like that launch a ball so high? He and the third baseman circled the ground, waiting for the ball to come down. Out of the corner of his eye, Roland saw Wade pass first base.

The ball kept drifting toward the outfield. "Mine! Mine!" called the left fielder, a girl with bright red braids.

But Roland kept running backwards, keeping his eye on the target. That little girl would never be able to catch this one. It was coming down too fast. "I got it! I got it!" he shouted, holding up his glove as the ball zoomed to earth.

It sank into the leather with a satisfying *thud*.

A body collided into Roland's back. He and the red-haired girl tumbled into the grass, arms and legs tangled. The ball popped out of Roland's glove and streaked across the field.

Wade's team screamed with delight. "Dropped ball! Dropped ball! Run, Shorty! Run!"

"I said it was mine!" the girl complained, rubbing her head. Her face twisted into a pout.

Baby-Face Shorty streaked past second base.

"Get off me!" Roland shoved her away and chased after the escaped ball. He landed face-down in the grass. His glove clamped over the ball, finally bringing it to a halt. He moved it to his pitching hand and looked up. Wade Erickson was already flying over third and his teammates were yelling, "Home run! Home run!" Roland pushed himself to one knee and threw the ball toward home plate and the catcher.

Time slowed. Both the ball and Shorty Wade Erickson sailed towards home. The catcher crouched with one foot on the plate, the other stretched forward toward the ball, his glove wide open. Shorty threw his legs out in front of him and went in for the slide.

His shoe hit the plate.

The ball sank into the catcher's glove.

"Safe!" Tommy yelled, throwing his arms out wide.

The kids erupted into cheers—both the team on the bench and the team in the field. Caps flew into the air. Players abandoned their posts. The whole lot of them ran to home and mobbed Shorty Wade Erickson.

Roland was left alone, still on his hands and knees. "I don't believe it!" he exclaimed, his jaw slack.

And it was true. He'd never seen a faster runner. Granted, he'd made mistakes with the ball. But for Shorty to make it all the way home? He forgot to be furious. He was simply amazed. And suddenly he felt like an idiot, all by himself on the edge of the diamond while the other kids swarmed their hero. He felt as if he were at home, listening to the empty echoes of a big house on the lake.

He pushed himself to his feet and joined the other kids. They slapped Wade on the back. The bigger boys lifted him onto their shoulders and chanted, "Shorty the Dash! Shorty the Dash! Can't tag him out—Shorty's a flash!"

Tommy watched the celebration and smiled, lifting his cap and settling it down again over his sandy blond hair. "Pity you dropped the ball, Roland. That would have been a perfect catch."

"What?" Roland asked, surprised to hear Tommy talking to him. When the words sank in, Roland was even more surprised to realize that Tommy was complimenting him on his play, even though he was from the opposing team. He blushed a little and shoved his hands into his pockets. "Aw, it was nothing. Wade scored that home run fair and square. You're right—he's pretty fast."

"Where'd you learn to catch so good?"

Roland stirred the gravel with his foot. "We have a pitching machine at school." He knew the real answer should have been that he played catch in the yard with his dad all the time. It wasn't like their yard wasn't big enough.

"Oh," Tommy said. "That's pretty swell." But he said it more like a condolence. He turned to him, his gray eyes bright as silver, his freckles smiling as much as his face. "You havin' fun?"

"Yeah," Roland admitted, eyebrows lifting. Way more fun than taking out his fury on tin cans and fuming about his dad—though he wasn't going to admit that to Tommy.

"You should play with us more often," Tommy said. "You're really good. Our rookie players could learn a lot watching you."

Roland frowned uncertainly. "You think?"

"Absolutely. Soon as Billy lets you out of right field." He winked.

Roland stared at him, realization slowly dawning that he would, indeed, be stuck in right field. To his surprise, he laughed. It *was* kind of funny.

"By the way, sorry about the other day," Tommy went on. "I hope your nose is all right."

"Aw, that was nothin'. I've had worse." In fact, he hadn't. He couldn't remember ever bleeding before in his life, beyond a scraped knee. But he didn't want Tommy to think he was a wimp.

Tommy stuck out his hand. "Pals?"

Roland stared at the offered hand. Was this for real? An hour ago, he would have spit in Tommy's eye. But in that moment, he realized why Billy had agreed to let him play shortstop. Because he and Tommy and the other kids were one team, not two. One team against Roland. Tommy had convinced his players to demonstrate that their little homegrown batter and runner Wade Erickson was twice the player Roland was, never mind all his big-city schooling and coaching. It had been the Lake Geneva Team against Roland—and they had won.

And now that they'd proved their point, Tommy was offering him the hand of friendship. A place on their team. Forgiveness for all past offenses. Roland struggled to admit how much he wanted that. Maybe those marble halls wouldn't echo so lonely if he had a friend over now and again.

He shrugged, hoping to look nonchalant. "Sure," he said. "Pals."

And they shook on it.

CHAPTER SEVENTEEN
ROLAND

✵

Sixty-three years later, Roland could still hear the laughter of boys running between sand bags, the crack of ball on bat. He could feel the gritty dirt press into his knees as he dove for the catch. Surely it had only been yesterday...

He swirled the ice cubes and orange twist in his Old Fashioned and stared out the picture windows of the Lake Geneva Country Club. The view over the lake was remarkable this afternoon—the piers a shining white, the sky and water both such a clear, bright blue as to challenge any artist's ability to capture it. His wooden runabout, a deep russet red, glowed in its slip below, one of a scant few watercraft tied to the country club piers today. Despite the fine weather, not many of his neighbors were taking advantage of the links. In fact, he alone occupied the dining room. It was just as well. He hadn't come here to socialize but to ruminate—and apparently to keep his distance from someone intending to kill him. It seemed like a ridiculous notion. But he imagined Monica Steele would kill him herself if she found him at home just now.

Since 1895, the year the club had been founded, this place had been as much a part of Roland's family history as the lake itself, going back three generations. Membership was highly selective, based primarily on your annual income, and any gentleman walking in without a proper shirt collar would be invited into his own private dressing room to change into something more appropriate. As relaxing as he found the club nowadays, he'd hated it as a boy. His parents rubbed shoulders with influential lake citizens, forming vital business connections while largely ignoring young Roland, unless it was to tell him to stop fidgeting in his chair.

He'd preferred to be on the baseball diamond with Tommy and Wade, or sailing the catamaran he had when they were teens. They'd lived under the summer sun, Roland and Wade going tan while Tommy's freckles deepened.

Tommy had given Roland an irreplaceable gift the day he'd thrown a ball into his hands and invited him to join the team: friendship and a childhood he could look back on with fondness. But that had always been Tommy's way, to extend a hand where none else was to be found. Forced into the role of man-of-the-house at an early age, Tommy had never had a proper boyhood himself. Yet he'd risen to every occasion.

It was impossible to think he wouldn't rise to this one. Now he lay in a hospital bed in Milwaukee, the victim of some lunatic's whim. And here Roland sat at the country club at the orders of police to abandon his own home. Lake Geneva had rejected friendship, youth, and happiness in exchange for bedlam. If events continued so, Roland feared life at the lake could approach a harrowing new brink, and the drop of a feather could tip it over the edge. Would the innocent and idyllic Lake Geneva everyone knew and loved survive?

Roland imagined he should pay Tommy a visit. But it had been years since they'd talked properly, beyond a brief hello as Tommy dropped off his mail. Roland had never thought poorly of his childhood friend. They'd simply grown apart—largely because, at some point, Tommy had been forced to choose sides: Roland or Wade. The rift had been that deep. But Roland had never begrudged Tommy his choice. Wade was like the brother Tommy had lost.

Roland adjusted his glasses and turned his musings again to the book in his lap, a biography of J. Robert Oppenheimer. He'd picked up a copy at the local library, spurred on by his new little project: Jimmy Beacon, the frustrated young scientist who would soon be entering his junior year at Badger High. Lucky thing Roland had stopped the troubled young man from blowing up his pier—a clear attempt to draw attention to himself and the broken world he struggled to live in. The boy reminded Roland all too much of himself as a lad: lost and alone. He needed shaping, that was all. Akin to the way Tommy had shaped Roland. The boy had so much potential...

Young Jimmy made no secret of his admiration for Oppenheimer, the brilliant theoretical physicist who had spearheaded the development of the world's first atomic bomb. Now, reading about the scientist's early life, Roland had no trouble seeing why Jimmy identified with him. Too brilliant for his peers, Oppenheimer had been an outcast, all the while craving their approval and recognition. Not unlike Jimmy.

Oppenheimer had ended a war that would have dragged on for years, and thus made his place in history. It had yet to be determined what young Jimmy could accomplish. With any luck, Roland could play a hand in the shaping of the boy's life.

"Roland?"

He looked up and saw Detective Monica Steele crossing the empty dining room toward him.

"Ah, Monica," he said. "Do join me." He folded his book and stood to pull out a chair for her.

Instead, she dropped into the one next to it and propped her elbows on the table, massaging her forehead. Roland paused awkwardly. He didn't imagine her slight was intentional. She seemed highly distracted. And come to think of it, had any of her male co-workers ever drawn a chair for her, she probably would have taken it as an insult.

To cover for the social faux pas, Roland assumed the empty chair himself. "Can I get you anything?" He observed her uniform—a black polo shirt and tan slacks. A badge and her service weapon were clipped to her belt. "You're on duty, of course. A soda water?"

She shrugged and tilted an eyebrow, as if forced to accept pleasantries foisted upon her. Meanwhile, she toppled over the linen napkin in front of her, which had been folded like a fan, and fidgeted with the hem.

Roland lifted his hand and called for the waiter. "James, a soda water for the lady," he said.

James nodded and hustled off to the bar.

"Well," Roland continued, folding his hands on the table and staring at Monica intently. He lowered his voice somberly. "How is he?"

She nodded, looking only half alive. "He came out of surgery okay." She quirked her mouth. "Now we wait."

"What was he able to tell you?"

"Nothing."

"Nothing at all?"

"Nothing that made sense. The medical gurus have him on every drug out of the pharmacy. It'll be a while before he can talk sense."

Roland nodded, his stomach sinking. "I see." He drummed the cover of his book angrily. "It infuriates me, Tommy being dragged into this. A better soul never graced our shores. He doesn't deserve this."

Monica looked up at him with bland eyes. "Roland, did you ever get your security cameras fixed?"

Before Fritz Geissler's body had been dumped at his pier a little over a week ago, the perpetrator had spray painted the lenses on all of Roland's security cameras. "The company's coming out Monday," he said.

"You have an alarm system?"

"Naturally. It comes on at nine every evening."

"You lock your doors?"

"Also automatic." He grinned. "An old man can't be expected to remember everything."

"Reset the system for twenty-four seven," Monica said. "I want your doors and windows locked and guarded around the clock."

As Roland stared at her, James set a glass in front of Monica, a lime slice seated on the rim. "Anything else?" James asked with a professional smile. A college student from the nearby town of Burlington, he'd mastered the old-fashioned customs and formality that reigned supreme at the Lake Geneva Country Club. The lad was a natural here.

Monica ripped open the lime and bit off one of the sections with her teeth, then dropped the remainder into her glass. She chewed without so much as acknowledging the waiter.

Roland tapped his book, then smiled up at James. "That'll be all, I think."

James nodded, bowed, and walked away, hiding a grin that looked uncomfortable—probably for Roland's sake. Beneath it, the boy appeared bemused.

"We're sending extra patrols past your house," Monica said. She eyed him sharply. "But we can't babysit you, Roland. We don't have manpower for that. Get those goddamn cameras fixed. See if the company can come out today. Or get a handyman and a can of paint thinner, dammit. Or leave town for a while." She drew circles in the air with her glass, her eyes glazed and distant. "There must be some vacation to Europe you've been planning."

Roland held up his hands to slow her down. "Monica, Monica... It's all right."

"No, it's not." She thunked her glass down on top of her crumpled napkin, sloshing soda water. "That's the part you don't seem to get. There's a killer running around here, Roland, bent on wiping out anyone remotely connected to the Markham Ring. It wasn't good enough to kill off the two surviving members; they're targeting next-of-kin, too. Why? What do you know?"

Roland stared at her, hurt. She was usually more tactful than this. *Markham Ring.* The sound of his own name—his son's name—attached to that atrocious business stung him like daggers. The implication—accusation more like—that he knew anything stung almost as deeply.

"Nothing, Monica," he said. "I know nothing. And that's where the problem always lay. Bobby was running around carrying off intricately-planned, high-end bank burglaries. And I didn't know. Because I didn't know Bobby. I didn't know my own son. I became my father, too busy with my own success to give a mind to my own flesh and blood. And now we are where we are." He breathed deeply and sighed. "Ultimately I suppose I'm to blame for everything."

Monica stuck her fingers into her glass, pulled out the lime, and bit off another section. "You won't do any good beating yourself up, Roland," she said, rolling the sour fruit around on her tongue.

"Well, neither will you," he replied.

She lifted bleary eyes to look at him.

"You take this all very personally, Monica. This is your town and you feel responsible for it. I suppose you and I both must learn to let lie what can't be amended."

Monica tossed back a drink of soda water as if it were hard alcohol and rose from the table. "You're right. But there's a lot I *can* do, and I don't mean to sit around letting moss grow on my rear." Eyes dramatically wide, she grinned like a lunatic and waved her hands about.

"Everyone seems to think this is still the quiet, idyllic, goddamn paradise it used to be. Well guess what: It isn't. Now if you'll excuse me, I've got a killer to catch." She walked across the dining room. "Hire yourself a fucking security guard, Markham," she called over her shoulder.

Roland lifted his eyebrows. Across the room at the bar, James turned his back to hide laughter while shelving tumblers.

Turning back to Oppenheimer, Roland shook his head and slipped on his glasses. As he found his page, he reminded himself it might not be wise to invite Monica Steele to dinner here with his lakeside peers—unless he intended to shock them with Bohemian language and manners.

SATURDAY
JUNE 28, 2014

CHAPTER EIGHTEEN
JIMMY

Jimmy Beacon paced up and down the Mailboat pier, trying to screw up his courage.

"Think with the heart," he muttered as the weathered boards creaked beneath his sneakers. "Tell her how you feel. How you feel *inside*."

He recited the expressions as if he were studying for a test. It was Roland Markham who had challenged him to cease thinking with the head—a nerve wracking proposition—and attempt to think with the heart. Seeking further explanation, Jimmy had turned to his fellow student and generally-acknowledged nice guy, Noah Cadigan. It was this young scholar who had proposed what Jimmy decided to label the Cadiganian Variation: To call a halt to his numerous experiments designed to impress Bailey and simply tell her how he felt.

Jimmy had spent the past three days since that conversation entrapped in excruciating turmoil, spending his nights staring at the glow-in-the-dark planetary stickers that had clung to his bedroom ceiling since he was five. Seeking direction, he had cast his glance between the glossy-printed gazes of Galileo, Einstein, Edison, and

110

Oppenheimer. But for the first time in Jimmy's life, none of them had offered inspiration.

He'd penned a dozen manifestos of his love. In them, he compared Bailey's unadorned beauty to the simplicity of E=mc2, her complexity to the theory of the multiverse, the way she made his head spin to the unpredictable behavior of an electron. But nothing he wrote came close to expressing what he felt. What he meant.

In the end, he'd decided to suck it up and wing it. Maybe inspiration would strike in the moment.

There was only one problem. She wasn't currently on the schedule at the Geneva Bar and Grill where she worked as a waitress and he as a dishwasher. So he'd resorted to her other job at the Mailboat. But it was 12:46 p.m., sixteen minutes past the time the boat was scheduled to return from its morning tour, and it still wasn't there. Just as peculiar, there was no one in queue behind the ropes, no one awaiting its next tour.

Tired of waiting, Jimmy turned on his heel and faced the boat moored on the other side of the pier, a gleaming white yacht with a single long deck and a cabin in the center—one of the old fashioned vessels the millionaires of the 19th century used to steam around in. Kids his age wearing red tee shirts and navy or white shorts bustled back and forth with tables, chairs, and plates of hors d'oeuvres, perhaps preparing the boat for a charter. In the midst of the activity, he spied an older gentleman, heavy-set and bald with important-looking but militarily inaccurate shoulder boards on his white button-down shirt. Embroidery over the pocket said *Captain Ben.*

Jimmy stood on the edge of the pier, his toes sticking out over the water, and spoke across the boat's railing. He clasped his hands behind his back. "Excuse me, sir. Where is the Mailboat?"

The man planted a clipboard on his hip and stuck a pen over his ear. "Sorry, tours on the Mailboat are canceled until Monday."

"Canceled?" Jimmy repeated. How could that be? He'd studied the schedule in detail. The boat clearly ran three times per day, every day—mail deliveries in the morning and regular sightseeing tours in the afternoon.

"Did you have a reservation?" the man asked. "We're happy to reschedule your tour or refund your tickets."

"What? No," Jimmy replied, his mind scrambling. He'd spent days working up to this. What was he supposed to do now?

Jimmy glanced over the young cruise line employees. "Uh... I don't suppose Bailey Johnson is here?" His heart pounded. It was one thing to ask for the Mailboat. It was another to ask for Bailey specifically. He'd had no intentions of speaking from his heart to a random old man, yet here he was: He'd as much as admitted that Bailey Johnson was the love of his life.

"I don't think she's here," the man replied. He turned to one of the kids. "Is Bailey here today?" he asked.

A girl with dark skin shook her head of exceptionally curly black hair and kicked out the legs of a folding table. "She's off until Monday—next Mailboat tour."

The old man shrugged at Jimmy. "Monday, I guess."

"Oh." Jimmy rocked on his heels. Well, this was remarkably inconvenient. Perhaps he could show up at her house, but he didn't know where she lived. With Bud Weber, of course. Wherever that was. Jimmy was quite sure he didn't want to know. Weber never failed to infuse him with the sensation colloquially referred to as "the creeps."

Other alternatives for opening his heart to Bailey: He could edit one of his fifteen-page manifestos and send it in a text...

"Can I pass along a message?" the man asked, interrupting Jimmy's concentration.

Jimmy's face flushed red-hot. "No," he said shortly. And then he turned on his heel and scurried away before the boat captain could propose anything even more embarrassing.

Great. It had taken him three days to accumulate the courage for this. And now he had to start from the beginning? This was too much work. Maybe he'd just go home to his laboratory and bury his head in flurries of engineer's paper. Design a new spacecraft. A new nuclear plant.

Maybe he'd go back to his designs for the Backfire Model, his alpha project, the bomb of all bombs—at least amongst those he'd designed and detonated himself. Jimmy had unleashed so many explosive devices against an undisclosed derelict barn that there was now no barn at all. The Backfire, however, was not designed for demolition.

It existed for but one purpose: Devastation.

CHAPTER NINETEEN
BAILEY

———— ❁ ————

The chair in Tommy's hospital room—the one I was sitting in—looked like it was trying to be denim, only it was green. And it wasn't denim. It was some kind of vinyl, and it left me wondering why in the world anyone would cover a chair in fake green denim. Also, why did I care?

Probably because Tommy's heart monitor had been beeping in my ear, over and over like a dirge that never ended, for three days running. I heard it in my sleep now. And then I'd wake up with tears on my pillow and a desperate plea that the beeping would never stop, even though it was driving me crazy.

For three days in a row now, Ryan had picked me up after his shift and driven me all the way to Froedtert. "I'll text you when I'm off," he'd messaged this morning. He just took our routine for granted now. Thank God. I think I would have died if I'd had to stay in Lake Geneva. Waiting. Wondering.

So I came here and sat with my hands in my lap and listened to Tommy's heart *beep... beep... beep...*

He rarely opened his eyes. Almost never spoke. When he did, it made no sense. He'd been really adamant

114

yesterday that we needed an accurate count of the ducks on the lake. I'd promised him I would get it. So I'd spent last night counting ducks. Six—though those were only the ones I'd seen from the railing overlooking the swimming beach and the Mailboat pier. If I hadn't been coming to the hospital again today, maybe I would have walked the entire Lake Shore Path and counted every duck in sight.

"Don't forget to talk to him," Ryan had told me just now as he left to speak with the doctor. "He needs to hear your voice."

So I talked to him. Only I couldn't drum up the courage to use my outside voice. So I used my inside voice, rambling the way I used to when Tommy and I were swabbing decks and sorting mail.

You know the strings of white lights on the boat that we turn on at night? I said silently as I sat in the chair with the fake green denim and looked into Tommy's sleeping face. *They look so quiet and peaceful, all glowy and everything, and the reflection sort of twinkles in the water, like a fairy dropped a load of stardust in the lake. I think it's one of the prettiest things I've ever seen.*

But the Mailboat isn't there now. It's up in Williams Bay, getting repairs. I know it'll be back soon, and all the other tour boats are there, of course. But it makes me really sad not to see it. It's always there. Just like you. It's like you're two sides of the same coin.

His face didn't change. My unspoken words had no impact on him. Just as I had no impact on him.

I'm just one of your mail girls, I said. *One of hundreds. I'm sure you barely know I exist.*

I love you, Tommy.

I shouldn't have said that.

My hands toyed with a ball chain necklace. From the end dangled a tiny silver helm. I didn't know why Tommy's son Jason had given it to me, moments before he died. I didn't know why I wanted so badly to keep it. Why I wanted so bad to belong to Tommy...

This was stupid. I shouldn't keep coming here. I'd been fighting with myself this whole time about what to do. And while it killed me, I thought I finally knew the answer. I should tell Ryan not to bring me back tomorrow. These last three days at Tommy's bedside could count as my goodbye. And then I should tell Ryan about Bud—everything about Bud. How he yelled at me, how he hurt me, how he maybe killed Tommy's son. And in doing so I would blow to bits everything that had been beautiful in my life. Ryan would take me to county social services in Elkhorn, where the case workers would make frantic phone calls to already overcrowded foster homes, trying to find me a new placement. Then Ryan would drive straight to Lake Geneva and throw Bud in handcuffs. And I'd never see Lake Geneva again. Or the Mailboat. Or Tommy.

It was time.

My heart cried inside.

I opened my lips, trying to find the courage to use my outside voice. To tell Tommy that I'd never forget him. I took one last look at the silver helm. I should leave it with him. Even though I wanted desperately to take it with me.

All of a sudden, Tommy took a deep, long breath, his chest rising and falling slowly. He stirred, and his eyelids fluttered.

I sat on the edge of my chair and froze.

CHAPTER TWENTY
TOMMY

I woke exhausted, as if I'd been asleep a thousand years. I half fought my way to the surface, half drifted, gradually finding connection with all my senses. First came the general realization that I had been asleep and was now waking. Then came auditory feedback—a distant beep wafting to my ears. Slowly it grew louder, closer. I didn't know what it was, but knew I should find out.

I forced my eyes open.

A tan shower curtain. At least, that's what it looked like. At second blink, I noticed it spanned a full wall. So no, it wasn't a shower curtain.

Where was I? Clearly not at home. I didn't know any room with a tan curtain.

Voices echoed in the background, hollow and hushed, as if wandering through a nursery full of sleeping children. The air was sickeningly sweet, the unique blend of illness and the various chemicals used to tidy up after it. I knew what it meant—*where* it meant—but couldn't grasp the words; words that should have been obvious and easy.

I hurt. Deep in my side. Every breath ached. At the same time, I felt as groggy as a sailor after a night ashore.

Someone was staring at me. Carefully, I twisted my head to the left. A girl with a wavy brown ponytail was perched on the edge of a chair, her eyes wide, her mouth slightly open as if she'd stopped breathing.

I parted dry lips and forced sound out of my rusty throat. "Bailey?" It hurt to speak, as if I'd swallowed broken glass.

She emptied her lungs with a rush. She really had been holding her breath. The expression of suspended animation was replaced with a brilliant smile. Sparkling eyes. "Hi," she breathed.

I glanced over my surroundings again. A bed with railings. A long counter and cupboards with a sink. A tall, wheeled rack with machines and equipment. Realization finally dawned, the words I'd been groping for finally coming to me. A hospital room. My hospital room. How had I gotten here? I tried to remember what happened, but it was like trying to capture a dream that had already vanished. What little came to mind was fleeting, abandoning me as quickly as it came.

"What happened?" I asked.

Her eyebrows dipped. "What do you mean?"

I closed my eyes again, irked. I was too exhausted to play ring-around-a-rosy. How had I ended up in a hospital? A simple explanation shouldn't be so much to ask for. Then again, it was hard to tell what Bailey considered obvious.

I searched my mind for my most recent memory, but everything was overlapped. I remembered arguing with Jason. I remembered Wade telling me Jason was dead. I remembered anguishing over whether or not to tell Bailey that she was my granddaughter. I was pretty sure I hadn't. I remembered burying my son, along with all his memories.

Specifics were gone, though—what had happened that brought me here; what I'd been doing just before. It was a blank. White fog. Based on my inability to remember and on the pain in my side and my throat, I guessed it must have been pretty traumatic.

I licked my lips. "Car wreck?"

Her frown deepened. Her eyes widened. She twisted her head. "You don't remember?"

I shook no.

She hesitated, her lips parted, as if uncertain how to tell me something she thought would be obvious. "You were shot."

I frowned. Shot? Was she serious? "How?" I asked.

She laughed nervously and nodded sideways. "That's what Detective Steele wanted to ask you."

"Monica?" Distant memory brought to mind a willowy teen with mahogany hair, jumping piers and delivering mail as if tasked with a life-or-death mission. I hadn't seen her much since then, but I knew she now worked for Wade as a detective on the Lake Geneva Police Department. "She was here?" I asked.

Bailey bit her lip. "You don't remember that, either?"

I shook my head.

"She was here Thursday. The police chief, too. Well actually, he's been here every day. But you've been pretty out of it."

I squeezed my eyes shut. Obviously. "What's today?"

"Saturday."

I'd been here three days? I glanced at the light in the room—dim, radiating softly off tan walls, encouraging sleep that was already far too willing to come and claim me.

I tried to smile at Bailey. "Shouldn't you be out jumping mail?"

She squirmed in her seat. "Brian's delivering it in the runabout. The Mailboat's up at the repair docks."

"Why?"

She hesitated again. Yet another thing that should have been obvious to me, but wasn't. She shrugged and lifted an eyebrow. "It was shot?"

I tried to string together everything she was saying, and suddenly the flashes of memory lasted a little longer. Came a little clearer. Sunk a little deeper. I remembered waking up, lying on the deck of the Mailboat. Finding Bailey leaning over me. Blood on her knees. Tears down her cheeks. *He's bleeding,* she kept saying into the phone. Calling for help.

Lost in the tatters of a forgotten nightmare, it took me a moment to realize Bailey was still talking in the current world. Chattering away, like she used to. The shy but apparently carefree girl I'd grown to adore. I was, of course, wiser now. *Carefree* was the last word to describe Bailey. She simply hid her wounds too well.

"...I mean, it's not like the whole boat is totaled, or anything. It's just the windshield and the front counter. And the sound system. The sound system's toast, actually. The boat won't be finished until at least tomorrow afternoon— or that's what Robb said—so there won't be tours till Monday. They're working straight through the weekend to fix it, but it took a while for parts. We've had to refund a ton of tickets. I heard somebody was being a total ass, 'cause they were all pissed about getting their ticket refunded. We offered a different day, of course, but whatevs." She rolled her eyes.

I grinned. This past week or so on the Mailboat, she'd been too quiet. Not her normal self. I realized I missed the way she rambled. I'm sure I didn't catch the half of what she said, and most likely it didn't matter. But I liked the sound of it. I wished she could be carefree in truth and not just in appearance. I laid back and soaked in the sound of her voice, of my granddaughter...

"Not that most people know why the boat's in for repairs. Officially, we're like, 'unscheduled maintenance.'" She made air quotes. "But word's gotten around. We've been getting a ton of phone calls at the office. And cards." She waved towards the other side of my bed.

I turned my head and was surprised to find a counter top bearing a flurry of greeting cards, balloons, entire bouquets of flowers. Did I actually know that many people?

But twisting my head reignited the ache in my windpipe, as if someone had punched me in the throat. I reached up a hand to rub the sore area, afraid of finding a bandage. But there was none.

"Um ..." Bailey gestured vaguely along the line of her own windpipe. "There was, like, a breathing tube," she explained. "You didn't really have it in all that long. Well, not long after surgery. But I guess they put it in just before the helicopter. So you had it for, like, several hours, anyway." She gave me a look of sympathy and absentmindedly rubbed her leg. "I guess that kind of sucks. I heard it hurts a lot."

I was still dwelling on the words *breathing tube* and *helicopter*. I'd almost died that day. But I hadn't. For whatever reason and despite all my past failings, providence had given me another go. Another chance to tell Bailey who she was. I'd better not ruin it this time. Not again. I doubted I'd be granted another opportunity to do things right.

I studied Bailey's face, scrutinizing it with new interest. The doe-like, deep brown eyes. The upturned nose. The small mouth that could spread into a surprisingly bright smile. The wavy brown hair. For the first time since I'd met Bailey, I saw what I'd overlooked for a full summer and a half.

Jason. He'd looked just like that at her age. They both took after Laina.

My glance dropped to the collar of her tee shirt, but the ball chain and silver helm were gone. What had she done with them?

I surrendered to the weight pulling down on my eyelids. But my mind kept rolling like waves on the lake—

small but persistent. *Don't waste another minute.* But what should I say? How should I tell her?

Bailey stirred. "We're supposed to call Detective Steele," she said. "She wanted to know when you woke up." She quickly rose from her chair.

I flashed my eyes open and forced words past my bruised vocal chords. "Bailey, wait." I was committed now. She wasn't going to leave this room without knowing.

She paused and lifted her eyebrows.

"Sit down."

She lowered herself into the chair again and clasped her hands in her lap.

My heart pounded. I grasped for a place to start. "What did you do with the helm?"

I thought her face blanched. "The helm?" she squeaked.

"Jason's helm."

I marked the change in her color for certain this time. She stared at me for a moment, as if all the cogs and gears in her head were whirling out of control. She turned over her palm, opening her fingers. A tarnished chain was balled up inside, the silver helm glinting on top. "I'm not even sure why he gave it to me. You're the one who should have it." She thrust it toward me.

"No." I closed her fingers over it and looked her steadily in the eye. "He meant for you to have it."

She glanced uncertainly between me and her closed fist. "You sure about that? 'Cause it seems pretty random to me. He knew me for, like, an hour."

I grinned, a pang of emotion stabbing me in the heart. "Yes, I'm sure." They'd only spent an hour of their lives together—but Jason had left her his entire genetic code. She was her father's daughter. He couldn't have missed it. I had no doubt that in that one hour, Bailey had stolen his heart just as she had stolen mine.

I released Bailey's hand, took a deep breath, and started. "The silver helm is a Thomlin family heirloom. My wife first gave it to me when I left for the Navy. I wore it every day until I came home. Then I gave it back to her, and Laina wore it every day, just like her wedding ring. When Jason left for college, she passed it on to him and told him it would always bring him back to us. That's what the helm means. It brings us home."

Bailey listened with blank face and blank eyes. But I noticed her fingers loosen from the helm as if preparing once again to let it go. No doubt, I'd only just confirmed her fears that she was unworthy of keeping it. She didn't yet know the last, all-important detail.

I filled my lungs. It hurt, but I kept drawing air into my chest, letting the pain fuel my resolve, mask my fear. I was still in no way worthy to be this girl's grandfather. Not when I'd failed so badly with her father.

"I spoke with my son the night before he died," I said.

The surprise was audible in Bailey's voice. "Jason?"

I nodded. "That was the first I'd seen him in seventeen years. He..." I paused. I really didn't want to tell her this part. But she had a right to know the full truth. "He was a fugitive." Try as I might, I couldn't bring myself to tell her why—to tell her all the things Jason had done. Stealing people's honest earnings. Killing a man to save his own skin and make good his escape.

"I read about it in the news," she said quietly. There was sympathy on her face, but of course no realization yet of what any of this had to do with her.

Mercifully, I didn't have to go into the details of her father's crimes. Good. I moved to the next part—his moral and personal failings. "He told me things I'd never known," I went on. "He'd been seeing a girl. He got her pregnant just before he skipped town seventeen years ago."

A little twist of her mouth. An, *Oh, that's a bummer,* expression.

Fear fluttered in my chest. There was only one more thing to say. One last piece of the puzzle and at long last she would know.

I licked dry lips. "Her name was... Kalli Johnson."

For several seconds, Bailey didn't move. Then she lifted her head a little straighter. Her eyes bored into mine. Her voice emerged half-whisper, half-whimper. "Kalli Johnson?"

I nodded.

"You mean...?" Her voice dropped so low, I could hardly hear it. "Jason was... my dad?"

Again, I nodded.

"So that means..." A tiny light dawned in her eyes, but her face registered shock. "You—?" She didn't seem capable of finishing the sentence. She sat as white and stiff as a pier post.

"Yeah." I answered her unfinished question. "I guess."

I waited for the shock to pass so I could see her secondary reaction. The one indicating what she really thought of having me as a grandfather. But seconds dragged by, and I wondered if Bailey had stopped breathing. Finally, one little sound slipped out of her wooden mouth.

"Oh."

That was it? Oh?

Exhaustion swept over me again. I fought to keep my eyes open. There was still so much to say. But I couldn't win this time.

"I'm sorry," I told Bailey, my voice losing volume. "I'm so tired." On top of that, my throat was ready to kill me. I'd pushed it too far. Tried to say too much.

She sat taller, as if stirring from a reverie. "No, that's okay. The doctor said you'd be pretty much wiped out. Um—" She dropped her eyes to her lap. To her fist, closed over the silver helm. "I'll let you sleep," she said in a whisper.

I nodded, finally allowing my lids to seal over my eyes. We would talk later. That would give her time to let the news sink in. It would give me time to figure out what on earth to do now that I'd told her. To figure out what this was all going to mean. For both of us.

I heard Bailey rise from her chair and make for the doorway.

"Bailey?" I said, looking again.

She stopped and peeked back through the tan curtain, appearing small and unsure. "Yeah?"

"Keep the helm."

I'd meant to pose it as a question. *Would* she keep it? I wasn't quite sure why it had come out as a command. Perhaps because I was exhausted and losing patience. Perhaps because I didn't want her to lose it—the most important piece of Thomlin family history.

Or perhaps I was simply giving her orders to come to home port. Tie down the moorings. End her life of drifting. I didn't want to lose her.

She didn't respond. Not so much as a blink. Seconds dragged by. Finally, the tiniest nod of her head, so small I thought at first I'd only imagined it.

She slipped away.

I'd finally told her. Perhaps things were going to work out, some way or another. We would find the answers. Maybe we would start by finding the questions. I sighed and fell into a cool darkness, drinking in the rest but uncertain what sort of dreams awaited me. Glints of light. The helm, dangling from the chain around Bailey's neck as I lay on the deck bleeding.

Other times, the flashes of light came from silver studs in a black leather vest...

CHAPTER TWENTY-ONE
BAILEY

❖

I pushed through the doors of the Surgical ICU and ran down the hall, the silver helm balled up in my fist. Adrenaline like a quadruple shot of espresso pounded through my system. The universe itself crashed down on me in a million blazing colors. I needed space. Air. I needed to run. China wasn't far enough. Africa. South America. Australia.

We have you, little one. The beautiful faces of the sirens morphed into wicked grins full of razor teeth. *You fool, we had you all along.* They opened their jaws wide and rushed to bite down on me.

I turned a quick corner by the main elevators and stumbled into the girls' bathroom. It was empty. For such a big hospital, it was funny how often this bathroom was empty. But there were no sirens in here. That was all that mattered. I slammed the door in their faces and felt their claws scrape against the paneling on the other side.

I flung the silver helm to the floor. It skittered toward the opposite wall, slid up the mop board, and collapsed again in a tangle. Grabbing the edge of the sink with one hand, I clapped the other over my mouth to stifle the sobs.

Bam. The waterworks hit like somebody had blown up a dam and the reservoir all came rushing out at once, tumbling over itself in giant foamy waves. I peeked at the girl in the mirror. Her eyes were shiny with tears, huge as if magnified by a lens. Her face was white. She trembled from top to bottom. That girl was stark terrified. And I was that girl.

Should I really believe anything Tommy had just told me? He didn't even have a clue what day it was. Couldn't remember that Detective Steele and Chief Erickson had been here. Twenty-four hours ago, he was freaking out about ducks on the lake, for God's sake. He was out of it. He didn't know what he was saying. It couldn't be true. I didn't want it to be true—which was dumb, because it was literally the only thing I'd dreamed of, ever since I met Tommy.

I leaned against the wall next to the paper towel dispenser and slid down to the floor, scalding tears streaming down both cheeks. I cried like never before, breaking world records, putting every previous cryfest to shame. I cried because it had taken us so long to find each other. A lifetime for me. A lifetime full of misery and longing and loneliness. I cried because we'd been right under each other's noses.

I cried because I knew, now more than ever, that I was going to lose him. It was possible he thought he'd told me something nice. He didn't know he'd shut us out from each other forever. Put the lid on the coffin. Hammered in the nails. Loaded the whole kit and caboodle onto a Viking longship, shoved it off, and set it on fire.

When had I ever been allowed to keep my own family? Demonic memories seared across my mind. My mom being dragged away by cops, calling that she would come back for me. She never did. My dad had never even bothered to show up at all. Or no—he did. For an hour. Just one hour. And he was literally shot down in front of me. That was *my*

127

dad, and the universe had made sure I saw him die. I didn't even have the emotional space left to let that one soak in.

I loved Tommy so, so much. All I'd ever wanted was a tiny fraction of his heart to call my own. But I knew now I'd only pretended to want it. Because now it was real and it was horrible. My mind conjured a million harrowing possibilities, worse than the hell we'd already been through. One way or the other, he would be ripped away from me.

I couldn't survive being abandoned again. Not by Tommy.

I would kill myself first.

I dried my eyes and stared across the tiles to where the ball chain sprawled like a body that had been thrown from a cliff. Life would be so much easier if I just died. Because more than anyone ever, I knew I could not survive losing Tommy.

CHAPTER TWENTY-TWO
RYAN

———— ✸ ————

I strode back into the SICU with a bounce to my step and a whistle on my lips. My chat with Tommy's doctor had left me hopeful. The captain's vital signs were growing stronger. I'd noticed myself, when I dropped Bailey off in Tommy's room a few minutes ago, that he had more color. If he would just pull through, maybe everything would be okay. Quietly fixing everything that was wrong with the world had long been Tommy's specialty.

It was clear to see that Bailey hung on his every breath. If she trusted anyone, she trusted him. Maybe she would finally feel secure enough to share her secrets with him and at long last I could swing a pair of handcuffs over Bud Weber's wrists. All I needed was a shard of an excuse to haul him in for questioning. Then I'd interrogate the crap out of him, pulling all his sordid secrets into the daylight. No one harmed a teenage girl during my watch and got away with it. Especially not Bailey.

I could never forget her the way I'd seen her first, a five-year-old child huddled in a closet. We'd just arrested her mom and her mom's boyfriend on drug charges. They hadn't come quietly. Bailey was dirty. Too skinny. I picked her up. She didn't cry. I put her in the back seat of my patrol car and drove her to Health and Human Services, where a social worker met me after hours. While the social worker put in calls to numerous foster homes, searching for an emergency placement, I gave Bailey a teddy bear. I always kept one in my trunk to help kids through hard times like this. Bailey sat in a chair, her tiny feet sticking over the edge. She held the bear's paws, staring into its glassy eyes as if a teddy bear were some strange new phenomenon. She never spoke. Never cried. Never asked for her mom.

I think I knew then that I'd never forget her. Those big, brown eyes. The silence with which she accepted the bad luck the world heaped on top of her. She had been born strong, that was clear. But what she needed most was the chance to simply be a little girl. I didn't think she'd ever experienced that yet.

I'd hoped and prayed that night that things would turn out okay. Her mom would get out on bail, dump her no-account boyfriend, stay clean, find a steady job, satisfy all the court's demands, and have her daughter back in no time.

Obviously, the reality had turned out far different from the dream. And when I found Bailey again, eleven years later, I was left feeling as if I'd somehow failed her—even though I'd simply done my duty.

But had I known that night that she'd eventually end up in the hands of Bud Weber, maybe I'd have done things differently—if it were only to check in on her. Now I had a mess on my hands, and I wouldn't rest until I'd fixed it, if I could.

Tommy had to be the key. I wondered what the odds were of his becoming a foster parent himself. I couldn't imagine any situation more fitting.

Arriving at his room, I slid aside the curtain and peeked in, expecting to find Bailey perched by his bedside, silent and watchful as she had been every day since I first started bringing her to Froedtert. Instead, her chair was empty. The captain was asleep.

Well, maybe she'd gone to the bathroom. I decided to wait a few minutes. Not wanting to interrupt the captain's rest, I stood outside his room and entertained myself scanning a rack full of brochures about surgical recovery practices. When I'd read every title twice and flipped through one or two, I realized Bailey wasn't coming back.

I left the SICU and wandered down the hall, drifting toward the main elevators. Maybe she'd needed to stretch her legs. Maybe she'd even taken a ride down to the lowest level to pick up a snack in the cafeteria. If a quick browse didn't turn her up, I'd text her. This was a huge hospital and she could have wandered anywhere.

Just as I rounded the corner to the elevators, Bailey herself emerged from the ladies' room.

"Hey, there you are," I said, grinning and hooking my thumbs in my pockets. "I wondered where you'd wandered off to."

Instead of replying, she kept her gaze on the floor and wiped at her eyes. Well, that didn't look good. Had she been crying? What on earth could she have been crying about? Was she worried about Tommy?

"I just talked to the doc," I said. "Good news—he says Tommy's vital signs are getting stronger."

She nodded but still didn't look at me.

I leaned my weight on one leg and rounded my shoulders, hoping to look sympathetic, hoping to maybe coax a straight answer out of her this time. "Hey, kiddo, what's wrong?"

"Nothing," she said.

Well, all right then. We were right back to square one. If we'd ever left it.

"How's Tommy?" I tried next.

She curled an arm around herself and rubbed her arm. "He just woke up," she said, addressing the carpet.

My heart leapt. In my head, I made a fist pump. But I figured I'd better keep my body language low-key. Despite the good news, Bailey was apparently still upset about something. Maybe these were tears of joy? "That's great," I said. "What'd he say?"

Bailey's mouth opened and closed silently like a fish staring at the side of a bowl. "Nothing."

I tapped the fabric of my jeans. For some reason, I didn't believe her. I wasn't sure how I'd expected her to react to Tommy's recovery. Sunshine breaking through clouds to the music of an angelic choir hadn't been out of the running. But this? Something was off.

"You don't look okay," I said frankly, drumming my fingers some more.

She glanced around, as if for an escape, and continued to rub her arm.

"Sure there's nothing you want to talk about?"

She shook her head.

I sighed, raising my eyebrows in surrender. "Okay. Tell you what." I pulled my phone out of my hip pocket. "I've got to call Detective Steele and let her know Tommy's awake. Why don't you go sit with him again? We can stay as long as you like."

She twisted a strand of her ponytail. "Actually, I was wondering if you could take me home."

That was not what I wanted to hear. "You couldn't have talked to him for more than a few minutes."

"I know. I just... I'm tired."

I stared at her with concern. What was going on behind those veiled eyes? Why did she cling to Tommy like a life ring... only to abandon him when it looked like he was going to be okay? It didn't make any sense.

I shoved the phone back into my pocket and reached out to touch Bailey's shoulder. "Bailey, what's the matter?"

She jerked away as if I'd tried to cut her arm off. She clutched her arms around herself even more tightly. "Don't touch me!" Her usually subdued voice leapt like a wildcat. Her usually emotionless face wrinkled into a ferocious scowl, though she aimed it somewhere past my left arm. She breathed through her teeth.

My heart leapt into my throat. I found myself crouching, making myself small and non-threatening. I reached out to her like I would to a stray dog. "Bailey, honey. It's okay."

"I want to go home," she said through a locked jaw.

"What happened?" I asked. What on earth could have gone on between her and Tommy?

"Please," she said, staring death threats into the floor. "I want to go home."

I sighed and backed off. Great. Somehow, I'd managed to ruin my perfect strategy for Bailey and Tommy, just as I'd somehow ruined things between me and Monica. And I still didn't know how I was pulling it off.

"Okay," I said, holding my hands up in surrender. "Whatever you want. I'll take you home."

I moved to the elevator and hit the down button. We waited for the lift side-by-side, studiously ignoring each other. It was back to the drawing board now. Square one. Visions of arresting Bud Weber faded again into an unreachable future—and along with it all my hopes for rescuing the girl beside me. She'd been born strong, all right. Too strong for her own good.

Just let me help you, I pleaded.

The bell dinged and we got into the elevator.

CHAPTER TWENTY-THREE
MADISON, WISCONSIN, 2004

Monica drove home with butterflies twirling in her stomach. This sensation was quite different from the general queasiness she'd been feeling lately, mostly in the mornings. This was joy. This was shock. This was wonder. Her heart skipped light and fast. Her hands shook with thrill. She hardly dared to believe. Not after all this time, all the times they'd tried, all the disappointments. She couldn't wait to tell Ryan. She was so happy she wanted to cry.

They really needed a bit of good news lately. They'd only moved to Madison a year ago, both of them having landed jobs in the Madison PD's Detective Bureau. Maybe it was the move. Maybe it was the stress of a new department. Maybe it was the increased caseloads, more demanding than the jobs they'd held back home in Lake Geneva. Whatever it was, it was draining, both mentally and emotionally, and it was telling on them both.

They'd never talked about it upfront, but Monica sensed life had gotten a little stale of late. Both too busy and too routine, all at the same time. They got up, they got to work, they worked late, they came home and crashed. Rinse and repeat. She couldn't even remember when exactly they'd gotten together long enough for her to become pregnant. Life was a blur.

But she was pregnant. *She was pregnant.* She nearly squealed like a girl.

At first, she hadn't let herself believe. It had to be a fluke. But she'd skipped two periods in a row. She'd chalked it up to stress. Her body rebelling against work-related exhaustion. But in addition to feeling queasy in the mornings, she'd been putting on weight—just barely enough to notice. She couldn't ignore the signs anymore. It didn't take a genius to figure it out. But she and Ryan had tried so hard for so long—and finally just given up.

That's why she hadn't told him she had a doctor's appointment today. She hadn't wanted to get his hopes up.

But the doctor had confirmed it.

They were having a baby.

They had a little time off coming to them. They should get out of town together for a long weekend. Go on a quick vacation. Door County, Chicago, wherever. Enjoy some fine dining, hole up in a hotel, watch a bunch of movies while cuddled in bed, lose themselves in each other while they still could, before Monica's soon-to-be-growing belly made intimacy a challenge.

As she turned the corner to their little gray ranch in the suburbs, images of furnishing a nursery playing through her mind, she glanced down the street and noted a red sedan parked in their driveway. She recognized it as belonging to Sarah McQuade, another MPD detective. Ryan had been working closely with her on a case. Monica sighed as she realized work had followed them home yet again. Shit. Her news would have to wait.

Sarah and Ryan's cars occupied the driveway, so she parked on the street and let herself in through the front door. Inside the house, she dropped her portfolio and keys on an end table. The great room—living room, kitchen, and dining room combined—was empty. They had probably taken their work to Ryan's office. Monica made her way down the hall quietly, not wanting to interrupt them if they were busy. She would just peek in to let Ryan know she was home.

But then she heard a laugh. A high, tittering laugh that morphed into a full-fledged giggle. Then a moan. The sound didn't come from Ryan's office.

It came from the bedroom.

Monica's heart pounded and her blood ran cold. This wasn't possible.

Something told her it was.

Monica fingered the door knob, for a few seconds questioning what to do. The romantic weekend was suddenly a ridiculous dream; the joy of telling Ryan her news, a cruel joke. The nursery faded away, with its crib and its stuffed animals and its hanging mobile that played soft lullabies.

In a flash, her mind was made up. There was no need to open that door to prove anything to herself.

She needed to open it to exact her revenge.

There was no point in sitting around nursing a broken heart. That had never been her way. She skipped straight ahead to phase two: the bitter resentment. How could he do this? How could he? She would make him pay.

She gripped the knob in an iron fist, twisted, and flung the door open. It hit the wall with a bang. Gasping in surprise, Ryan and Sarah McQuade twisted around to look. McQuade pulled up a sheet to cover herself.

"Monica," Ryan muttered, his expression dumbstruck.

Monica stared at McQuade and pointed down the hall toward the front door. "Out!" she yelled, her voice weighted with authority.

McQuade leapt from the bed, taking the sheet with her. She picked her clothes up from the floor, then rushed past Monica out the bedroom door. She still had the sheet. Monica didn't care. The bitch could keep it.

Ryan jumped up and pulled on pants. "Monica, I can explain."

Oh, really? That was rich. Exactly what kind of explanation did he have in mind for what she'd just seen? She pointed toward the door again, her glare intense. "You, too," she said. "Out."

He pulled on a shirt. "Okay, we'll talk about it later."

She leaned in, nose-to-nose, and glared him in the eye. "I mean *out*. Go move in with your girlfriend. You'll hear from my lawyer in the morning."

"You don't have a lawyer."

She shifted an eyebrow. "I will in the morning."

Ryan stared in shocked disbelief. But Monica meant every word. She had trusted him. Implicitly. Since they met in kindergarten. Since they started dating in high school. Never once had he given her reason to doubt his loyalty. A trust like that, built up over a lifetime, couldn't be trampled underfoot as if it meant nothing.

Not today, when their life together had finally become complete. She fought back the tears. She wouldn't let them show. Not now. Not ever.

Ryan finally grabbed his car keys off the dresser, pulled an overnight bag down from a closet shelf, and threw some shirts, pants, socks, and underwear inside. He paused in the bedroom door as if looking for one more thing to say. But nothing came to him. He walked out in a stewing silence.

Monica waited until she heard his car leave the garage. Then she screamed and tore apart the bedding, flinging blankets and pillows everywhere. She screamed until her voice was sore. Then a wave of nausea hit her. Apparently baby didn't like mama's mood. Monica scrambled to the bathroom and made it just in time. She heaved into the toilet. When she was done, she closed the lid and leaned her head on her arm. With the other hand, she rubbed her belly.

MAILBOAT III

How could this be happening? How could Ryan have so utterly ruined the most perfect day of their lives?

How was she supposed to go on from here?

CHAPTER TWENTY-FOUR
MONICA

———— ❈ ————

I lay on my sofa staring into the ceiling, memorizing the dots that patterned the plaster. One hand cradled the back of my head. The other drew little circles on my belly, over and over...

I had found a divorce lawyer that night. He served papers on Ryan the next morning. We were on record for the quickest divorce in the state of Wisconsin. Ryan didn't try to fight it. Just another sign his heart had already left me.

I conveniently forgot to mention to anyone that I was pregnant. I didn't need Ryan's input on the fate of our child—or the court's or anyone else's. I knew from the start what I had to do. Four weeks into the divorce process, just as I was starting to show, I terminated the pregnancy. Because I could never think of it as anything but our pregnancy. Our child. And I just didn't have the strength to raise that child without the love of my life at my side.

I knew I would look into her eyes and see nothing but her father.

Of course, I never knew officially whether it was a boy or a girl. But in my heart, I knew. We would have had a daughter. She would have been beautiful and talented. She would have been at home in sports, like both her parents. She might have taken up music, like me. Obviously, her grades would have been better than both of ours put together—because we had both sucked at school. And we would have mutually banned her from a career in law enforcement because we never would have let her risk her physical and emotional health in a job like ours.

But if she'd rebelled and taken the badge anyway, we would have been the proudest parents in the world.

Beyond that, the questions reamed endlessly. Would she have inherited her father's knack for pranks and hijinks? Or would she have been kick-ass and stubborn like her mother? I hoped for the former. Maybe then she also would have been kind and forgiving—unlike me.

This summer, she would have turned ten years old. I saw her constantly. Her ghost grew up by my side. I watched her, robbed of any chance to touch her. To hold her. To love her. She stared back, smiling but hollow. Sometimes I thought she didn't know who I was.

Giving her up was my one and only regret in life. Regardless of kicking Ryan's ass to the curb, I should have kept her. I shouldn't have given up on her like I did. It had been selfish. And now I was nothing but a hardened shell around an empty center. A center that could have revolved around her instead.

I turned my face into the pillows and let the hot tears glide down my cheeks.

My phone rang. I let it ring.

It was Saturday, my day off. Neumiller, Lehman, and I were taking turns spelling each other, making sure the case was never dropped. But I had no temptation to go into work anyway. In fact, it had taken a Herculean effort to get from my bed to the sofa this morning, where I'd been lying ever since. The coffee I'd brewed hours ago sat cold and untouched on the kitchen counter. Breakfast was still just a thought in the fridge. And it was now seven at night.

My Wall had finally collapsed, built of nothing but hatred and venom, and I was nothing without my exoskeleton.

I'd never told him. I'd never told Ryan. The most perfect day of my life had been ruined by the realization that I was all alone in the world and this child would never have a father worthy of the name. He hadn't deserved to know. But from the moment I gave up my baby, I made it my business to hate Ryan Brandt as much as possible. That mission had only grown daily, especially since he'd come back to Lake Geneva.

The phone kept ringing and I finally picked it up to look at the screen. Caller ID said it was Ryan. I nearly threw the phone across the room. But then my hand found a chunk of the Wall, warped, twisted like shrapnel. I tested its weight, then picked up the phone. "What?" I snapped.

The background was filled with the distinctive hum of a car in motion. "Tommy's awake."

I closed my eyes. The relief of the news was diluted by the fact it had come from Ryan. "Is he coherent?" I asked.

"I don't know. I didn't see him. Bailey... uh, Bailey isn't feeling well, so I'm taking her home."

"Well, ask Bailey, then." I flipped my palm in the air.

I heard Brandt mumble something away from the phone. This was followed by such a long pause, I wondered if they'd both been taken by aliens and left the car to coast down the Interstate unmanned.

"Brandt?"

"Sorry, Monica. I'm still here."

"What did she say?"

"Um... nothing."

I tapped my foot on the armrest at the other end of the sofa. "Well, this is a lot of help. Am I supposed to make a trip to Milwaukee or not? It's my only day off, for God's sake."

"I can call the hospital."

I savored the cower in his voice. "Forget it. I'll call them myself and make sure I actually get some information." The Wall was coming back together. I was beginning to feel stronger.

"I'm sorry, Monica," Brandt said.

"Yeah, whatever. I gotta go." I hung up.

I got off the sofa. Grabbed the coffee mug from under the Keurig and popped it into the microwave. From my pocket, I took an elastic band and yanked my hair into a tight ponytail. It was time to get back in the trenches and fight the world. Spit in its hand. Piss in its eye.

Markham was wrong. Ryan's dad had been wrong. I wasn't a cop because I gave a shit about the downtrodden and victimized. I was a cop because it was a legal way to take out my fury on the world. Clap my fellow mortals in irons. Slam them behind bars. Fill their dreams with nightmares.

I drank my coffee hot and black, savoring the bite. I needed my Wall. I was dead without it.

CHAPTER TWENTY-FIVE
TOMMY

When I woke again, I looked immediately to the chair where Bailey had been sitting—but she wasn't there. Anticipations crashed. I'd just assumed she would come back. That we'd talk. That I'd find out her true reaction. But she was simply gone. A wave of intense loneliness washed over me. Maybe this *was* her answer—to vanish. To walk away. I couldn't blame her. Not after telling her I'd raised her father to be a criminal.

Or had I told her at all? Maybe I had dreamed Bailey sitting in the chair beside me. That I'd told her about her dad. My head swam and my memory mixed dreams, wishes, and reality like an illusionist deftly working his curtains and mirrors.

One question at a time. I thought I remembered Bailey telling me I'd been shot. I gingerly reached my hand to my side where a dull ache throbbed. My entire midsection was wrapped in bandages.

Maybe it was true, then. But if I'd really taken a bullet, you'd think I'd remember such a thing. Even at seventy-five, I never lost my keys or forgot an appointment. Always the curious sort, I'd made a point of learning something new every day. Reading something. Hearing something on the radio. Learning a new skill—mostly related to boat restoration and repair. All that mental activity had kept my mind sharp and young and it was unusual for me to have simply blanked out an entire day and its events. The memories had to be in there somewhere.

I closed my eyes and mulled around through the magician's stage props, searching for the truth. I'd buried my son. I'd felt guilty for not telling Bailey that the man whose death she'd witnessed was her own father. I'd come to the Mailboat early, unable to sleep. And then—

—*the sunrise glittered through the windows. It was quiet. Still. The boat rocked gently beneath my feet. A mountain of a man faced me, feet spread, a gun held in two hands. Flashes of light spit from the muzzle. Pop, pop, pop...*

"Damn you," the man fumed, "What's it take, anyway?"
Another pop from the gun.

Fire seared through my belly and I hit the deck hard, face-down on the pine wood planks. I stared at the grooves between the floorboards, panicking. Bailey... I had to warn Bailey...

Heart pounding, my eyes flew open. I heard voices. They chattered over an intercom. Gym shoes padded softly but quickly over tile. I looked left and right. An IV stand. A heart monitor. A hospital. *The* hospital. I was still in the hospital. Wasn't I? What was real? What was imagined?

My breath rushed in and out through my mouth. I felt tied-down. Restricted by the needles taped into my skin, the wires and tubes draped over the bed railings and screwed into the machines. I was trapped in a web. I couldn't run. What was real?

A knock sounded on the door frame. My eyes shot to the curtain, a flimsy barrier that protected me from nothing and exposed me to anything. The curtain began to draw aside. Sweat broke out across my forehead. I gripped one of the railings. Tried to think of some way to defend myself. Prepared for the shooter to appear...

A thin woman with long brunette hair slipped through the curtain, smiling. "Knock, knock, anybody home?"

Monica?

Monica Steele. I knew her. She was safe. Maybe this part was the reality, not the dream. I took a few slow breaths to calm my nerves. Shook the fog from my head and loosened each finger from the railing. For a moment, a shooter appearing in the doorway had been the only reality worth planning for. But maybe there was no shooter. At least not now.

I licked my lips. Tried to converse normally. "Monica," I said, my voice hoarse. "Haven't seen you in a while." In fact, I hadn't seen her regularly since she was in college. She'd been my mail jumper every summer until she landed an internship with the Lake Geneva Police Department just before her senior year. The summer after that, she and her boyfriend Ryan had gotten their first temp jobs as patrol officers and quickly moved into full-time positions.

I blinked and stared down at the hospital blanket, a tan waffle-weave. Clearly my memory was fine. Put to the task, I could probably write a one-paragraph bio about every mail jumper I'd ever worked with. And yet, until a moment ago, I hadn't remembered being shot?

But the reason was clear now.

I didn't want to remember. Those memories lived in a dark place—a place full of fear, terror, and hate. A place no living being should ever go.

I glanced up at Monica. It dawned on me she wasn't here on a social call. She had questions. She wanted answers. She had a criminal to track down. She needed those memories of mine.

This could get problematic.

She stepped further into the room. "Haven't seen you in a while either, Tommy. You didn't have to land yourself in the hospital, though. I would have settled for coffee."

I grinned, but without heart in it. I waited for her to cut to the chase. My hands were shaking. I slid them under the folds of the blanket.

She drummed her fingers on a leather portfolio in her hands. Her face turned serious. "I'm here on business," she said.

"I know," I replied. My heart was still racing from when she'd knocked on the door. Was there any good way to do this? To stir up the memories she was looking for? My mind scrambled for a solution.

She dropped into the chair and laid the portfolio on her lap. Gripping the edge of the leather binder, her eyes bored into mine. "Give me a name, Tommy."

I filled my lungs slowly, gingerly. Pain radiated through my belly. It felt like someone had cut me in two. I embraced the pain. It kept me grounded.

I shook my head. "I don't have a name." Granted, I hadn't so much as tried to remember one. Mostly, I was wishing my adrenal glands would finish flooding my bloodstream with their nerve-jangling concoction. There was no shooter. Not now.

"Never seen him before?" Monica continued.

I had to slow my mind down. I had to think this through. I measured my breaths. Focused on the footboard at the end of the bed. I could do this. It was important. Monica wouldn't be asking these questions if the shooter was in custody. He was still at large. God, I shouldn't dwell on that. I needed to focus. I let my mind edge toward the memories of that morning on the Mailboat. I saw the sunrise. I felt the waves—

I saw the muzzle flash and felt the bullet tear into my flesh.

My heart jolted back to the jackhammer rhythm. I snapped my eyes to the marker board on the wall and began to read voraciously. The name of my doctor. The name of my nurse. My room number. My medications. There were a lot of them. A fresh load of adrenalin was dumping into my system. I forced my mind on something irrelevant—untangling the doctor's illegible scrawl. Anything but the memories...

But they were eager from the invitation, however slight. The memories were pressing at the edges of my mind. Grasping. Reaching. They were a trap. A Pandora's box. If I dared crack the lid open, there was no guarantee I'd get it back on. I couldn't control the thing. There was no going near it without it sucking me in.

"Tommy?" Monica prompted. "Have you seen him before?" she asked again.

"No," I said. And that was going to be the answer to all her questions. Right or wrong, I didn't remember anything.

And I wasn't going to.

But she kept right on asking. "Description, then?"

"I don't remember."

She narrowed her eyes. "You were facing him. He was standing fifteen feet from you. And you didn't see him?"

It was eerie to hear her describe an event she hadn't witnessed—an event I couldn't even remember. But I knew she could read a crime scene. The formation of a blood drop could tell her where in a room it had come from; what direction it had traveled; the force with which it had moved; the type of weapon that had been used, whether gun, knife, or blunt instrument. So she knew where I'd been standing.

Depending what she'd picked up on the ground—spent shell casings, actual bullets—she would know something about the gun. From interviewing my doctors, she would know the trauma the bullet had caused—info I wasn't even privy to yet. With this information, she would know how far the round had traveled, the velocity with which it struck me, and from all this, where on the Mailboat the shooter had been standing.

Wade had explained crime scene reconstruction to me a long time ago. Nothing was a mystery to her—except what the man had looked like. Apparently he hadn't left footprints, or Monica would have told me his height and weight, based on his shoe size.

But she knew I'd been facing him. She knew I must have looked at him. I couldn't simply feign ignorance.

I ground my teeth. Glanced at the box of dark memories. The sides were opaque. I could see the general shape of things without looking the contents full in the face. "He was... big," I said. "Tall."

She flipped open her portfolio and jotted it on her notepad. "Hair color? Outstanding features?"

That much I couldn't see through the walls of the box. I shook my head. "I don't remember."

She looked up, dissatisfaction etched in every line of her face. The way my drill sergeant used to look at me every day, even if I'd out-performed every other man in my unit. She rapped the end of her pen on her notebook. "Tommy, who won the World Series in 1938?"

I wasn't sure what on earth she meant by such a question, but I answered truthfully. "The New York Yankees. That was the year I was born."

"When did Joe DiMaggio retire?"

"Nineteen fifty-one."

"Who had more home-run hits in a single game than any other player?"

That's when I realized she didn't even know the answers herself. She was making up these questions on the fly. But she knew I would know. "There were eighteen," I said. "Each of them scored four home runs. The first was Bobby Lowe, 1894. He played for the Boston Beaneaters." I had a nagging feeling I knew the point behind these baseball trivia questions.

She raised an eyebrow and tapped her pen a little more slowly. A little more distinctly. "Tommy, do you mean to tell me you remember all that—but you don't remember anything about the man who shot you?"

My jaw tightened. I didn't question for a moment my ability to drum up every relevant shard of evidence in excruciating detail. But I didn't dare. Neither did I care to explain why I wouldn't.

"I don't," I simply said. "I'm sorry. The whole thing is just... a blur. Bits and pieces." And it would stay that way until I chose otherwise.

She studied my eyes carefully, suspicious. I dropped my gaze to the waffle weave blanket again and set my jaw.

"Maybe if we start from the top," she suggested. "The last thing you remember clearly. The rest usually fills into—"

I glared at her, my nostrils flaring. "It's not there, Monica. I don't remember."

She didn't buy it. She shook her head. Her expression turned to one of pleading. "Tommy, you're the only one who's seen him."

So this was the same man she'd been looking for? In that case, she was too tactful to say things bluntly: I was the only one to have seen him and lived.

She chewed her lip. Glanced over her notes as if looking for advice. Finally, she ventured ahead. "We picked up .22 shells and rounds from the scene. Same as at Jason's. Whoever shot you—it's probably the same person who killed your son."

I closed my eyes. Hot tears formed beneath my eyelids. I wouldn't let them fall. What good would it do to find justice for my son? It wouldn't change the seventeen years he'd betrayed me and his mother. The seventeen years he'd lived on the run, not even aware he'd left a daughter behind.

"He threatened Roland, too," Monica said, as if she were playing her last card.

Roland. An old friend I'd barely spoken to in twenty years. But did I want him to suffer a fate similar to mine—or worse?

I breathed deeply and eyed the exterior of the box. Reached for the lid at arm's length. Cracked open the top a hair's breadth. A quick peek suggested the beginning of the tale wasn't too hard to handle. I'd try.

"I was early," I said, picturing the deeply slanting shadows across the pier. "I unlocked the Mailboat and went in." I paused, waiting for the reel of memories to feed out a few more frames. I found myself wanting to play them more quickly. "He came in behind me. Through the open door." How could he have just shown up without my noticing him coming down the pier? I didn't want to know. To remember. His appearance had been from nowhere. Ghostlike. It was unnerving. I had to move on. "He asked if I was Tommy," I said.

Monica looked up from her notes, eyes narrowed. "He knew who you were?"

That would imply I knew him, too, and I was quite sure I didn't—though I was staring through the blurry sides of the box again to get that information. It was one of those bits I didn't want to stare at directly.

Which meant I did know him. Somehow. I frowned, not even sure what I meant. I knew him, but I didn't know him.

"He knew my name," I finally answered. It was the best I could do. Or the best I would do.

"Then what happened?"

I tried to slip back into the box and pick up the reel where I'd left off. But the ribbon was tied in knots. Looped in piles of bunny ears. I tried to feed it through the projector anyway. It whirred. It zipped. It banged.

Light flashed from the end of the muzzle. Pain stabbed through my belly like a sword.

I dropped.

"Tommy?" she prompted.

I opened my eyes and stared into space. The projector was smoking. The box sat empty. The film was gone.

"He shot me," I said.

I was never opening that box again.

CHAPTER TWENTY-SIX
MONICA

I rolled the pen between my fingers uncomfortably. This wasn't the Mailboat captain I'd known most of my life. Tommy had always been a straight shooter. He said things like they were. He didn't have time for games or even niceties half the time. But now he was evading my questions. Why? Had the perp threatened him? Or were the memories still too raw? Was I pushing him too hard?

But I had to push. This whole event sickened me. Infuriated me. I was a firestorm of death to anyone who harmed someone I had cared about, even as a teenager. So I needed the facts. I needed to find that sick son of a bitch who had shot Tommy and whack him in the nuts with the entire penal code—large-print edition.

I needed Tommy to remember, and I needed him to tell me.

"He just made sure it was you, then pulled the gun?" I prompted.

Tommy nodded.

Once again, I was convinced he wasn't telling me everything. His eyes had gone cloudy, as if fixed on something a million miles away. A sheen of sweat glistened across his brow.

I tilted my head. "Tommy?" I called softly.

He shook his head as if waking from a reverie. Looked at me as if surprised to find me there. I didn't like it. Maybe I'd mention it to the hospital staff. But it was becoming clear this was all I was going to get out of him for now.

I bit back my impatience, folded the cover of my portfolio over my pen, and leaned forward. "We aren't going to let him walk free," I said. "We're going to catch him and lock him away until no one so much as remembers he existed."

Tommy nodded.

"Do you have anything else for me? Anything else at all?"

He rolled his eyes toward the opposite wall and sighed. He was silent several moments, and I thought he'd simply close up and say nothing. But then he spoke. "I remember..."

My ears pricked eagerly. "Yes?"

"He was wearing a leather vest."

My body froze solid, except for my eardrums. They hummed with anticipation. A leather vest? That's what Bailey had said: The man who killed Jason Thomlin had been wearing a leather vest. "What color?"

"Black," Tommy said. "With silver studs."

I stared at him for the span of several universes. A black vest with silver studs. I wrapped my hands around the evidence and enfolded it to my chest. At last, proof. These weren't isolated incidents. It was all connected. It all went back to the same person. The same .22 rimfire. The same black leather vest.

My tone dripping with eloquence, I dropped a gem-encrusted f-bomb.

MONDAY
JUNE 30, 2014

CHAPTER TWENTY-SEVEN
BAILEY

Monday arrived all blue and beautiful, big, billowy clouds puffing across the sky like exploded marshmallows. The petunias that hung in pots from the light posts glowed neon pink. My backpack was slung over my shoulder and I was wearing my extra-grippy shoes for mail jumping, tightly laced. It was like a dozen idyllic summer days I'd experienced in this town, one of a thousand beautiful days that marched across Lake Geneva's history.

Only it wasn't.

It was finally the Monday the Mailboat was back.

I crossed the courtyard in front of the Riviera, the stones already warming in the morning sun. The water splashed and sparkled in the fountain, shaped like a layered pastry stand with an angel on top. A robin sat on the lower tier, sprinkles raining down on him from all directions. He alternately flapped his wings, flinging water everywhere, and sat all fat and cross-looking as if he were stuck there against his will. Only I was pretty sure he wasn't. Yet he didn't leave.

You and me, buddy, I said to the robin. *Both of us trapped someplace we love. Who'd have thought, right?*

He frowned at me and splashed some more.

I was the robin and the fountain was the Mailboat. The Mailboat's presence had always washed over me like a refreshing rain, letting me fling aside the dirt of my life while bathing in a thrilling cold shock of exhilaration—literally, if I fell in the lake.

But today I was stuck. Trapped in the place I loved. I wanted to stay. I wanted to go. Everything that had once been clear was now an oozing fountain of mud.

Robb Landis had called yesterday to confirm that the Mailboat would be back at the pier today and resuming tours. *Yes, sir,* I said, *I'll be there.* I was on the schedule, after all. It was my job to be there.

Technically it was my job to be there on time, too. Except that I wasn't.

But as I walked under the arches, I didn't bother checking the time on my phone. I figured I was somewhere between fifteen and twenty minutes behind. I didn't need to confirm the fact and make me feel any more miserable about myself. I didn't even run to catch up or plan on apologizing to Brian, the captain who'd be driving the boat today.

Everything had changed.

I reached into my pocket and touched the silver helm necklace. Wearing it right now felt as impossible as abandoning it in the bottom of a drawer. So I was back to carrying it in my pocket, stuck between worlds just as I was.

Maybe those ancient Greek philosophers who said that nothing was real were right. Or maybe we were just brains in a jar enjoying hallucinations at the hands of a mad scientist. Or maybe aliens were running experiments with us, but the experiments were all going wrong and so the aliens were going to scrap us and start over.

Any of these options seemed more likely than that Tommy was really my grandfather—and that this could be a good thing.

Family are people who leave you. Unless you leave them first. Sometimes taking the initiative seemed like the right thing to do.

Hence I wasn't sure what I was doing here. Hence why I was late. Neither here nor there. Trapped in between.

The escape route was obvious. Just tell Ryan. Yes, Bud hurts me. Yes, Bud yells at me. Yes, Bud makes me have sex with him. I've heard people say all those things are bad. Are they? I guess it's all I've ever known. He wasn't the first to treat me like this, and I never really imagined he would be the last. Lots of people have yelled at me and hit me. My own mom did, and she always said she loved me. Mostly I believed her. And sex? Honestly, I barely remember being a virgin. It started with one of my mom's boyfriends. An older boy in another foster home carried on the tradition. And now I have Bud.

Far as I could tell, this was just what life was like. Love always includes hate. Men always want sex. Isn't this why we have make-believe? Isn't this why people make pretty books and movies that make you cry? Isn't this why we invent virtuous heroes and heroines? Because life sucks so bad everybody just wants to kill themselves? I never fooled myself that real life could be pretty.

Maybe that's why I never thought twice about the possibility that Bud might be the guy who killed—

Who killed my dad.

I stopped under the second tower and planted my forehead on the brick pillar. I hadn't had the brainpower before to deal with this new twist. Apparently it decided to sink in now, under the shadow of the Riviera when I was already late for work.

Jason Thomlin was my dad. The man I'd tried really hard to save that night... had been my dad.

158

My heart pounded then exploded into a million pieces.

That's why Jason had asked me so many questions at the diner. That's why he'd wanted to know all about my college and career plans. That's why he'd left me a hundred-dollar tip under a coffee mug.

Because he was my dad.

But it was worse than that.

He'd been so nice to me. He'd *died* for me. He looked an awful lot like a virtuous hero. Even though he'd been bad. Even though virtuous heroes weren't supposed to exist.

But... why hadn't he *told* me? Why couldn't he have just told me he was my father? Tears squeezed out of my eyes and I ground my forehead into the coarse bricks. I would have turned into some sort of crime-fighting cyborg. I would have torn Bud Weber and Charles Hart's arms from their sockets. I would have bitten their heads off with my bare teeth. I wouldn't have been halfways useless, like I actually was. I would have done anything to save my dad. Just like I had always dreamed he'd do anything to save me—which is exactly what he did.

Maybe it was obvious why he hadn't told me the truth, even as he lay on the street dying. I remembered his tears drawing lines on his face through dirt and blood as he looked up at me. I remembered it like I was still there. Right now. Maybe he hadn't wanted to tell me he was a criminal. He was supposed to be one of the bad guys. He took people's money. He killed a cop to get away. It hurt so much to have to believe it.

And so he'd given me the silver helm and died, maybe hoping I'd never have to know.

But I knew.

Still, how could any son of Tommy's be bad? I tried really hard to smash the pieces together, to make them fit, but they wouldn't go. In my heart, my dad had always been my hero. My pretty story. The thing that kept me from killing myself a long time ago. And even now, knowing what I knew, I couldn't picture him any other way.

I pictured him now the only way I'd ever actually seen him. Asking me all about myself at the diner. Standing up for me during the gun fight in the street. And I knew what I'd always known.

He loved me. He actually loved me. And it hurt so, so bad. It hurt to finally be loved. It hurt to know that at least one pretty story had actually been for real, if only for an hour.

And it hurt to know for sure and for certain that I wasn't allowed to keep pretty stories. That I wasn't allowed to keep my own family.

Why was I trapped wanting what I already knew I couldn't have?

I dug my forehead into the corner of a brick and let the hot tears fall.

CHAPTER TWENTY-EIGHT
JIMMY

———— ❈ ————

Jimmy stood on the sidewalk across the street from the Riviera, strategizing furiously but resisting the urge to pace. This was the day. Monday. Peering around the side of the building toward the lake, he confirmed that the Mailboat was back at the pier. His heart rate accelerated and his palms perspired. A handful of people milled about—cruise line employees. He had not yet verified whether Bailey was one of them, but if he could trust the word of the boat captain he'd spoken with the other day, she was supposed to be here.

It was time to act. It was now or never. If he lost his nerve, he'd never regroup for a second assault. He adjusted his cap, pulled his feet up from his spot, and crossed the street.

It was time to test the Cadiganian Variation: To speak from the heart.

He crossed the courtyard and passed under the curved arches. When the Mailboat came into full view, he stopped. There was Bailey Johnson herself, bearing her red and white backpack, stepping onto the boat. The sunlight caught the brown and gold highlights of her hair, cascading down her back in a wavy ponytail. His mouth went dry.

Your beauty defies the laws of science, he said in his mind, practicing. *The curvature of your smile is geometrically perfect. I'd like to measure the amount of light reflected by your eyes.*

Despite staying up all night to tweak the lines, he knew the instant he looked at Bailey that they still fell far short of how she made him feel. In no way did they capture the way the sight of her warmed his heart. Helped him forget everything he hated about the world. Even suggested to him that he could have something as scientifically unprovable as a soul.

He contemplated scampering back to his lab and re-writing the words for the hundredth time. But he'd already put off this moment for days, and been foiled, and had miraculously screwed up enough courage to try again. If he didn't go forward with it now, he never would.

He closed his eyes. Breathed deeply. Remembered Noah Cadigan's advice. *Tell her how you feel. How you feel inside.*

He squared his shoulders, cracked the vertebrae in his neck, and stepped onto the quay. Quite possibly, this day would go down in history.

CHAPTER TWENTY-NINE
NOAH

Noah Cadigan knelt on his hands and knees on the bow of the Mailboat, white and warm in the sun, and scrubbed away a dusting of fingerprints on the new windshield. The guys at the cruise line's repair shop in Williams Bay usually gave their work a final polish, but Noah couldn't blame them for missing a few spots; the Mailboat repairs had been dropped in the middle of their usual work schedule. Under the circumstances, they'd done a top-notch job with the entire project. First thing this morning, Noah and Brian had tested the new sound system and examined the way the hole in the counter top had been filled with sawdust, the splinters glued down, and the whole thing re-finished. The floor had been scrubbed clean, as well. You couldn't tell what had happened here just four days ago.

The latest news was that Captain Tommy was doing well, too. Noah couldn't imagine he wouldn't be back to work sooner or later.

So Noah scrubbed the windshield and tapped his foot on the bow, bobbing his head to the music blaring over the boat's speakers. He'd plugged his phone into the jack and started up his favorite play list. Hey, they had to make sure the sound system was doing its thing.

But between each new wad of paper towel, Noah checked his black digital watch. It was twenty minutes past seven. Where was Bailey? He was supposed to be the one who was always late, but she'd just broken his all-time record. Did she forget she was on the schedule today? Maybe she thought the boat was still at the repair docks? Brian had tried calling her, but she hadn't picked up.

Then again, Noah couldn't blame her for dragging her feet. He hadn't seen what happened here. But she had. She was the one who'd found Captain Tommy. Noah knew she really looked up to him. He couldn't imagine what that experience had been like for her. Terrifying, probably. And right on the heels of finding that body at the end of the pier two weeks ago. Things were getting weird around here...

Noah squirted the last section of window and scrubbed it down rapidly. He had to keep moving. If Bailey didn't show up soon, they'd have to call somebody else in. But what if no one could come last-minute? He'd have to stock the snack bar *and* go to the post office to sort the mail. Brian was hustling through his own checklist, too, in case he needed to pitch in with Noah's chores. What if Noah ended up jumping all the piers today by himself? He liked to think he was up for that.

But not at the expense of Bailey. Hopefully she was okay...

The windshield done, Noah swung down from the bow to the rub rail. When he glanced over the pier—there she was. She'd made it! He grinned wide. It was funny the way the sight of Bailey gave him a little jolt of joy. But she always had, ever since she'd started attending Badger High School two years ago.

Grabbing the railing above the window, he leaned over the open water that ran between the pier and the boat. "Ahoy!" he shouted above the music, making a salute with the spray bottle. "We were about to send the lifeboats. I figured sharks grabbed you on your walk across town."

She glanced at him and flashed a tiny smile but kept her head down. Without a word, she walked past him and through the doors of the Mailboat.

Wow, did she look down. She was always quiet and shy, but not like this.

He swung his leg through the mail jumper's window and straddled the sill, setting the spray bottle and paper towel in front of him. A delicious summer breeze moved through the boat, warming him through his tee shirt. He watched Bailey walk up the aisle and drop her backpack into a chair near the front counter. He peeked at her eyes. They were damp and red. She'd been crying—a lot, by the looks of it.

He wasn't going to tease her anymore for being late. He gave her kudos for showing up at all. What happened four days ago had to have been a nightmare. A nightmare she was maybe still living.

He leaned further into the boat and grabbed his phone off the counter, then dialed down the music. It throbbed quietly in the background, then died all together as he pulled the jack. He tossed the phone into his open backpack, sitting in a nearby chair. His sketchbook peeked out of the main pocket. It was full of a lot of new drawings, several of which he was going to submit to a sci-fi and fantasy art competition. He couldn't wait. He'd even thought about showing them to Bailey for her opinion. But not now. She clearly wasn't in the mood. He leaned back against the windowsill.

"They fixed it up," he said, nodding generally toward the front of the boat where the damage had been concentrated. "Did a nice job with it."

She ignored him resolutely, unzipping her backpack and digging around inside. She pulled out a stretchy

165

headband, slipped it on, and tucked the loose strands of her hair underneath it.

Noah rubbed his thumb over the spray bottle trigger, letting his nail snap off the end without pushing hard enough to activate the spray. She was so hard to get through to. He bit his lips together, bowed his head, and looked at her meaningfully. "Just tell me if you need anything, okay?" he said in a low voice.

She stopped mid-tuck. Froze, staring down the length of the boat. Her eyes shimmered with new tears. Looks like he'd made her cry again. Maybe that was good? His mom always said it was better to cry. Punch a pillow. Whatever. Just get it all out. And don't break anything.

"Hey, it's all good," he said. "Go cry in the bathroom for a while." He threw a casual hand aft, towards the two heads. "Go home if you need to. We'll be fine."

She looked up at him, eyes glittering, but said nothing. She was so tough, always holding it in. That was probably why she seemed so shy. He'd always thought there was more, though. It had to be hard to be a foster kid. Even though his parents were divorced, he really couldn't imagine life without either one of them.

He pulled his other foot into the boat and slid off the window. "Hey, look," he said, closing the distance between him and Bailey. "We're all here for you, okay? In case you hadn't noticed, we're kind of a family around here. If one of us is hurting, we're all hurting. And this has been a hell of a sucky start to the summer, for you more than anyone." He shrugged. "Well, other than Tommy."

Bailey stared at him blankly, as if he were speaking a foreign language.

He looked into her brown eyes and couldn't help but smile. She was so fascinating. Deep. A lot deeper, he thought, than the other kids at school ever gave her credit for. And she was really, really sad. Not just now, but in general. The thought of taking away a little bit of that

166

sadness, of showing her how beautiful the world could be, brought a warm, tingling feeling to the pit of his stomach.

He reached forward. Touched her hand. It was like touching the sun itself, despite the clouds that shrouded her life. His heart thrilled in a way that felt totally addictive. His mind skipped to ideas of walking hand-in-hand with her along the Shore Path at dusk.

But first things first. Right now, all she needed was a friend. There was no reason he couldn't be that for her.

He looked into her eyes again. "I'm here for you, okay?"

CHAPTER THIRTY
BAILEY

I looked down at my hand in his and felt it shaking. I'd worked super hard to stop crying before walking up to the boat, but now I wanted to cry all over again. My brain screamed at me to get my hand back. That Noah wanted what all boys wanted.

But my heart whispered that I'd known him for two years and he'd never been like that. He'd never eyed me. He'd never made suggestions. He'd never tried to get me alone.

Were virtuous heroes real, or did I merely want to believe in them?

What was real? What was the lie? Why was everything to do with the Mailboat so confusing now?

CHAPTER THIRTY-ONE
JIMMY

————— ❈ —————

With the assistance of corrective lenses, Jimmy had never had reason to doubt his vision, the primary sense of the human species.

But as of the present moment, he could not believe his eyes.

Jimmy stood just off the quay in the shadow of the tower, his jaw hanging open. Through the windows on the lower deck of the Mailboat, he could see Bailey clearly. And with her, Noah Cadigan.

Holding her hand.

Fury boiled up in Jimmy's chest. That slimy double-crosser. Cadigan had pretended to offer council on the wooing of women, only to casually make the move first. Jimmy had never discussed this scenario with either Cadigan or Markham, nor had he outlined it in any of his designs. But he was pretty sure that bombarding the test subject with two Openings of the Heart—simultaneously from two different suitors—would result in a system overload and utter failure of the experiment.

The Cadiganian Variation, indeed. The dirty little con artist had planned this all along, the intended outcome obvious: To humiliate Jimmy in front of the object of his affections, thus ruining any hope of courtship.

Jimmy contemplated how to proceed. He should disappear, robbing Cadigan of his chance to undermine him in front of Bailey. But that was the passive answer. And Jimmy was tired of standing by, letting all his classmates trod him underfoot.

Something snapped inside his heart like a glass stirring rod—once delicate, now razor-sharp.

He huffed several breaths of air. Rolled up his sleeves. Stormed down the pier and through the door of the boat.

"Cadigan!"

The thief looked up and Bailey whirled.

Cadigan grinned and casually dropped Bailey's hand, looping his thumbs in his shorts pockets. "Hey, Jimmy, what are you doing here?"

"This is neither the time nor the place to 'hey' me." He crossed the deck and pointed at him and Bailey. "What do you call this?"

"Uh…" Cadigan's eyes flashed uncertainly between Jimmy and Bailey. "Call what?"

Jimmy gestured at them wildly, hands flopping. *"This!"*

Cadigan shrugged and pointed a thumb at Bailey. "I'm… talking to Bailey?" he suggested.

"'Talking to Bailey,'" Jimmy repeated mockingly. "An Opening of the Heart." He leaned into his opponent's face. *"A Cadiganian Variation!"*

Cadigan produced an expression akin to both confusion and amusement simultaneously. "A what?"

"Don't pretend you don't remember our conversation from the other day," Jimmy said, "how a hypothetical young male entering reproductive maturity can attract a young female, also entering reproductive maturity."

Bailey's eyes widened as they darted between Jimmy and Cadigan. "What are you guys talking about?"

"You, Bailey!" Jimmy shouted, flinging his arms towards her, like an engineer unveiling a groundbreaking new prototype. "We were talking about you!"

Cadigan's eyebrows lifted with apparent enlightenment. He held up his palms in a manner designed to elicit pacification. "Whoa, dude, I didn't know you were talking about Bailey. You never said."

Jimmy flapped his hands overhead, cognizant of a possible parallel to the mannerisms of a green frog puppet on a certain TV show. "Wasn't it obvious? Have you never seen my pupils dilate when Bailey is nearby? Have you never noticed the increase of my heart rate, as evidenced by the throbbing of my temporal arteries?"

Cadigan shifted his weight back on one foot and planted his hands on his hips. "Wow, now that you mention it, I'm not sure how I missed that." His brows were growing heavy—an expression of impatience Jimmy had never seen him use before.

"Are you being sarcastic?" Jimmy inquired.

Cadigan narrowed the distance between them and shook his hands. "Of course I'm being sarcastic!"

"Your temporal arteries are throbbing."

Noah Cadigan's face reddened and his nostrils flared. "Knock it off, Jimmy."

"You might consider working on your anger management issues."

"I *said*, knock it off! My God, you wonder why people don't like you!"

Jimmy's mouth snapped shut as the words hit him like a pressure wave. In the back of his mind, he heard the kids at school laughing at him. His mother dismissing his scientific pursuits from time immemorial. Bailey making excuses not to go out with him. The fact that Bailey was standing right there made the collective situation infinitely worse. What he felt right now was, quite possibly, what some labeled "embarrassment." Or perhaps "humiliation to the extreme."

Jimmy turned to a nearby backpack which he recognized as Cadigan's. As was often the case, a zipper was open and a ring-bound drawing pad hung half-way out. Jimmy observed a pencil sketch of a castle full of tiny, hapless people bravely fending off an attack from a giant, horned monster that looked like a cross between a hippopotamus and a triceratops.

Jimmy snatched the drawing pad from the backpack, gripped the top few sketches firmly in both hands, and ripped them in two.

Cadigan's mouth fell open. "Hey! Why would you do that?" Staring in dismay, he gripped his hair.

Jimmy let the halves of the sketchbook drop to the floor. What he said next, he said slowly and clearly and right in Cadigan's face.

"Bailey is mine."

"Stop it! Stop it!" Bailey closed her eyes and clenched her fists. Her face had morphed into a shade of pink and her eyes were wet with tears. "I am *not* your girlfriend, Jimmy." She whirled on Cadigan. "And I'm not *yours*, either. And *no one* is going to be… *reproducing* with me. So just stay away from me! Both of you!"

She ran out of the boat with tears running down her cheeks. In the doorway, she nearly collided with a tall, thin elderly man.

The gentleman in question glanced from Bailey to Jimmy and Cadigan, his expression bewildered. "What's wrong? What happened? I heard a lot of fuss."

Cadigan spoke to Jimmy through his teeth. "I think you'd better leave now."

Jimmy elevated his chin. "I will. I think I've made my point." He nodded curtly and made for the door.

"Jimmy," Cadigan called.

He turned.

172

"In case you didn't notice... your experiment has failed."
He shifted an eyebrow. "Like, epically. I thought I'd better
point that out, since there's a good chance you didn't get
the memo."

Jimmy shrugged. "I'll redesign the experiment and try
again."

Cadigan pointed a finger. "Stay away from her, Jimmy."

"Only if you do."

"I work with her."

"So do I."

Cadigan sighed and closed his eyes. "Just go."

Jimmy turned and walked off the Mailboat. He passed
the tall old man without a word. Once on the pier, he
glanced around for Bailey, but she was nowhere in sight. So
he headed for the street, for home and his secret lab. His
fingers itched for his drafting paper and protractor, his raw
building materials, his wires and batteries, his chemicals,
his detonators, his explosives. They were just waiting to be
turned into something useful. Something that could blast
away the anger still rushing through every extremity of his
body.

Jimmy spied a family of ducks dabbling just off the
quay, exploring the long lake weed that grew between the
piers and the tour boats. The little ones practiced diving
like their parents, sticking their heads under water and
pointing their fuzzy tails in the air.

Jimmy grabbed his cap off his head—the one with his
name inscribed inside the headband—and flung it into
their midst. They scattered in all directions, the ducklings
making helpless peeps while the parents squawked in
alarm, rounding up their young and staring daggers at
Jimmy.

He watched his own name vanish beneath the waves.

CHAPTER THIRTY-TWO
JIMMY

Jimmy measured ingredients for his next experiment precisely, leveling his eye to the graduated cylinder on the workbench as he poured a glittering clear liquid. A milliliter's error in either direction, and his experiment would be ruined. There was nothing like the rigors of science to clear one's head. In the laboratory, there was no room for emotion and other weaker human states.

Yet his thoughts returned in pulses, like an electromagnet, to the incident that morning aboard the Mailboat.

Having filled his cylinder, Jimmy sighed and looked over his shoulder at his design sketches pinned to the opposite wall, layer over layer. He knew what diagram lay at the very bottom, and it seemed to beckon him. He ought not to succumb to temptations. If anything, he ought to rip that drawing from the wall and incinerate it. From this day forth, it no longer held relevance to his life.

Yet perhaps there was beauty even in heartache.

He sighed, capped the bottle from which he had filled his cylinder, and crossed the room. Pausing first to observe a moment of reverence, he lifted several upper layers of paper to one that hugged the very struts that constituted the rough-hewn wall.

Bailey stared back at him in black and white, locks of summery hair curling around her face. Technically accurate in detail, the portrait still fell far short of her actual beauty. As he examined it, he determined there was something lacking in the eyes. Didn't they say the soul was in the eyes? He didn't know how to draw soul.

A knock sounded on the door of the lab. Jimmy glowered and hustled back to his chemistry set. He poured the cylinder into a beaker and mixed the contents with a stir rod, observing the reaction beneath the gooseneck lamp which illuminated his nocturnal experiments.

"No admittance without a valid password!" he growled.

"Is 'hello' a valid password?" a voice replied from the other side of the door. Jimmy knew who it was. Roland Markham.

He sighed. Markham wasn't the kind of man easily dissuaded. The first time they'd met, Jimmy had been on the verge of blowing up Markham's pier, and the old man wouldn't leave until Jimmy had accepted a glass of iced tea and shown the curious old geezer how the bomb worked.

Resigning himself to this ill-timed but unavoidable social call, Jimmy set down the beaker on the workbench and crossed the rough wooden floor. He stepped over the oil and grass stains where the lawn mower used to sit, back when the laboratory had been a backyard garden shed— back when his family had owned a lawn mower. He slid aside the deadbolt and yanked open the door without bothering to remove his goggles or gloves. Markham stood outside in grass up to his knees with fireflies blinking around him.

"What do you want?" Jimmy asked. He may be stuck with Markham, but he didn't have to be polite.

The old man grinned in the flickering light of the bulb that hung by a wire outside the door. He scanned Jimmy's attire. "My apologies, young sir. I appear to have interrupted you during your intense scientific processes."

"How does one draw soul?"

He raised his eyebrows. "I beg your pardon?"

Jimmy flapped his hand. "Forget it." He returned to his chemistry set and finished stirring the beaker. He noted the change in color in his ledger.

Markham invited himself into the lab and closed the door behind him. Hands clasped behind his back, he tilted his head to observe Jimmy's face. "I take it things aren't going well today?"

"I tried to think with my heart."

"Oh!" Markham hitched his trouser legs and sat on the tall bench by the drafting table. "And?"

"Botched. An amateur interfered and ruined the entire experiment. The damage may be irreparable." Jimmy emptied the contents of a test tube into the beaker. The color changed from pink to orange and effervesced. Jimmy scribbled more notes.

"Oh, I see," Markham muttered. "May I ask what happened?"

Jimmy peeled off his goggles and launched into the whole story, leaving out no detail. "Cadigan was nothing but a lying thief. He made his move on Bailey and forced me into the position of a court jester. It was..." He spread his arms. "Humiliating!" He picked up his beaker again and punctuated the air with the stir rod. "I'll never forget this. Not even after I'm recognized as the greatest scientific mind of our generation. In years to come, historians will talk of how I was rejected by my peers, rejected in love, yet overcame all to earn my place in the hallowed halls of greatness."

Markham tapped his thumbs thoughtfully. "You're afraid Bailey will never give you another chance?" he asked.

"The probability is essentially zero. I calculate that by the time she reaches the half-life on her current state of emotional instability, we'll both be old and feeble."

"Well, that is pretty dire." Markham tilted his head. "There are other girls, surely? Someone else you've met in school, perhaps? A neighbor?"

Jimmy felt his face burn. How dare he suggest that Bailey could be so easily replaced, as callously as one changes out a pair of socks. "I never abandon an experiment," he said.

Markham leaned forward, frowning intensely. "Then you will die a lonely and warped old man. You are young now. You have many years ahead of you to find the right woman. And there are literally millions of girls you've never met. You can't stand there and say with any certainty that Bailey is the *only* girl for you."

Jimmy logged a new sensation. Something akin to tissue being torn in the region of his cardiac muscle. It was the worst feeling ever. And sadly, it was not the first time he'd observed it in himself. He turned away from the old man and stirred his beaker with a vengeance.

"Tell me about your sister," Markham said.

Jimmy grunted and talked with his back to the old man. "Samantha? She's a self-important senior, too absorbed in the shape of her own butt to earn a decent grade in any subject. Her personality is best likened to that of a female dog—pardon the expression."

Markham's gentle tone didn't change. "I meant your other sister."

Jimmy froze as if the temperature of the universe had dropped to absolute zero.

"Amelia was her name, wasn't it?" Markham went on.

The sound of her name ripped through the air like lightning. Jimmy turned slowly, all his joints loose, particularly those of his jaw. "How do you know about her?" he asked.

177

"I was chatting with your mother just now. It came up."

Really? But his mother never spoke of Amelia. No one did. His entire family had thrown her memory out in the gutter and barred the door as if she were a street urchin they couldn't bother with.

Jimmy set down the beaker and planted his palms on the workbench. He stared past the streaks of dirt on the cracked and cobwebbed window. Stared into the darkness outside. Listened to the crickets chirp. Studied a fat, black spider in the windowsill who seemed equally intent upon those innocent, happy, Orthopterian voices...

"She was three years younger than me," Jimmy finally said. "She was always following me around and I pretended I hated it. But she thought I was the world. I'd read my science magazines to her and she'd make me stop and explain everything. I repeat: Literally everything." He smiled at the memory. At the time, he'd pretended to be annoyed. But in reality, he was pleased. While enthusiasm didn't make up for natural talent, she'd soaked everything up like a sponge. Who knew where her curiosity and a degree of tenacity may have led her, given the chance? Jimmy shrugged. "I showed her how to do some simple experiments. She wasn't very good at it, but she liked it. She used to tell everybody I was going to be the greatest scientist in the world."

"And what happened to her?" Markham asked.

Jimmy swallowed hard and tears pricked the corners of his eyes. His grip tightened around the edge of the workbench. Perhaps some of these memories were in fact better off left in the street. Yet Markham had calmly opened the door and beckoned them back in, as innocently as if they were a hungry stray dog. Tail wagging. Disease-ridden.

Jimmy grit his teeth, the fury rekindling. "Somebody picked her up," he said.

He stopped there, the words hanging emptily in the room. The expression perhaps held ambiguous meaning on its own. But after seven years of silence, he found it oddly challenging to speak in specifics. He waited to see if Markham inferred the full and proper meaning without assistance. Jimmy would have preferred it that way. But Markham said nothing. Jimmy got the impression he was waiting.

He swallowed and said it again. "Somebody *picked her up* while we were at the playground." He drew breath from between his teeth. "They found her body a week later in the woods. What was left of it. Someone had beat it to pieces." Under his breath, he added, "She was six."

Markham allowed a reverent silence to linger. Then he said quietly, "I'm very sorry."

Jimmy swiped his nose with the back of his hand. "We were only down the street from home." His throat felt strangely spasmodic and his voice wavered. "I was supposed to watch her."

"Mmm," Markham said, a sort of sigh that was perhaps expressed empathetically. Beyond that, he said nothing, as if leaving space for Jimmy's memories and remorse.

Jimmy could see the tiny, smiling face of his little sister, the way he had seen her last. *"Close your eyes, Jimmy, and count backwards from one hundred by twos while I hide."*

She loved it when he counted backwards from one hundred by twos. If he tried to count by fives, she would catch on in a moment and yell at him for cheating. To this day, he couldn't count backwards without thinking of Amelia. She'd hid, and he had searched for her long and hard, but never found her. He should have told his mother sooner, but he was afraid she'd be mad at him. He was supposed to watch her...

Markham's voice broke into the reverie. "I hope you don't blame yourself, Jimmy."

He whirled and snapped back, "Who else is there to blame? I was supposed to watch her! And instead, I let some sick bastard kidnap her, rape her, and beat her to death. One stupid afternoon at the playground, and I got my sister killed."

"You were only a child at the time."

Jimmy leaned forward and jabbed a finger into his own chest. "I was the greatest mind of any kid my age. Every year, my teachers advised my parents to let me skip the next grade—the next *two* grades. And I couldn't figure out a temporary position as a babysitter. Ask me to recite the entire periodic table of the elements and I won't miss a single atom. Ask me to solve a page-long equation and I'll have it done in five minutes." He felt his face burn red hot. "I could build freaking Tsar Bomba if I had access to the equipment and materials." Short of breath, he spat his final thought out through impassioned spurts. "But I let... a pervert... steal... my sister!"

He wanted to detonate something, but none of his bombs were ready. Instead, his eye landed on the chemistry set, just one of the many symbols of his supposed brilliance. He swept his arms across the workbench. The system of metal supports and glass instruments crashed to the floor and shattered. His half-finished experiment spilled across the ground, leaving a stain in the floorboards that overpowered the grass and oil spot that had resided there before. He knew this new blemish would be permanent; a constant reminder of this moment, which would, by chain reaction, remind him of Amelia. Jimmy threw the beaker and stir rod down on top of the rest of it.

Markham didn't move from his bench. He simply sat with his hands in his lap, as cool as a summer breeze across his pier, and stared in silence at the wreckage.

Jimmy panted as the adrenaline came down. The secondary reaction would be tears, but he struggled to prevent their manifestation. He grit his teeth instead. "That's why everyone hates me. I'm an idiot."

Silence lingered. The crickets sang. Jimmy glanced at the corner of the window and saw the spider furiously wrapping silk around a struggling moth.

Markham finally spoke again. "Did they ever find him— the man who took your sister?"

Jimmy shook his head.

"I thought not," said Markham. Then he drew breath as if to explain something. "You see, your story is not unfamiliar to me. I remember reading it in the paper back when it happened. I never realized you were her brother."

Why would he bring that up—the fact he had read it in the paper? The deepest agony of his life felt suddenly cheapened—a penny horror sold on every street corner. *That's right, friends. Read it here—a chilling thriller, this is. Beautiful maiden; bloodthirsty monster—the lot. Hot off the press!*

Markham studied the broken chemistry set in silence as if contemplating something he considered keeping unsaid. But at length, he spoke. "Do you know, I heard a rumor once..."

"Yeah?" Jimmy asked, his voice deadpan. He didn't want to hear the gossip from the streets.

"Mind you, it's only a rumor. About a man with..." He grimaced as if an unpleasant taste had entered his mouth. "With a questionable taste for... young girls."

Jimmy's skin crawled. As he watched, the spider in the window hugged its prey close, piercing it with its incisors, pumping more venom into its struggling victim. The moth squirmed, then ceased its struggle.

He wished Markham would shut up. He'd make him shut up with a shard from the chemistry set in a minute.

But the old man went on. "A man," he said, "I think you may know."

Jimmy frowned. Who in the name of Isaac Newton did he know who was sick enough to kidnap and murder little girls?

And then it came to him.

He *did* know someone like that. A person who drowned him in creep so vile it was suffocating. One man he could believe was completely capable of murdering a helpless child. Truth bubbled to the surface and with it came indignation.

Bud Weber.

Out of nowhere, the moth sprang back to life, kicking a renewed attack against the spider. Refusing to die.

CHAPTER THIRTY-THREE
RYAN

———— ❄ ————

Finding Bill Gallagher's house wasn't challenging, a two-story home with white brick and gray siding. As promised, the wrought-iron lamp post in the yard was lit. So were the solar-powered lights along the walk and two brass wall lanterns on the porch. I climbed the steps and lifted my hand to ring the bell, then paused at the sound of children's laughter inside. The sound dug to the heart of everything that was on my mind tonight. Everything I'd come here to talk about.

I peeked through the stained glass sidelight and made out a blurred image of Bill on his hands and knees in the living room, roaring like a bear while two children, a boy and a girl, climbed and jumped on him. Bill's wife, Peggy, sat on the sofa wrapped in a fuzzy blanket, purple and periwinkle, a bowl of popcorn in her lap. Beside her sat a girl, thirteen or fourteen, similarly cocooned in pink and white, a TV remote in her hand. The teen cast a glance at the brawl on the rug, smiled with a mild air of superiority, and turned her attention back to the TV.

I grinned. Bill's grandchildren? Feeling a little guilty for breaking up this moment of domestic bliss, I pushed the button. A bell rang inside the house. Bill's voice sounded through the door.

"Okay, okay, lemme go. I gotta get the door."

The children giggled. "No! No! We have to capture you!"

But Bill peeled them off with the assistance of some well-deployed tickles and snuck away to the foyer. He swung the door open and beamed at me. A knitted hat was parked on top of his head with a lion's nose, eyes, and ears, red yarn sticking out in all directions, corded ties dangling down past his shoulders. "Ryan, my man! Come on in."

Before Bill could move to let me pass, the two smaller children, maybe seven or eight years old, attacked from behind. The girl wrapped herself around his leg while the boy leapt onto his shoulders.

"We've got you! We've got you!"

Bill grasped the arms around his neck and groaned. "Oh! Oh! I'm wounded! I'm done for!" He spiraled slowly to the rug in the middle of the foyer, moaning melodramatically. Once on the floor, he rolled as if to pin the kids underneath him while giving them plenty of time to scramble out. "Ohhh, I'm done for!" He sprawled full-length on his back and stared at the ceiling.

The kids giggled until they couldn't breathe, their small faces turning pink. I grinned and tried not to laugh out loud.

Bill sat up, back rigid, legs straight out in front of him, his face as serious as a stone statue. He placed a hand on the boy's shoulder and spoke in a deep tone. "Congratulations, my young warriors. You have conquered the Wicked Beast of the Wood. The two of you now must reign together as King and Queen of the Jungle." With the formality of a pope crowning a monarch, Bill removed the fuzzy hat and placed it in the children's upturned hands. "Rule well, my children. The entire Magical Kingdom of Stuffed Animals now looks up to you."

They laughed all the more.

Bill broke his serious expression and tousled their hair. "All right. Go set up your kingdom. I've got to talk to Ryan here for a while."

They tugged on his sleeves. "But we want you to come with us!"

"Oh, I'll be along in a bit. I expect you to have organized your royal court by then and maybe gotten started on a cavalry."

"With unicorns?" the girl asked.

Bill rubbed noses with her. "Yes, with unicorns!" He turned to the boy. "And dinosaurs! Now go on upstairs. I'll be along in a bit."

"Yes, Bill," they both said and scrambled up the stairs. The lion hat became a hand puppet and roared all the way up the railing.

Bill watched them, laughed, then groaned. "Ohhh, Ryan, give an old man a lift." He held up his hand.

I grasped it and pulled him to his feet. "Your grandkids?" I asked.

Bill planted his hands on his hips and stretched his back. "Naw, the newest pair of fosters. Brother and sister. The wife and I said we were gonna quit, but we just couldn't say no. They would have been broken up otherwise. Social services couldn't find anyone to take 'em both."

Bill's words raised my eyebrows. "You're a foster home?"

"Hell, didn't you know that? Tyler and Teresa are the sixty-third and sixty-fourth kids we've taken in since we started in 1989." He pointed over his shoulder into the living room, where Peggy and the teenage girl were discussing the TV show during a commercial break. "Missy's number sixty-two."

I shook my head. "That's a lot of kids."

Bill cast his eye around the foyer, the stairwell, and the hall. Every wall was plastered in photos of children, from newborns to teenagers. "It sure is," Bill said, pride in his voice. "Angels, all of 'em." He pointed to a family portrait. "That's us with our natural-born kids—Andrew, Grace, and Jordan. They're all grown up now." His finger moved to another family portrait, but bigger. "And here's us with the three of them plus the ones we adopted. Titus, Laquisha, Allie, Krista, and Josh." He chuckled. "Anyways, the ones we've adopted so far. Never say never, eh?" He patted my shoulder. "Looks like Missy might moving to an aunt's house soon. But these two—" he glanced up the stairs where the two little voices continued to chatter. "I don't know. If their mom gets things back together, they'll be going home. But if not, Peggy and I may have to consider it..."

I shook my head again. "You like to keep busy."

Bill put his hands in his pockets and shrugged. "Most of the kids only stay with us briefly. Their parents hit on rough times—get in trouble with the law or drugs or family disputes—and just need a chance to sort things out again. Then the kids go back home. But a few bounce in and out of the system. And a few more never make it back to their own families." He shook his head. "Those are the ones that break your heart."

I stared at the photos, unable to speak. I realized now that I'd underestimated just how appropriate it would be to talk to Bill tonight. The words all wanted to come rushing out of my mouth, yet none of them volunteered to go first.

Bill slapped me on the arm with the back of his hand. "Let's go into my office. We can talk freely there."

He led the way down the hall. My eye fell over faces of all ages, shapes, and colors. Some of them looked shy, scared, or confused. Yet they offered a smile for the photographer. Some of them positively beamed.

"We take lots of photos while they're here," Bill rambled on. "When they leave, we send the photos along with them. Some kids, it's all they have besides the clothes

186

on their backs. They get to have their pick from the Magical Kingdom of Stuffed Animals, too, or whatever they liked to play with while they were here." He paused and rubbed his chin. "Gotta wonder how much of that stuff stays with them. Some of those kids move around a lot. We had one boy twice. Gave him a dump truck he loved to death. He told us he got moved out of one home so fast, he didn't have a chance to take it with him. Poor tyke. We couldn't buy the same truck again, so we got him a new one with flashing lights."

I grinned. If an angel ever walked the earth, it was probably Bill Gallagher.

Bill pushed open the door to his office and motioned me in. The desk was a gleaming cherry wood, buried in loosely-organized papers, a well-thumbed Bible, and another spray of framed photos. The desk was outfitted with a comfy leather office chair behind it and a set of upholstered chairs in front of it. But Bill guided me instead to a heavy leather sofa and an armchair. Between them sat a gas fire, flames licking warmly against a fake log.

"Take a load off, Ryan, and tell me what brings you here tonight. Want anything to drink? Beer? Wine? I can mix a bad cocktail. Water's on the menu, too, if you ain't comfortable drinking alcohol in front of a preacher."

I laughed. In addition to volunteering as our police chaplain, Bill had his own flock to tend at one of the local churches. Yet his clerical collar was deceptive. People approached Bill as if they had to be paradigms of perfection; model Christians, or even model fake Christians if they weren't religious. But Bill was a chameleon, adapting himself to whatever company he was in. When visiting little old ladies, he pet their cats and sipped their tea. But among cops, he drank and cussed as comfortably as the rest of us. "I haven't been struck down by lightning yet," he'd say. "But if Jesus appears to me on Broad Street, I s'pose I'll change my ways."

"I'll take a beer," I told him.

Bill clicked his tongue and winked. "Beer it is. You're an IPA person, aren't you?"

"Yes, sir."

He grabbed a bottle from a small fridge on a countertop and popped the lid with a bottle opener. He handed me the beer, then chose another one for himself. "Well, what's on your mind, Ryan?" he asked, settling into the leather armchair.

I took a sip then leaned forward on my knees and rolled the cold bottle between my palms. I exhaled slowly. Now the hard part. "God, I don't even know how to say this."

Bill drank from his wheat lager. "Well, say it badly, then we can figure how to say it better."

I grinned. Plunge in anywhere, I guess. "Well, there's Monica."

"Yeah? She still giving you grief?"

My heart pounded in my chest as I paged through my thoughts. Everything that had happened over the past few days... The things we'd said, both good and bad... Those moments we'd shared at the hospital in Milwaukee... I finally looked up at Bill and went for broke.

"I'm still in love with her." I locked my jaws together and waited for his response.

Bill smiled and lifted his brows. "Well, don't that beat all. Have you mentioned it to her?"

I shook my head. "That sounds like a bad idea."

"She still kicking you in the nuts for showing your face in town again?"

I nodded. "I mean for a moment, I thought maybe..." I rolled the beer in my palms again. I couldn't say it out loud—everything I'd been dreaming. I was an idiot for even hoping. I couldn't even bring myself to say the words. Yet the ache... That horrible emptiness Monica had left behind...

But Bill lifted his head. "Go on."

I sighed and studied the brown, black, and cream rug beneath my shoes. "Every now and again, we actually sort of get along. And then I get my hopes up. But then I don't know what I do wrong. I'm trying my hardest to not be an idiot. To take things slow. To give her room to breathe. But next time she looks at me, *bam.*" I snapped my fingers. "We're back to full Monica-hates-Ryan mode."

Bill nodded. "Some hurts take a long time to forgive. Monica, she's real tough on the outside. But that's just to make up for being so sensitive on the inside."

I sighed. "I should just leave her alone, shouldn't I?"

"Is that what you want?"

"I don't want to keep making her upset."

"Okay, that's what you don't want," Bill said, "but that's not what I asked." He leaned forward and pointed a finger at me. "What do you *want?*"

I opened my mouth, but no words came out. Forgetting Monica seemed like the right thing to do in so many ways. But it was definitely not what I wanted. Not by a long shot. I wanted her in my arms again. I wanted her at my back again. I wanted our lives to revolve around each other again. I wanted everything we once had—but without me being a dick.

"I want…" My insides writhed at the thought of putting these feelings into words. It felt so wrong. "I want *us* to be happy."

He merely nodded again. Waiting for more. So I said it all. "I want us to be happy again. Together. Like we used to be."

"And you feel that desire is wrong," Bill said. "Why?"

The man was a mind-reader. But wasn't the answer obvious? "Because I don't make her happy." I held up my hands, palms facing, as if indicating a measurement. "I'd say I put her somewhere between mildly annoyed and raving mad."

"She's told you as much?"

I actually laughed out loud. "In everything she does. Everything she says."

He held up his hands. "She's told you, 'Ryan, I hate you and you make me miserable.'"

I thought back on all the conversations we'd had since I moved back to Lake Geneva. I shook my head. "No, I guess not."

"Uh-huh. And on top of that, you say there are times when you two get along just fine."

I nodded. Tried to predict where he was taking the conversation next.

Bill sat back in his arm chair and studied me. "Have you ever considered maybe it has nothing to do with you?"

I turned that over in my head, then pulled an exaggerated frown and nodded, feeling sarcastic. "Considering she curses my name every time she sees me, that would be really ironic." I tilted my head and lifted an eyebrow to let him know I didn't buy it. "Come on, Bill, everyone knows she hates me."

Bill flapped a hand. "She treats everybody the way she treats you."

I opened my mouth, but no words emerged. He had a point. "But," I ventured, "I'm the reason she treats everyone the way she does."

Bill sat up taller and stared at me down his nose. "Ohhh, it always comes back to you, does it? Lordy, aren't you high and mighty."

This time, I really was speechless.

Bill grinned. "You know people are complicated, Ryan. There could be a lot of factors in play here. More than you ever dreamed. For instance, she might be feeling guilty."

I sneered. "Guilty? About what? I'm the one who cheated on her."

Bill shrugged. "Throwing you out. Never hearing your side of the tale. Not giving you a second chance. Could be lots of things she regrets. Or it could be entirely unrelated and blowing steam at you is simply convenient." He leaned forward and took a sip of his beer. "All I'm saying is, you've only got one half of the story. Your half. Monica hasn't volunteered hers. Maybe she never will. But until you have that second half, all you have to work with are guesses. And those guesses could be so far from the truth, they're not even relevant."

I nodded slowly. The man's words made sense. Maybe I'd assumed I knew how Monica felt. Betrayed and hurt were a fair wager. But could there be more?

"So here's an idea," Bill continued. "Let's say you proceed with the understanding that your wish—your deepest desire to be happy together with Monica—isn't a bad thing. In fact to be in love, to forgive and be forgiven, to maybe even have a second shot at a relationship—" he sat up and spread his arms. "These are all great things! Nothing wrong with any of 'em." He leaned forward and lifted a finger. "But you will never get there without hearing Monica's half of the story. Maybe she'll never tell you. Unfortunately, you can't force her to. But what you can do is foster an atmosphere that welcomes her to share. Be open. Be understanding. And most of all, be patient."

I thought that's what I *had* been doing. But come to think of it, my focus had mostly been on myself. I wanted Monica to forgive *me*. I wanted her to come back to *me*. I wanted her to make me feel better about *me*. Wow. I was such a selfish bastard, I was even selfish when I was trying to be unselfish.

I closed my eyes and tried to picture myself shifting my concerns from my own scrapes and bruises to hers. Scared as I was of rejection again, terrified as I was of learning all the ways I'd hurt her, the truth was that I wanted to know. Everything. The whole story. I wanted to know how she'd found it so easy to give me the boot so swiftly, after the lifetime we'd shared together. Maybe there was more to the

191

story than me being an asshole. Maybe there were things that had been left entirely unsaid.

Leather squeaked as Bill leaned back in his chair. "So what else is new? How's Project Bailey going?"

I grinned at the name he'd assigned to my little mission, then looked down at my beer, which I hadn't touched since our conversation began. My mouth was dry, but my head was so focused on the conversation I couldn't bring myself to interrupt it by taking a drink. "Yeah, that's not going so well, either," I said.

"Uh-oh. Tell me more."

I explained what had happened at the hospital earlier. How Bailey had apparently talked to Tommy, then insisted on leaving. When I'd tried to get more information, she'd turned into a terrified, furious animal.

"She wouldn't talk to me the whole way home," I said. "Hasn't talked to me since. I've called a couple times. Texted." I shook my head. "Not a word." I sank into the sofa and raked a hand through my hair, forcing a laugh. "Is there any explanation for women?"

Bill pulled a frown and shook his head. "None at all."

"I thought I had it all figured out," I went on. I sat up and motioned with the beer. "Bailey trusts Tommy. Great! I already know Tommy's concerned about whoever's abusing her. He was the one to report it. So all I've got to do is make sure Bailey and Tommy are together. Wait for her to finally tell him that her foster dad's abusing her. Presto-magico! I have a case. I can get Bailey out of there—I don't know, foist her off on you—"

Bill grinned. The glint in his eye suggested the offer of another foster child was better than a plane ticket to the Caribbean.

"—and then I can throw Bud Weber in a dungeon where he'll never see the light of day again." I slouched back into the sofa and stared at the ceiling. "But now she's not talking to Tommy, either." The frustration built up

inside my chest as if I were a human pressure cooker.
"What am I doing wrong, Bill?"

Bill was silent before replying. "You say she's been in
foster care how long?"

"Since she was five," I said to the ceiling.

Leather squeaked as Bill shifted his seat. "Now, it's not
like I'm an expert on foster kids or nothin'..."

I laughed and tilted my head down so I could look at
him.

"And I've only spoken with Bailey the once," he said.
"But I might be able to tell you a thing or two to shed some
light on the matter."

I sat up again. "I'm all ears."

Bill nodded. "Do you feel like, no matter how nice you
are to her, she just shuts you out?"

I lifted my eyebrows and made a circular nod. "Yeah.
Definitely."

"Like she's even angry at you?"

I clamped my jaws. Had Bill been listening in when
Bailey blew up at me? "Yeah. She looked like she wanted to
punch me back at the hospital."

"Did you in fact believe she might punch you?" Bill
questioned.

I nodded. "If I'd kept pushing her."

Bill shook his head. "Ooh. She's got it bad."

"Got what bad?"

"I call it Foster Care Syndrome. Seen it a hundred
times." He sat forward and framed the air with his hands.
"Now, Ryan, I want you to try to put yourself in her shoes
and see if this makes any sense. Let's say your very earliest
memory is of your daddy and mommy bein' taken away
from you."

"Okay." In Bailey's case it was her mom and a boyfriend.
I didn't have a clue who or where the father was. But since I
wasn't sure where Bill was going with this, I didn't
interrupt.

"And let's say you were dropped off at somebody's home. They treated you nice and everything, but they were strangers. And you're real young. At that age, you just wanna be with your parents. But Mom and Dad never show up again."

For some reason, Bill's words triggered a completely new line of thought. My own father, rarely home. Always working. Too tired and cross afterwards to throw the pigskin in the backyard. Wasn't even there for my high school graduation. He'd taken the day off—supposedly so he could be there. Instead, he got drunk the night before. Was in bed sleeping it off the next day. Missed the whole thing. Left the house before the party that afternoon.

There I went thinking about myself again. I put my thoughts back on Bailey.

Bill went on. "And just about the time you get used to your new digs, decide maybe these strangers are okay, *bam!* With no explanation whatsoever, someone comes along and takes you away again. Maybe you go on to a new foster home. Or a group home. But you never see that particular family again. And this keeps happening. Maybe sometimes you stay with relatives. Maybe you even stay with mom or dad again and you figure everything's finally gonna be all right. But no. The cops come an' take 'em away, just like before. And you keep moving. Home to home. Family to family. You know what that does to ya, Ryan?"

I wasn't sure I wanted to know. The picture Bill painted was already bleak. But I followed along anyway. "What?"

"You learn," Bill said slowly, "that you can't hang on to nobody. You learn that nobody's gonna be there for you no matter what. You learn that you're alone in the world, and you can't depend on anyone but yourself. And it don't matter how nice someone seems. Don't fall for it. 'Cause they'll be gone tomorrow. Peggy and me, we try to make this house a refuge from the storm. We try to make the kids forget that their mommy and daddy yelled at each other.

We try to make 'em forget that another foster family kicked 'em out because they were 'difficult children.' And you can see for yourself, the kids do all right here. But you know what? We see a kid again that we had maybe six months, maybe a year ago. And you know what they say?"

I shook my head.

"'Why'd ya leave us, Peggy and Bill? Why'd ya let us go?'" Bill shook his head. "And boy, if that don't cut you to the heart. But ultimately, no matter how much we love them, we don't have a say in what happens to them. The court does. And we gotta abide by what the court says, even if it's monkey business half the time. But as far as the kids are concerned, we abandoned them, just like everybody else did.

I nodded, soaking in what Bill was saying. Trying to see things from Bailey's point of view. "That makes sense."

"Well, that's only the first half. Here's the second: The stuff you learn when you're little sticks with you forever. They talk about a child's mind being like a blank slate and you can write on it whatever you want. Well, that's true— only we don't have any chalk. It's all permanent marker. And Bailey's slate says, 'Don't trust people. They'll be gone tomorrow.' It's all she knows. So you know what she's doin', when she's shutting you out and having meltdowns and threatening you?"

"What?"

Bill jabbed the air with his finger. "She's givin' you every reason to leave *now*, rather than later. She *wants* you to abandon her. 'Cause it'll hurt less now than after she's had a chance to get attached to you. In her world, the idea of somebody sticking around long-term doesn't exist. It's never happened before. She's thinkin', 'This guy can abandon me now... or he can abandon me later.'" He waved his hand, as if clearing a table top. "There ain't no other option in her world, ya see?"

I rocked in my seat and studied my toes past my beer bottle. I felt like I should have been able to put all that information together myself, if I'd merely thought for a minute. Thought about Bailey rather than me and my need to help her. My need to make up for putting her in foster care in the first place.

Maybe the time for thinking about me was over. It's all I'd ever done.

"So what do I do?" I asked.

Bill made a long sigh through his nose and stared at me from under arched brows. He was sizing me up. Weighing whether or not I was in any way qualified for the job he was about to propose.

"There's only one cure," he said at last, "and it don't always work."

That sounded foreboding. "What is it?"

Bill paused. He leaned forward in the arm chair. "You have to love her *relentlessly.*"

Relentlessly. I tried to imagine the definition of "relentless love," but wasn't sure I grasped it. So I asked. "What does that mean?"

"That means that when she runs from you," he drew a line through the air with one pointy finger, Bailey running away, "you have to follow her." His other pointy finger caught up and the two touched. I ignored the beer bottle in the second hand—the one that represented me. Bill next lifted his hands, palms out, the bottle pinched between his thumb and first finger. "When she pushes you away, you have to pull her close." He made fists and drew them into his chest. "When she spits in your eye, you have to look at her and say, 'Bailey,'" he bobbed a finger. "'I'm not gonna leave ya.' Because when she seems to be rejecting you the worst, that's when she needs you the most."

I pondered Bill's words with a sinking feeling. I didn't have a great track record for being there for people, if my marriage to Monica was any example. Bill was literally asking me to do the one thing I'd never succeeded at. Relentless love. Love that pursued, even when it was rejected or hurt.

"Now, that's a tall order for anybody," Bill said. "Been there dozens of times. Hell, I had a teenage girl throw a knife at me and it stuck in the wall. And you know what I did?"

I shook my head.

Bill reached behind him to his desk and turned around a photo frame. A girl with black skin and curly dark hair beamed out at the world like a homecoming queen. "Foster failure number two," Bill said proudly. "I adopted that little girl. Proved the shit out of her that I wasn't gonna leave her." Grinning happily, he took the photo off the desk and smiled down at it. "She's a commercial pilot now. Got married last year. And even when I gave her away, I told her, 'If he does you a bad turn, I'm takin' you right back.' She knew by then I meant it." He kept smiling into the photo. "Relentless love. Yes, siree. Takes a lot out of ya, but it gives a lot back."

I swallowed carefully, rolling the beer bottle in my palms. "But I'm leaving Lake Geneva at the end of the summer. I'm only a reserve officer. My position goes away middle of September." Suddenly, I was grateful. I'd come here with the hope of finding a way to stay, but not anymore. If anything, this conversation had firmed up my thought of leaving. This didn't take a lot of deep contemplation. I already knew I wasn't capable of the kind of relentless love Bill embodied. As soon as I felt someone didn't like me, I was out of there.

But Bill shrugged. "You have a cell phone. The opposite end of the world is just a text message away. But Ryan." Bill leaned forward over the photo of his adopted daughter and crossed his arms, elbows on knees. "Remember this: A child's heart is a delicate thing. Especially when it's already been broken. Be careful what you do. You can't fence sit on this one. You can't turn your back on her half-way through."

But isn't that exactly what I would end up doing? Wasn't that simply my nature? I finally asked the question outright. "Am I capable of relentless love?"

Bill left me waiting for an answer. I heard neither breath nor the squeak of leather. Just a long, hollow silence.

"We all are," Bill said. "If we want to be."

TUESDAY
JULY 1, 2014

CHAPTER THIRTY-FOUR
JIMMY

---※---

Jimmy cracked open the back door of the restaurant and peered in. From the door, he could sight up the long, narrow kitchen, all the way past the ovens and grills to the pickup window at the front. In the middle of the kitchen stood Bud Weber, pulling buns out of the oven and replacing them with sheets of rolled dough yet to be baked. He smacked the door shut and slammed trays down on the counter.

As if equipped with a sensor, he looked directly at the door. "Yo, you're late," he barked. "I got a stack of dishes a mile high back there. Get your ass in gear."

Today, Bud's usual tones of dissatisfaction passed over Jimmy's head. "Yes, sir," he said, stepping through the door and closing it behind him. As Bud turned to a kettle on the stove, Jimmy gave him a sneer. What secrets was that fat bastard hiding? Jimmy would find out. Soon. The minute he got a chance.

Jimmy stepped into his dish room and strapped on a clean white apron, soon to be stained with the leftovers of a hundred meals. It was only three days before the Fourth of July, and the town was already buzzing for a Tuesday.

People's families were arriving in town. No one would want to cook. They would come here, sate their hunger, and shove their dirty dishes at Jimmy, the unknown face behind the dish room wall.

Jimmy attacked the mountainous mess Bud had created from preparing specials all morning and watched the kitchen carefully. At approximately 10:15, Bud would leave his stovetop and grills to arrange the walk-in cooler. At 11:20, he would step out back for a final cigarette before the rush. And if he was drinking beer at his regular rate, he would relieve himself at least twice between now and lunch.

But today, Bud seemed determined to remain in his kitchen. The hands of the clock above Jimmy's dishwasher slowed, a warping of the space-time continuum, marked only by innumerable loads of dishes. But Bud never removed himself from his hot and greasy domain.

Hours later, his emotional state vastly decayed, Jimmy carried a stack of pots and pans into the kitchen and hung them over the stove.

Bud shouted. "Hey, quit fartin' around, old man!"

Jimmy jumped and whirled to give Bud a scathing glance, ready to argue that he had been applying himself industriously all morning. But the man's back was turned, arms folded over the pickup window as he conversed with a patron in the lobby. Bud was simply exchanging banter with a regular—unfeasible as it was to think of Bud having friends or even people who liked him. Jimmy sighed. False alarm.

As he returned to hanging the cookware, Jimmy observed that Bud's conversation, far from terminating, merely extended. Bud's companion came behind the front counter and leaned on the opposite side of the window, making himself at ease.

Wait. Maybe this was his chance? Palms perspiring, Jimmy observed Bud and the customer for another few seconds. They didn't seem in any hurry. Jimmy glanced at the clock above Bud's head. In less than twenty minutes, the doors would flap back and forth on their hinges, setting off an annoying bell every 10.6 seconds (average), and the dining room would fill for lunch with ravenous *homo sapiens.* If Jimmy was going to act at all, he should act now.

Heart pounding, he slipped into the storeroom and approached the door to Bud's office. He touched the doorknob but paused. This room always filled him with dread. Once he had heard what sounded like people in coitus—and Rita the head waitress had walked out afterward straightening her skirt and blouse. On a separate occasion, it was a man who had emerged, old and bald-headed but looking rather satisfied. Jimmy never entered this room without listening first. But intimate relations were not all that transpired behind this door. Just last week, Jimmy had caught Bud stashing not cash but a gun and what looked like a black leather jacket in the vault.

Jimmy had concluded long ago that it would behoove him to keep his nose to his own business if he wanted to remain bodily intact around this establishment. Now, with his hand on the knob, primal survival instincts objected against his entering Bud's office.

He did it anyway.

Slipping over the threshold, he pulled the door shut behind him. The place was a rat's nest of papers and empty booze bottles. While Bud Weber never left a streak on a stove top or a smudge on a shot glass, he apparently didn't give a damn about his personal spaces. The dingy drywall and the industrial carpet stank like grease from the deep fryer.

Jimmy approached the desk and began to shuffle through the papers. What did he even seek? Anything that might tie Bud Weber to more nefarious business than operating a bar and grill. But the documents were nothing but bills to be paid, magazines from restaurant supply companies, and a lot of junk mail.

Jimmy shuffled through the drawers but with no better success. Pens. Files. Paper clips. He did find a box of bullets in the bottom drawer. But even bullets and a gun meant nothing on their own. Bud had a Constitutional right to protect his place of business.

Jimmy knelt on the desk and searched the shelves overhead. Nothing but beer steins, a lot of dust, and a dead fly. He sorted through a stack of envelopes. But hope and time were both running thin. What if Bud had concluded his conversation with the restaurant patron? What if he had relocated to the storage room? Jimmy would be trapped in the office.

Jimmy was about to descend from the desk when he noticed something out of place. One of the beer steins sported a thin layer of dust on the lid. Had he forgotten to clean this container the other day? But no, he never would have risked Bud's wrath by overlooking the proper cleaning of one of his prized possessions. If a stein was still dirty, it was because Bud hadn't given it to him in the first place. But why would Bud have left one out?

Jimmy pulled the stein off the shelf and flipped open the lid.

Inside was an odd array of small items. A necklace of large pearls, probably plastic, with a set of earrings to match. A tube of deep maroon lipstick, the case scratched, the cake of makeup inside dry and cracked. A black, eight-sided locket with a glittering silver spider sprawled across the lid. A pocket knife.

Jimmy dug through them all until he reached the bottom.

And there he found it. A silky pink bow, faded and filthy.

Jimmy removed it. Fastened to the back of the bow was a hair clip. Attached to the top was a white butterfly. Not an original piece of the hair accessory, the butterfly was secured un-artfully with a dried-up rubber band. The winged creature clearly wasn't even meant as a decoration. It was a plastic model like the ones Jimmy used to buy at one of the gift shops, though his personal collection had consisted primarily of grasshoppers and spiders and other more fascinating species. Displayed in large bins, you could choose the ones you desired at the reasonable price of twenty-five cents apiece.

In fact, Jimmy *had* purchased this butterfly at the gift shop. When he was nine.

He'd given it to Amelia because she didn't like his grasshoppers and spiders. They creeped her out. But he had wanted to show her that insects, too, were worth her study. So he'd bought her the butterfly. He was somewhat put off that she turned it into a hair accessory instead of observing the number of spiracles on its abdomen and thorax, through which it breathed; the construction of its antennae, which it utilized for both smell and balance; its curled proboscis through which it drank nectar. But at least she liked it. It had made her really happy.

She was wearing it the day she disappeared.

Jimmy's hand shook while tears stung his eyes. After all this time… It was like holding a piece of his sister again. A piece of his sister that cried out for justice. For revenge.

Jimmy had tested Markham's theory, and it had proved correct. The villain who had killed Amelia had been right under Jimmy's nose all along. But Bud Weber had gotten away without punishment far too long. He'd gotten lax. He'd kept something from the day of his kill. A souvenir. Twisted minds did things like that, did they not? Kept mementos of their murders so they could relive the day? No doubt, this explained the random assortment of mostly female objects hidden in Bud Weber's beer stein.

Jimmy thought of everything Bud had done to torture and kill his six-year-old sister and the fury built in his chest. He gripped the bow in his fist. Bud would regret keeping this. He'd regret kidnapping Amelia. He'd regret treating Jimmy like trash this whole time. He'd regret everything.

Jimmy finally understood the purpose for which his bomb, the Backfire Model, had been designed.

FRIDAY
JULY 4, 2014

CHAPTER THIRTY-FIVE
RYAN

———— ⚓ ————

Mounted on my patrol bike, I inched through the pedestrian and vehicular traffic in the tourist district. The Fourth of July fell on a Friday this year, making for a long weekend and plenty of work for the LGPD. The celebrations were all on the outskirts of the city at the Grand Geneva Resort and the Geneva National Golf Club. But by appearances, plenty of Chicagoans agreed that a day on the lake was a prime way to celebrate the nation's birthday. And when they weren't in their boats or on the beaches, they were in the streets perusing the gift shops and restaurants.

So I stood on my bike pedals, pulling off an impressive balance at snail speed while creeping around hand-holding couples, children with ice cream cones, and tiny dogs on threadlike leashes. In between scanning the streets for disturbances, I concentrated on how badass I looked in this stance, my bike and I held aloft by the hand of God—or finely tuned muscular adjustments, take your pick. Focusing on my own coolness was better than replaying my conversation with Bill Gallagher, which was stuck in my head like the spinning wheel of a crashed bicycle.

His challenge, *relentless love,* rang through my head like a taunt. Was I capable? Could I even picture a world in which I was there for Bailey and Monica in a way I'd never been for anyone before?

But I already knew the answer. Why else had I spent my morning before my shift filling out applications to other departments, all of them far, far away? I was a drifter. That was my nature. For Monica or Bailey to rely on me was about as advisable as relying on that crashed bicycle. Why should I expect them to do such a thing? Especially Monica?

Yet if I was a drifter, I wasn't sure why I'd paused, mouse over the "send" button on the applications, and never submitted them.

I rode up the handicap-accessible dip in the sidewalk on the northwest corner of Broad Street and Main and crept expertly between the light pole and an elderly lady with shopping bags over her arms. I searched for problems requiring a hero on a bike: traffic violations, pickpockets, medical emergencies in the July heat.

"Hey, Brandt!" a voice yelled over the din.

A man in his thirties pushed through the crowd, thumbs tucked into the straps of a backpack-style child carrier. The little boy seated inside wore a white bucket hat and a blank expression as his big blue eyes soaked up the shapes and colors around him.

"Schultz," I greeted the man carrying the baby. I let one foot off the pedal. Mike Schultz and I gripped each other's hands then bumped fists and made the "watching you" gesture, forked fingers pointed at eyes, then at each other. He had a secret handshake for every cop in the department, even Monica. In a little stroke of brilliance, he'd designed a handshake for her that drew from her usual stash of fury; it started with punching each other in the shoulder and ended with simultaneous karate kicks.

Ours, on the other hand, was developed after we were nearly shot down in the street together, two weeks ago to the day. If Schultz hadn't been watching my back, I would have been dead.

"What are you doing, man?" I asked. "Lucky enough to get the Fourth of July off and you're just wandering around town?"

"I know, I'm an idiot, right?" Schultz agreed.

I whistled low. "You should have run away. Minnesota or something."

"Oh, South Dakota, at least," Schultz laughed.

A woman with long, straight black hair caught up and slipped a hand in his. A straw bag slung over her shoulder was stuffed with rolled-up towels, snorkels, and a set of inflatable arm bands. The toddler at her side took one glance at me then hid his face in her breezy white dress, deciding to be shy. The woman stroked his messy, dark hair.

Schultz motioned to the woman. "Oh hey, Ryan, this is my wife Nicole."

I grinned and shook her hand. "I know. Mike only talks about you non-stop. I've seen your pictures."

She laughed, an easy, relaxed sound paired with an equally lovely smile. "Nice to meet you."

I eyed the kids. "And these must be Jackson and Aiden." Jackson, the three-year-old, dipped behind his mother's dress again.

"Both guilty as charged," Schultz confirmed, beaming down at the boy.

"Braving the beach, eh?" I asked and jabbed a thumb over my shoulder. "Have you seen how crowded that place is? You'll be lucky to get a six-inch-wide strip to unroll a towel."

Schultz shrugged. "Eh, I packed the OC spray."

I laughed. Oleoresin capsicum—better known to civilians as pepper spray.

"You're tempting fate, man," I said, shaking my head. "You know you'll get called out." There's no one more superstitious than a cop. Never say "It's quiet today." Never

210

start your shift without your lucky pen. And if you miraculously get a red-letter day off—a holiday, a festival, whatever—go out of town. It's guaranteed something big will pop up that requires extra manpower.

Schultz shrugged, his gesture bouncing the baby carrier on his back and the baby inside it. "Eh, it's a risk I'll take. Besides, I don't want the only time people see me to be when I'm in uniform."

I nodded my head. "Yep. Definitely got a screw loose. You live outside of Chicago, not Mayberry."

Most of us preferred it if no one knew what we did for a living. At parties, your friends introduced you as "the cop" and half-baked jokes about us arresting their buddies ensued. On the flip side, you never knew when you'd bump into someone with a chip on their shoulder. Things could get icy and dicey real quick when all you wanted was to relax and enjoy a drink. The lofty thinkers in law enforcement talked about improving relationships between communities and their police departments—getting out of the patrol cars and into the street, being present on duty and off. But the real world wasn't made of roses. Any cop who'd been on the beat for half a day knew that. We became aliens when we took the badge, understood only by each other.

But Mike Schultz smiled at me. "This is my town, man. I don't like to hide from it. I live here twenty-four seven, not just when I'm on duty."

His optimism was so shiny it hurt to look at it. It dawned on me then that there was a reason everyone voted him "most likely to be promoted to sergeant." He was the epitome of everything a police department hoped to be. If his ten years wearing the badge hadn't rinsed the scent of roses out of his nostrils, perhaps nothing would. I hoped not.

I quit arguing and simply bumped him on the shoulder with my fist. "Okay then, poster-boy cop. Have fun in the six inches of sand and sunshine you get out there on the beach."

He laughed. "We will! That one's turning into a good swimmer." He pointed to Jackson.

One eye peeked out from behind the dress.

"Oh, I bet," I said with a smile for the kiddo. Then I turned to Nicole. "Good to meet you."

She smiled that serene, winning smile. If being a cop's wife and raising two small children was stressful, her demeanor didn't show it. "Good to meet you, too."

Mike Schultz and his family rejoined the flow of foot traffic. To my surprise, the three-year-old looked behind him and waved. I smiled and waved back.

As I watched them, Schultz's words mingled with Bill Gallagher's and the truth was as obvious as a dead body in my own locker: Mike Schultz embodied what Bill had been talking about. Relentless love. My brothers and sisters in blue became quickly disenchanted after a steady diet on the dredges of humanity, topped off by a legal system too slow, often unjust. My own dad—my boyhood hero—had broken under that pressure, under the disparity between the good he wanted to do in the world and the tides of evil that beat him down.

But in the face of those same tides, Mike Schultz just forged on, loving relentlessly. There went a man capable of embracing his little family, his town, and the whole world by appearances, regardless of the circumstances. I hoped he'd never quit.

I asked myself again whether I was capable of that kind of love. But the answer came back the same. I couldn't find that kind of hopeful courage in me. For better or worse, I was my father's son. I broke the hearts of the people I cared about. I was a drifter. And it was time to drift again.

I resumed my tedious pedal through the swarm of people I'd sworn to protect—all of them strangers to me. All of them preferring to keep it that way. I was the foreigner. The alien. The strange one in the uniform with the lights on my handle bars that flashed red and blue. These strangers would call me when they needed me, I'd sort things out, and then we'd go back to whatever we'd been doing before.

That's all my acquaintanceship with Bailey was meant to be. I was supposed to drift in, fix her problems, and drift out. Not love her relentlessly. I'd made my dad's mistake and cared too much. Coming home to Lake Geneva had tempted me with shiny possibilities. Lofty ideas. Too many things that were too good to be true. But as with most of my ideas, it was probably straight out of the toilet.

I filled my lungs. Steeled my mind. Tonight I would submit those applications. In a couple weeks, I'd have a new job lined up somewhere else. I'd explore another part of the country. Surround myself with new strangers whom I'd swear to protect and to serve.

It was time to leave. To get out of Monica and Bailey's lives.

No doubt they'd both be thrilled.

CHAPTER THIRTY-SIX
JIMMY

❖

The dishwasher churning, Jimmy Beacon glanced at the clock above his sink for the hundredth time. Twelve thirty. He'd been calling Bailey all morning, but she wouldn't pick up. Perhaps she was still so emotionally distressed from Noah Cadigan's blunder that she refused to communicate. But it was imperative he talk to her.

She couldn't come to work today.

Jimmy glanced at the red and black backpack stashed under the metal counter. Inside the main pocket was the Backfire Model. It was ready. Today was the day.

Jimmy shoved another tray of dishes into the washer, then dried his hands on his apron and tiptoed to the door to the dining room. Every table and chair was filled. Thanks to the national holiday, Lake Geneva had grown to three times its normal size and a proportional number had squeezed through the door of the restaurant, increasing the operations of the bell to every 3.53 seconds. From his dish room, Jimmy could see straight across the dining room to the bar. Bud Weber stood behind it, a centerpiece crafted of rough-hewn timber like a ship's gunwale, but marred by stickers advertising various beers. Between pouring the drinks, Weber chatted up his group of usual comrades, four men Jimmy often saw here. They appeared to be in high spirits.

Laugh on, Jimmy thought. *You don't know what's coming.*

The setup was ideal. What Bud Weber had done in secret would now be made public. The man's friends would know. His patrons would know. The whole world would know. And Amelia's death would finally be avenged. Jimmy fingered the pink bow in his jeans pocket and let its satiny texture fuel his fury.

But Bailey was due to walk through the door any minute. Jimmy didn't want her getting hurt—killed. He could attempt to turn her away at the door, but he risked the possibility of her interfering with his plans. Holding him up with useless attempts to talk him out of it. Warning Bud. Ruining his opportunity.

No, he had to stop her before she ever arrived.

Jimmy pulled his phone out of his pocket. He had to try one more time.

CHAPTER THIRTY-SEVEN
BAILEY

❋

There's no mail on the Fourth of July.

You probably knew that.

What I meant to say was that, ironically, there's still a Mailboat tour on the Fourth of July. But without the mail. We still deliver the newspapers, because if there's so much as a post card to drop off, by George, we'll deliver it. We're dedicated like that. And there's tickets to sell, so we're all about that.

Anyway, the point is that I was on the Mailboat that morning. After we returned to the Riviera docks, I tucked myself into one of the tiny bathrooms on the boat to change out of my mail jumper's uniform—red tee shirt, white shorts—and into my waitressing clothes. Today's ensemble was a maroon tee shirt that said "Badger High" and khaki shorts.

Slipping through the lines on the pier, I made my way to the bike rack beside the night watchman's hut on the corner of the quay. Getting to the bar would be slow going today, but Bud would want me at the restaurant pronto to help with the extra people. I blew a strand of hair out of my eyes as I worked my bike lock. Bud would kick my butt if I was late. More than ever, I wasn't keen on crossing him. Not if what I suspected was true.

Not if he was the one who'd killed my dad.

The thought made me feel cold and numb inside like ice. Like an animal trap with claws made of cold steel, digging into my skin. If it had really been Bud... I didn't know what I'd do. Probably something stupid. Brave but imaginary me wanted to confront him. Blow up in his face with accusations. Slap his cheek, then turn on my heel and storm from his house, never to return. But the truth was that he'd just beat me into a pulp before I reached the front door.

Good thing brave me was only imaginary.

There was no point saying anything to Ryan or anyone else. I couldn't swear it was Bud. It had been so dark that night... Everything had happened in an eye blink... Besides, why would Bud Weber want to kill my dad? It made no sense. There was no "motive," as they said on TV.

Then again, he'd killed my mouse Humphrey... Bud didn't really need a motive to be cruel.

I sighed and wrapped my bike lock around the handlebars. My brain was full of so many crazy ideas these days. All I wanted was to forget them and go to sleep and never wake up.

Before I could get on my bike, my phone rang. I fished it out of my backpack, hoping it wasn't Bud calling to yell at me already.

But the screen said it was Jimmy.

I groaned. I'd been hopeful we'd never have to talk to each other again beyond a few words at work. *These clean? Yep. Okay.* I considered throwing my phone back in its pocket without answering. But I would see Jimmy soon enough. May as well get this out of the way rather than answer a dozen questions when I got there.

I picked up. "Yeah?"

"I've been endeavoring to call you all morning," Jimmy said, his voice terse.

I rolled my eyes. Apparently there was no dodging the accusations. "I was working," I said. "Besides, I don't get great reception on the lake."

"Oh." He said it abruptly, as if he hadn't thought of those possibilities. Not surprising. Sometimes he started the dishwasher without putting the dishes in.

"What do you want?" I asked. "I'll be at the restaurant in fifteen minutes."

"That's why I called," Jimmy said. "You can't come in today."

Okay, now he was really pushing the limits. I'd never had a spine, but I was beginning to consider getting one. I tapped my foot. "Bud will roast me if I no show. Did you forget I live with him?"

"Don't worry about that. There will be no Bud."

I frowned. Had Jimmy gotten into the whiskey? He was usually impossible to follow, but this time he was breaking his own records. "What are you talking about?"

Jimmy's voice came over the line flat and featureless. "I have a bomb. I'm going to set it off in precisely nine-point-six minutes. Don't come to work today."

CHAPTER THIRTY-EIGHT
JIMMY

Jimmy let the words swirl around in his head a few more times, like a flask of glittering chemical compounds. *I have a bomb. I'm going to set it off.* Far from feeling overwhelmed by an overactive neural state, he was calm. Collected. Relieved. Especially now that he'd told Bailey. This was real. It was happening. It felt so right. The timing. The setting. The situation. Finally, something in his life was perfect.

Bailey's voice squeaked in his ear. *"What?"*

Jimmy sighed and rolled his eyes. Apparently it would require some effort to bring her up to speed. He ducked further into his dish room, away from the dining room door. He let the churning of the dishwasher hide his voice from prying ears. "I'm going to kill Bud Weber, Bailey," he said, each word slow and distinct. "I'm at work, I have a bomb, and I'm going to kill him."

"You're kidding, right? 'Cuz that's not really funny."

Anger burned. She didn't understand. Jimmy clutched the phone in both hands. "This isn't a joke, Bailey. He killed my sister. I have proof. Weber's gotten off scot free for far too long. But not anymore. Today he pays for it."

"Umm... Maybe we should call the police? I have someone's number..."

Jimmy hissed into the speaker. "They had seven years to find my sister's killer. They failed. I'm not letting him slip through their fingers again."

He paced to the door and peered toward the bar, relieved to see Bud still chatting with his friends. Jimmy didn't have time for pointless arguments. His own opportunity could vanish.

"Look, Bailey, I called to warn you. I'd prefer you avoided any risk of personal injury." He swallowed hard, images of everything he and Bailey could have had together flitting through his mind: Studying together. Achieving great scientific breakthroughs together. Some day, attending awards ceremonies side-by-side. Maybe even going to the movies.

But those dreams were pointless now. Mere flights of fancy, never meant to come true. The space-time continuum was a book already written, with no past and no future. Somewhere in the universe, he was always killing Bud Weber, not living a life full of accolades.

"I know you think I'm an idiot." He fought a catch in his throat. His eyes were warm and scratchy. What were these? Tears? He wiped at them angrily. Even now, he struggled to admit how deeply he desired for Bailey to simply understand him. "Everyone thinks I'm an idiot. But that no longer matters. I don't intend to survive this encounter. This is my suicide note, Bailey. My final words. Tell the world why I killed Bud Weber. It was for Amelia." His jaw clenched. "I loved her." He didn't think he'd ever said those words out loud. Certainly not to his parents and not to his sister Samantha. He sucked in a breath through his nose, flaring his nostrils. "And I love you."

There. He'd done it. He'd executed an Opening of the Heart. A Markham Challenge. A Cadiganian Variation. In the end, it hadn't been so hard. But maybe that was because nothing mattered anymore.

There was a pause on the other end of the line. Finally, Bailey started to speak. "Jimmy—"

But Jimmy pulled the phone away from his ear. The hesitation in her voice said it all: She did not love him back. He pressed the button to end the call. His phone beeped and he heard her voice no more. He dropped the phone into his trash bin. Words were pointless now. There was nothing but action. One final action.

He knelt under the counter and opened the zipper on his red and black backpack. For years, he had diagrammed, drafted, and updated the Backfire Model, an FAE, or fuel-air explosive. It operated according to the same principles that had wreaked devastation in historic flour mills and coal mines: Infuse the air with a highly flammable substance, then light it afire. The pressure wave and fireball were devastating—the closest effect you could achieve to detonating an atomic bomb, if you didn't have access to radioactive materials.

The device inside his backpack, however, was not the Backfire Model. Acquiring enough explosive fuel and rendering it easy to transport had proved problematic. Worse, a test run would have been his only run. It was hard to conceal a mushroom cloud. It was perhaps fortuitous he had considered that latter point.

Instead of the Backfire, Jimmy had been forced to construct a device infinitely more simplistic. In the bottom of his pack rested a plain metal pipe filled with a deadly hardware store cocktail: nails, nuts, bolts, ball bearings. In no way did this device showcase his true intellect. But perhaps there was beauty in simplicity. Amelia herself had embraced that particular virtue, simultaneously reveling in the infinite wonders of the universe.

Across the pipe, Jimmy had stenciled its name: *Amelia's Revenge.*

221

Last night, he'd practiced at the abandoned barn on a group of watermelons and had coated the yard in a glorious fruit salad. In addition, his prototype had shredded three layers of plywood to splinters. Jimmy had watched from behind a tree at one hundred yards and found a nail embedded in the bark afterwards, not far from his right hand.

This was a fundamentally different bomb from any he'd built before. This was not designed to bring down structures, like the barn or Roland Markham's pier.

It was designed to tear through human flesh. To take life. To bottle up the pain and fury he'd suffered for seven years and broadcast it across a densely populated area—with Bud Weber in the middle, where the devastation would be most concentrated.

He made sure the batteries were seated tightly and the wires secured.

He flipped the switch that turned off the security.

The Revenge was ready.

He'd never felt so alive in his life. Nothing had ever felt so right.

CHAPTER THIRTY-NINE
BAILEY

The phone line beeped in my ear—that same, happy little beep it makes every time you end a conversation and say goodbye. Only this time, the happy little beep sounded like an idiot. Like it hadn't heard what Jimmy and I had just been talking about.

I glanced up and down the piers, taking in the usual sights and sounds of tourists browsing the little gift shop on the quay, buying tickets, lining up for a lakeside cruise. Smiles. Sun hats. Cameras. Down the shore, kids laughed on the beach. Out on the lake, dozens of power boats zipped around, kicking up spray.

Was Jimmy being for real? I knew he was always a little off, but... a bomb? He was always talking about random science-y stuff, but did he even know how to make one? Granted, it would be kind of convenient if someone killed Bud for me. But what if other people got hurt? And for real, the thought of someone murdering Bud was more comfortable as a fantasy than a reality. There'd been way too many murders lately—and I still wasn't sure how I'd gotten sucked into literally all of them.

My heart fluttered as I tried to think what to do. Go to the restaurant? Try to talk Jimmy out of whatever craziness he was up to? Maybe just call him back? I mean if he really had a bomb, it might be smarter to talk to him over the phone than in person.

What had he said, nine minutes? Great. That didn't give me much time to figure out what to do.

I paced a tiny circle beside my bike and twisted the end of my ponytail. In class once, some terrorism expert guy had talked about stuff like this. If anyone we knew ever talked about bringing guns to school, tell a teacher. Tell your parents. Tell someone.

But this wasn't school and there were no teachers. There had never been parents in the first place—not for me. I glanced at the Mailboat and for a fleeting moment I wished I could tell Tommy. But even he wasn't here. And Brian had to take the next tour. They were loading passengers now.

I stared at my phone. I could simply call the police station. Talk to someone I'd never met and didn't know. But for real, I was sick of talking to cops.

On the other hand, Ryan's number was in my contacts. He was a cop, too. But I'd also seen him in ratty jeans and a tee shirt with sandwich wrappers littering his car. And I felt like I knew what he'd do. He'd, like, make sure I was okay and stuff, then go be a badass.

Opening my contacts app, I found his name beside a photo of a serious-looking German Shepherd in sunglasses. I'd pulled it off Google to use for his avatar. The pic felt appropriate somehow. My thumb hovered over the call button.

God, I didn't know what to do. What if this was all a mistake? A joke? What if there was no bomb? But I guess I'd rather make an idiot of myself in front of Ryan than some random police dispatcher.

I tapped on the German Shepherd.

CHAPTER FORTY
RYAN

───── ⚙ ─────

As I pedaled down Wrigley Drive past the Harbor Shores
Hotel, my eye drifted to the public access boat ramp on my
right. The textured pavement dipped into the cool waves
and I considered plunging my bike in at full speed, yelling
at the top of my lungs. It was the Fourth of July, after all, not
to mention hot enough to fry an egg on the sidewalk. But I
restrained myself. Instead, I squirted a shot of ice water
into my mouth from my water bottle while I rounded the
crowd, thinner here on the outskirts of the tourist district.
To my left, children laughed in the swimming pool outside
Harbor Shores.

My cell phone rang. Appreciating the excuse to pause in
such a recreationally tempting area, I set a foot down,
pulled my phone out of my shirt pocket, and looked at my
screen.

The caller ID said Bailey Johnson. I lifted my eyebrows.
Drift in, drift out, one voice commanded.

*Yeah, and what if her foster dad's beating the crap out of
her right now?* another voice asked. *You're a cop, Brandt.
Pick up the damn phone.*

I picked up the phone.

Resting a hand on my duty belt, I tried to sound relaxed. "Hey, Bailey, how's it going?" God only knew what this was going to be about. The last time we'd talked, she'd wanted to punch me. One foot still on a pedal, I practiced keeping the front wheel balanced with no hands. I told myself I wasn't fidgeting. I was fine-tuning my motor skills.

"Hey!" Bailey's voice chirped on the other end of the line, and at the sound of it all my resolves to leave Lake Geneva wavered. "Uhhh... good," she said. "Well, actually not good. I mean..." I could picture her button nose crinkling as she concluded with, "I don't know really."

In good news, she didn't sound pissed anymore. The tension in my shoulders and biceps relaxed. If I was lucky, I wouldn't blow this thing again.

"What's up?" I asked.

She huffed a breath. "Okay, so... there's this boy I work with at the restaurant. His name's Jimmy. Jimmy Beacon. And I mean, he's always been a little funny, but this is like, extra weird, even for him."

This was a business call, then. The fact she would contact me directly instead of the Communications Center sparked a flash of hope. Was she starting to trust me? Maybe Mike Schultz had something going with his cop-community relations idea...

"Yeah?" I said. "What's weird?"

"He..."

Bailey hesitated. Over my shoulder, a kid made a cannonball into the swimming pool. Children yelled and water washed over the concrete. On the lake, boats zipped and zoomed, cutting up the surface, turning it dicey. I listened closely for Bailey's answer.

"He said he was going to set off a bomb," she finished.

A bomb? My brain clicked into full cop mode. I pulled up a mental checklist of vital info I needed to gather. "Where?" I asked.

"At the restaurant."

"Bud's place?"

"Yeah."

"When?"

"Like, in nine minutes."

"Nine minutes?" A sign of a person's intent to actually commit an act of violence was to announce a date and time. Nine minutes was chillingly specific—not to mention near-at-hand. "Bailey, where are you?"

"At the Riv. Jimmy said not to come to the restaurant."

"Yeah, don't." The thought of her being anywhere near that place and a potential bomb froze my bones.

I twisted my head and swore silently at the pavement. There I went caring about her again. No wonder I hadn't submitted any of those apps.

"Bailey, stay on the line," I said. "I'll be right back. Okay?"

"Okay," she said.

I put her call on hold and grabbed the mic clipped to my shirt. "Forty-four thirty-seven. Citizen reports bomb threat at Geneva Bar and Grill, suggested to go off in nine minutes."

Steph was working the radio again. She hit the emergency tone and repeated my message, requesting all units to proceed to the location. Mounted on a bike, I knew I'd arrive laughably late. I'd let the vehicle units spearhead the initial response and join them later. Meanwhile, I'd gather information from Bailey. I didn't trust anyone else to talk to her, knowing her penchant for not talking at all.

I tapped her held call and fished a pen and pad out of my pocket. "Bailey?"

"Yeah?"

It was a minor miracle she was still there. I pinched my phone between my shoulder and my ear. "What kind of bomb are we talking about? Where specifically might he have put it?" My pen hovered over my notebook.

"Um... I don't know. I think he has it with him, actually. He sounded like he was going to, like, commit suicide. Oh, and kill Bud."

Kill Bud? Well, at least the kid's heart was in the right place. I pushed my morally questionable happiness aside and returned my mind to the interview. "Why does he want to kill Bud?"

Bailey inhaled, then paused again as if considering the potential ridiculousness of what she was about to say. "He said Bud killed his sister."

It was telling that I didn't even question whether Bud Weber was capable of such a thing. My distaste for the man skyrocketed—and my worries over Bailey along with it. If this was true... My God, how on earth could Bailey have ever been placed in his home? But I already knew the answer. I'd run a background check on Weber myself. His record was clean. Whatever crimes lurked in his past, they were buried under secrets, lies, and years.

Dire possibilities for Bud's future—and brighter ones for Bailey's—danced before my eyes. If we could just navigate this situation successfully. Stop the alleged bombing. Safely take the boy into custody. Launch an investigation into Bud's past. Put Bailey in a temporary placement until we could revoke Bud's foster license. Drag him to court. Slam him in prison. Let him rot.

But where would Bailey go after that? I was the one who'd put her in foster care in the first place, and look where that had gotten us.

Best to work this out one thing at a time.

"Bailey, describe Jimmy for me."

"Um, skinny. Short. Dark hair. Big glasses."

I scribbled in my notebook. "Age?"

"Sixteen. Same as me. He goes to Badger High, but he's in a lot of the advanced classes."

"Do you have his address and phone number?" With his number, we could start pinging his phone and verify his location—provided he hadn't shut his phone off.

"Uh... yeah. Hang on a sec."

The sound from her end became more echo-y, more noisy, and I assumed she'd put me on speaker phone so she could open her contacts app. A moment later, she read off his information. I jotted it down.

My radio squawked. "Forty-four thirty-seven."

"Hang on, Bailey." I put her on hold again and pressed the button on my mic. "Go ahead."

Steph sounded awkwardly apologetic. "Our other units are stuck in traffic. You currently have the shortest ETA."

My jaw dropped. Was she kidding me? My gut told me she wasn't. In Lake Geneva, all roads led through downtown—which was nothing but a tangled mess of pedestrians and vehicles right now. That's why we had a bike patrol in the first place—to keep the patrol cars out of the impassible human blockade. But if our vehicle units were north of downtown, or if one or two had dipped their toes into the morass, they'd have a time of it trying to get through. Was I seriously the only one patrolling south of the divide?

"Where's forty-four thirteen?" I asked into the radio—Ted Franklin's call sign. "Isn't he patrolling the south side of town?"

The radio clicked. "He's broken down," Steph said. "Changing a flat."

Christ Jesus, this wasn't happening. I checked my watch. Two minutes were already lost. I had a horrible fear of arriving to nothing but a smoldering ruin.

"Ten-four," I told Steph. "En route."

I pushed off, hitting the buttons that activated the lights and siren mounted to my handlebars. Navigating with just one hand on the grip, I picked up Bailey's call again. "Bailey, I've gotta go. Stay at the Riv."

229

"Okay."

I hung up and shoved my phone back into my pocket. It was an abrupt goodbye, but I could apologize later. Right now, I had a bomb to stop.

I grabbed both handlebars and leaned low. The best speed I'd ever clocked was thirty-one miles per hour, according to the speedometer on the stationary bike at the police department gym. I tried to factor in distance, grade, traffic...

I was never good at math. I just hoped I got there in time.

CHAPTER FORTY-ONE
JIMMY

Spine straight, Jimmy strode up the two steps into the bar.
The straps of his backpack dug into his shoulders, the
Revenge weighty on his back. It was loud, everyone talking
over everyone else. The room was dim. A pair of sea
lanterns above the bar flashed red and green. Two separate
baseball games played on two separate TVs. Laughing with
his friends, Bud Weber leaned on the counter. He wore a
black tee shirt, a white towel slung over his shoulder.

Weber believed he was in his element right now. At the
height of his kingdom, his success, his popularity.

He was wrong.

Jimmy navigated between the tables to within a few
feet of the bar. There, he stopped. Planted his feet. Stared
daggers at the man. He waited for Bud to notice. To realize
that something within his realm had deviated from the
norm.

But Bud never looked up. He took a swig from his beer
glass. Made a joke. The four men sitting before him laughed
as if it were their job to laugh at Bud Weber's jokes. As if it
were the popular thing to do. As if they were in a freaking
high school.

Jimmy cleared his throat but the sound was overwhelmed by the noise. He did it again—louder. He imagined he was behind the podium of a lecture hall and someone in the back row had fallen asleep.

Bud looked up and frowned. "The hell? Why aren't you washing dishes? You see how busy it is in here? They'll be stacked to the ceiling if you don't get a move on." He waved his hand as if shooing a dog. "Get back to work."

But Jimmy wasn't going anywhere. Bud Weber had intimidated him many times before, but not today. Jimmy held the power now. All the power. He thumbed the small activator that fit in the palm of his hand. A wire ran under his arm, over his shoulder, between the zippers of his backpack. A click of the button and Bud Weber wouldn't live long enough to regret his actions.

But Jimmy held back. He *required* Weber to regret. To regret, and then to die.

Jimmy reached into his pocket. Slowly pulled out Amelia's bow. Balancing it on his palm, he held it up for Bud and his friends to see. "Do you know what this is?" Jimmy asked.

Bud squinted at the bow, then scowled and shook his head dismissively as if it meant nothing to him. "Tie your hair up with it and get back to your dishes."

His cronies laughed.

Jimmy's face went hot and his nostrils flared. He would not be humiliated. With every ounce of solemnity he owned, he stood taller, stared Bud Weber in the eye, and announced the charges he had come to bring against him. "My sister was wearing this the day she was murdered."

The smiles faded away from the four men's faces. They glanced nervously between each other and Bud. Gradually, the rest of the bar seemed to understand that something unusual was happening. Something big. One by one, the conversations on bar stools and booths died. Eyes turned toward Jimmy and Bud.

Cool vindication washed over Jimmy's skin. This was everything he'd dreamed of. He had the room's attention now. Soon, he would have the world's. He pictured the headlines. *100 Wounded, More Killed in Deadly Blast...* He would never go down in history as a brilliant scientist. There would be no statue of him in the park. But go down in history, he would.

Bud laughed. "I always knew you had a screw loose, Jim. Your sister probably killed herself because she couldn't stand to look at you. Throw that thing in the trash and get back to your dishes."

Fury flashed through Jimmy's veins. How dare he? How dare Bud Weber look him in the eye and disparage his sister's death? This man knew full well—better than anyone—how Amelia had died.

Jimmy grabbed a bottle off a nearby table—to the surprise of the person who had been drinking out of it—broke it on the table edge, and threw it at Bud, the jagged edges flashing ominously as they rotated through the air, flinging droplets of beer.

Bud ducked, far more quickly than Jimmy thought him capable. The glass smashed against bottles on a back shelf. They tottered and fell, then hit the floor behind the bar with a crash.

Bud glanced down at the place where the liquor had fallen, then turned to Jimmy, his face a study in rage. "Why, you little—"

To Jimmy's shock and horror, Bud planted his hands on the bar and swung his legs over the top, leaping the obstacle like a gorilla. His comrades scrambled out of the way, knocking over their stools. Bud landed heavily on the other side, grabbed Jimmy by the straps of his backpack, and shoved him like a train sweeping away a car on the tracks. Jimmy's backside bashed into the table behind him. It flipped on its end. He fell into a chair and it toppled sideways, one of its wooden legs snapping at the joint.

Jimmy landed on his back on the floor, his knees draped over the seat of the broken chair.

As he landed, Jimmy heard something thud to the floor behind him and roll away. He craned his neck backward to look. From this unusual angle, the restaurant appeared upside down. He searched for the source of the thud, his heart beating with dread. He had a suspicion, which was quickly confirmed.

It was his bomb. Sitting three feet away, the steel pipe alternately reflected red and green from the flashing sea lanterns. In hindsight, there existed a high degree of probability that he had forgotten to close the zipper after arming the device. On closer inspection, the situation was worse than first appeared. One of the wires feeding into the pipe had become detached. The bomb had no juice. It was dead.

Jimmy hazarded a glance at Bud.

Towering overhead, Bud Weber scowled down. "What's that?"

Jimmy's mind scrambled. "It's mine," he said. In hindsight, it was a less than stellar answer. Granted, it was already obvious that the device belonged to him; it had emerged from his backpack. But if he had hoped to avoid identifying what the item was, he was doubtless out of luck. He had a feeling Bud already knew.

The man's expression evolved to one of disbelief. "You *dare* bring a bomb into my bar?" His voice was somewhere between fury and hurt, as if Jimmy had threatened his only child. He wondered if it was the building Bud loved or the liquor. Probably the liquor.

Bud's face darkened like a thunderhead. Jimmy observed every muscle in the man's body go rigid. First the legs. Then the torso. The shoulders. The arms. The neck. Bud's face turned blood red. The jaw and temples went tight as steel bands. The nostrils flared and the hands balled into fists.

Jimmy hazarded an objective observation and concluded he was about to be murdered.

Scooping up his broken bomb, he scurried to his feet and ran. Dodged between the tables. Jumped down the stairs. Made for his dish room and the door at the back of the restaurant. The floor pounded like a drum behind him and he knew Bud was right on his heels.

He had to get away. Hide somewhere. He had to fix his bomb. He was dead without it.

Skidding on the tiles in the dish room, he paid a not-so-fond farewell to his last load of dishes, currently churning away in the washer. He knew he'd never be back to sort and stack them. Despite the fact that Phase One of the Plan had proved a debacle, it remained the best way ever to hand in one's resignation. Jimmy claimed it as a win.

He swerved into the kitchen, ripped the back door open, and leapt down into the sandy parking area. The state park wasn't far. He'd make for the woods. Vanish in the trees. Restore his bomb.

While the current situation was distressingly inconvenient, not to mention strenuous on the lungs, he remained resolute. He would not falter. He would see this through to the end, one way or another. He would make adjustments to The Plan, just as any good scientist would abandon a faulty hypothesis in favor of a new, more promising one.

Only one thing mattered now: Living long enough to kill Bud.

CHAPTER FORTY-TWO
RYAN

※

At the wail of my tiny siren, cars moved aside on the less-crowded streets outside of downtown. I strained my ears for the sound of an explosion. But I felt no vibrations in the ground. Heard no screams. When I finally skidded to a stop in the parking lot in front of the Geneva Bar and Grill, I was relieved to note there still *was* a Geneva Bar and Grill. Not that I had any fondness for the place or the man who owned it. I leaned my bicycle against the wall, drew my service weapon, and crept up to the bank of paned windows with the neon signs advertising popular brands of beer.

I peered through the glass. The dining room was packed, just as I had expected for a holiday on the lake. But something wasn't normal. It took me a second to realize what it was. Every head in the room was turned toward the back of the restaurant and what looked like a swinging door to the kitchen area, flapping on its hinges as if recently used. Up in the bar, people were on their feet. A table and stools were overturned. Diners glanced at each other as if deciding what to do.

I didn't see any skinny kid with dark hair and big glasses, nor did I see Bud Weber. But my gut instincts read the rest of the scene like a book. I doubted I'd find Jimmy or Bud here.

I holstered my weapon but kept a hand on the grip as I walked into the restaurant, making my way to the bar where the action seemed to be centered. Up close, I observed scattered stools. Shattered and tipped bottles on a shelf behind the bar. In the middle of the wreckage stood a waitress I recognized from previous visits, a middle-aged woman in a snug skirt. Arms folded, she snapped pink bubble gum and shook her head, talking with four men.

I approached the group. "What happened here?"

She eyed me up and down. "Well, you got here fast. I didn't even call you." Her voice was low and gravelly, a smoker's voice.

There was no time for chit-chat. "Where's Jimmy?" I asked.

"You know Jimmy?" Her penciled eyebrows arched. "He been in trouble with you boys? Christ Jesus, don't Bud ever run background checks on these kids?"

I stuck to the topic. "I got a call about a young man named Jimmy threatening to set off a bomb."

One of the men snorted. "A call from who? God?"

I gave the man a closer look. Late thirties. Dirty blond hair. Unshaved jaw. A tattoo of a skull on his right forearm. The skull bore a rose on its right temple, which was turned toward the viewer. I'd seen this man around here before. One of Bud Weber's usual cronies. The other three behind him looked like they'd do whatever the first one said. The whole lot of them were posturing, standing up to me as if they were Bud's personal army. God, I didn't feel like a bar fight today. Not with a crazed teen running around with a bomb.

"Just tell me where Jimmy is," I said. "Or Bud. Is Bud here?" At least Bud Weber pretended to get along with me.

The men stared. The woman snapped another bubble.

A shaking voice piped up from behind me. "That way," he said.

I turned and saw a thin, sixty-ish man in a plaid button-down shirt. He stood next to a shaking woman and the overturned table. That was probably his steak and potatoes all over the floor.

"They went that way," he said. He motioned away from the bar and towards the door in the rear of the dining room. "The bartender chased a kid out of here. The kid—" He nodded, his face white. "The kid had something in a backpack that fell out. A pipe of some sort. The bartender said it was a bomb."

Shit. A pipe bomb—nasty buggers designed with one intent: To blast itself into shrapnel, spray any other deadly contents it may contain, and tear human flesh.

I nodded to the man. "Thanks."

Not bothering to say goodbye to Bud's gang, I ran down from the bar and across the dining room. At the swinging door, I stopped and drew my sidearm once again. I peeked through the porthole window into what looked like an empty dish room. Entering quickly, I cleared left and right, letting the nose of my gun lead the way. The room was empty. I moved on to the next doorway, which I assumed led into the kitchen. I could hear the grills and the deep fryer.

Peering left over my sights, I observed a round little man with a walrus mustache turning burgers on the grill. My motion of entering the doorway must have caught his eye. He glanced down the length of the narrow kitchen. At sight of me, he squeaked and held up his hands, grill flipper and all, then pointed wildly the opposite direction. "That way! They went that way!" he said.

I looked over my shoulder and observed a door to the outside swinging lazily on its hinges, revealing a view of a sandy parking lot and a dumpster.

"Left or right?" I asked the cook.

He trembled, apparently not understanding my question.

I didn't have time to figure out a more eloquent way of asking. "Left or right?" I demanded.

"Left!" he squeaked.

I rushed out the door and turned left. There was no one in sight. Just an empty parking lot that butted up against trees. I ran into the woods and reached for my radio mic again. My own voice vibrated with every footfall, the words coming out in spurts between breaths.

"Forty-four thirty-seven, in foot pursuit. Subjects not in sight, but possibly headed for the state park. Teenage subject is confirmed to have what may be an explosive device."

"Ten four," Steph said.

Big Foot Beach State Park was a small campground and trail system uniquely located within city limits. In fact, it was within our patrol jurisdiction. The fact that it was named after its beach was laughable. If you laid down with your toes in the lake, you could stretch your arms above your head and touch South Lake Shore Drive, a well-trafficked roadway at that point. But even that narrow strip of sand would be packed with tourists today.

We were far from the beach here, though. If Jimmy and Bud were in the park at all, they'd be in the woods. I hoped I could trust that the cook hadn't just sent me on a wild goose chase. There was no telling who was my friend and who was my enemy at the Geneva Bar and Grill.

CHAPTER FORTY-THREE
JIMMY

Jimmy dashed through the woods, his feet following a trail he didn't know. Deciduous forests had never been his natural habitat. Bud's heavy breath sounded mere inches behind him. How could a fat man run so fast? Jimmy pushed harder, his broken bomb secured firmly in one fist. He found an intersecting trail and turned. It went around a bend. At the next crossroads, he turned again, selecting his path at random. He stole a glance over his shoulder and saw to his relief nothing but a dirt path and thick woods pressing in on either side. No Bud. He'd finally lost him.

Jimmy slid into the thick underbrush like a runner to home plate. He rolled over onto his stomach. The vegetative cover didn't look nearly as thick from below as it had from above. He shimmied backward, still clutching his bomb. He held his breath. He wouldn't move until he was sure Bud Weber was gone.

A tree branch rustled behind him. Jimmy's heart leapt into his throat. Barely daring to move, he glanced over his shoulder, fully expecting Bud to fly at him from behind.

Instead, Jimmy spied a deer with a mouth half-full of grass, sunlight dappling its back through the canopy. It lifted its tail and pranced away. But then, as indecisive as all members of its species, it paused and looked again, waiting to see what Jimmy would do.

Jimmy rolled his eyes. The stupid animal had caused him an excess of unnecessary cardiovascular distress.

No sooner was the thought out of his mind than footfalls beat down the trail. Jimmy caught his breath and stared through his curtain of leaves. That was no trail runner. He could hear Bud panting and growling under his breath.

Jimmy begged the deer not to move and draw Bud's attention. The creature complied. It flipped its tail up again, but stood rooted to the spot, examining the oncoming runner with first one eye, then the other.

The pounding footsteps slowed. Crept. Then stopped. Right in front of Jimmy's nose. Jimmy held his breath. What had given him away? Did Bud have a sixth sense? A more scientific approach brought to light a more reasonable cause: a broken branch amidst the underbrush where Jimmy had dived in.

Bud's shadow leaned forward. Jimmy's heart pounded in his chest.

Snap!

The deer had finally had enough. It sprang away, leaping over bushes and branches. Bud's shadow backed off.

"Damn deer," he said under his breath.

And he took off running again.

Jimmy exhaled. That had been the proverbial "close call." He owed much to that deer.

He waited approximately four point three minutes, then backed further into the woods, further away from the path. Finding a thick shrub for cover, he sat down and assessed his broken bomb for damage. To his relief, he only had to reconnect a wire where it had detached from the pipe. He disarmed his device, then utilized a sharp-edged

241

stone to bare the wires and twist them back together, feeling much like his ancient ancestors who first used sticks as tools, though to less impressive effect.

Perfect. He was armed again.

Now all he had to do was catch up with Bud.

Somewhere in this overgrown deciduous forest...

CHAPTER FORTY-FOUR
RYAN

I'd been meaning to put in a jog at the state park, but this wasn't quite how I'd pictured it. For starters, I wouldn't have been wearing body armor and a duty belt—an extra twenty-six pounds together. Also, I might have chosen a better time of day than the heat of a muggy afternoon while dressed in black. Finally, I don't think I would have run every trail twice—which I'm pretty sure I did by the time my radio squawked with the joyful news that my backup had arrived and established an Incident Command in the parking lot of the Lake Geneva Middle School, northeast of the park. I considered my cardio done for the day—maybe the week—but I hadn't found a single trace of Bud or Jimmy.

I dove off the trail in the general direction of the school and found myself crashing through thick overgrowth, followed by a chain link fence. I scaled the fence, dropped down on the other side, pushed through more trees and scrub, and finally toppled out onto Wells Street near the school's track field. I jogged across two baking-hot parking lots before sighting the big black truck with the words "Mobile Command Unit" painted in white.

The big, black truck was surrounded by various patrol units. In addition to our own, I counted two from the Walworth County Sheriff's Office, one from State Parks and Rec, and another pair from neighboring towns. SMART had clearly been called out—the Suburban Mutual Aid Response Team, a collaboration between area emergency services in southeast Wisconsin. It was nice having our brothers and sisters from other departments at our back.

Officers from each organization were congregating around the sergeant's car, strapping on tac vests, checking gear. The middle-aged gal who manned the park entrance booth was talking to the sergeant, wearing her Smokey Bear hat. One of the Walworth County sheriff's deputies, feet spread, stood in the shade of the truck next to a German Shepherd sporting K-9 body armor, its ears erect while its tongue panted in the heat.

I pulled up to the group, huffing.

"Report?" Sergeant Burns asked. Burly, sixty-something, tough as old leather.

I shook my head. "No sighting."

Someone handed me a water bottle. I took it and looked at the man in the navy blue uniform who had given it to me. Mike Schultz.

"Told you," I said. I screwed off the cap and guzzled.

Schultz only smiled. "The beach was too crowded anyway."

One last car, an unmarked SUV, pulled up and two people descended from the front seats. Monica and her partner Stan Lehman were dressed in tan slacks and black polo shirts. I tried to catch Monica's eye, but she slipped on a pair of black sunglasses as she and Lehman joined our circle. Her face was directed toward the sergeant, not me. I shouldn't have been surprised.

"Give us the details," Sergeant Burns said now that I was breathing a little easier.

I reviewed everything that had happened, from Bailey's call to the apparent row at the bar to my jaunt through the woods. I finished with a description of Jimmy and the phone number and address I'd jotted down in my notebook. Around the circle, pens scratched on paper. The K-9 licked his nose and glanced to his human partner, checking for commands. When none came, he went back to eying a squirrel harvesting acorns on a nearby strip of lawn. But the dog never broke his sit-stay.

"Any results from pinging the boy's phone?" I asked.

Burns nodded. "We found his mobile in a garbage can at the restaurant."

"What about Bud's?"

"In his office."

Well, that was a big help.

The sergeant unfolded a map of the state park on the hood of his car. It was nothing but a paper print out from the ranger booth, but it showed all the roads and trails. He pointed to various intersections around the park. "Our inner perimeter is here." He pointed to the intersections at South Lake Shore Drive, South Street, and Wells, and the southern corners of the park, where there were no intersecting streets. For each intersection, he assigned a patrol unit. "We have more SMART teams establishing an outer perimeter as well." His finger traced the map. "We also need a checkpoint at the park entrance. Franklin, Doyle, you two are in charge of that. We'll send out a text alert notifying campers to evacuate the area." He looked to the woman in the Smokey Bear hat. "Can I have your people back that up with a PA?"

The ranger nodded. "Yes, sir."

I anticipated that park visitors would be told to find something to do outside the park and to watch our social media pages for updates as to when the park would reopen.

245

"At the checkpoint," the sergeant continued, looking at the assigned officers, "make sure Jimmy or Bud don't slip through without our notice."

Burns turned his eye to me, Schultz, and a few other officers, including the man with the dog. "I need all of you to stand by. The lieutenant's on his way with the drone."

We nodded. One of our more epic departmental purchases, the drone had proved its value more than once in both search and rescue and the odd manhunt. Equipped with a camera as well as thermal imaging, it could give us a bird's-eye view of the park without any of our personnel having to go in.

"Once the drone clears the open areas of the park, if nothing turns up, we go in and start clearing buildings, tents, and RVs."

We nodded. The K-9 quirked his head as if aware that he'd been issued his orders.

Burns continued, "The Milwaukee County Bomb Squad has been notified. Their ETA is one hour." He looked at Monica and Lehman. "I have patrol units and a second SMART team proceeding towards Jimmy's house to establish a perimeter and help clear the neighborhood. That's where I want you two. Talk to the family. Find out whether this kid is even capable of making a bomb or if that was just a prop he was seen with. Figure out where Jimmy might have run away in a pinch. A light search of his house is all—don't go poking underneath things. Leave that for the bomb techs."

Monica and Lehman nodded.

"Chief's up to date?" Monica asked.

"He's been notified," Burns answered. "He's in Milwaukee, but he's on his way back."

Monica nodded. The sunglasses masked any reaction in her eyes, but she held her head erect. Even without details, she and I were both aware that Wade was at Froedtert visiting Tommy. No sooner had one crisis been addressed than another reared its head. We weren't even allowed a few days to catch our breath. To assess. To process. On the one hand, this was the kind of adrenaline-pumping adventure that cops lived for. On the other hand, I wasn't sure how I felt about feasting on it here, in my hometown. I expected this sort of thing in Minneapolis, Austin, or any of the other big cities I'd worked for. Not here. The Lake Geneva I'd come back to was not the Lake Geneva I'd left.

"We're organizing on Tac-1," Burns said. He tapped his hood. "All right, let's do this."

The group broke up towards their various vehicles, turning dials on their radios.

Schultz elbowed me in the arm and nodded to his car. "Let's get you in a tac vest."

I nodded and turned to follow him but dared a final glance at Monica. To my surprise, she was looking back at me, over her shoulder as she made for the SUV. Her eyes were still masked behind her sunglasses. Her lips, straight as a slab of concrete, betrayed no thought or emotion. But I knew the expression. I'd seen it many times before. The brief, silent exchange of glances had always been one more goodbye before a mission, deep with feeling but innocuous enough to express in front of our fellow officers. A silent reminder to be careful. To come home safe when it was all over.

Monica turned and stepped up behind the driver's wheel. The door closed, the engine turned, and she pulled away.

I was reading too much into it. I must have been. But like a poker to dying embers, the glance had prodded the ache in my chest, sending up a renewed flame.

I sighed. Look at me: I was failing with my resolve to leave Monica, just as I was with Bailey. Classic example of my wandering ways. I even wandered away from my vows to wander away.

CHAPTER FORTY-FIVE
MONICA

———— ⚓ ————

While it pissed me that Ryan had caught me looking at him, it pissed me more that I had looked at him in the first place. I wasn't trying to invoke old habits or memories. You'd think it would be easy to ignore a man I despised, yet here I was. Just as the ghost of our child haunted me at home, Ryan haunted me at work. I couldn't escape either.

Fingers laced behind his head, Lehman lounged in the passenger seat as we headed for Jimmy Beacon's house.

"So," he said, watching the scenery, "we've got a kid running through the streets with a bomb. I suppose this wins a place in your conspiracy theory, too?"

"What conspiracy theory?" I asked, slanting my eyes. "The murder victims and the assault victim are all connected by a common history, the Markham Ring. Two of our crime scenes are connected by .22 caliber bullets, as well. That's not a conspiracy theory. It's good police work."

"Good police work with one big, fat problem," Lehman said. "When that boat captain was shot, the members of the Markham Ring were already dead—all three of them." He waved his head side to side as he counted off the names. "Bobby? Slug to the noggin, compliments of our own chief of police, circa 1990-whatever-it-was. Fritz? Knifed, choked, and drowned, then tied to a pier post for the fishies to feed on. Jason? Remodeled into a strainer, chock full of bullets. So..." He turned to me and stared, expressionless, through a pair of orange sunglasses. "Who shot the captain?"

"The same person who helped Charles Hart kill Jason," I said. "Somebody with a .22 and a black leather vest. That's all we know."

"Mmm-hmm." Lehman pursed his lips. "I take it our suspect isn't a sixteen-year-old kid?"

Now he was just pushing my buttons, making fun of my theories—a pastime of his. "Bailey said the man who killed Jason was big and tall," I replied. "She also said Jimmy is short and skinny." I gave Lehman a glare. "So no. The killer isn't a sixteen-year-old kid."

"Oh, good." Lehman drew a circle in the air with his finger. "This bomb thing is unrelated, then?"

"We don't know that. We don't know anything yet about Jimmy Beacon."

"So it *could* be related?"

"Three homicides and a shooting, followed by a bomb threat—all in the course of two weeks? That's pretty coincidental. I'm not ruling it out."

Lehman grinned and stared out the windshield again. "Lake Geneva, Wisconsin: bedrock of intrigue and evil." He clicked his tongue and shook his head. "You do love you your conspiracy theories, Monica."

I ignored him in hopes he would shut up. More than once, I'd considered pinning a sign to his cubicle: *Don't Feed the Troll.*

After fighting our way past the bottleneck of downtown, we entered a quiet residential neighborhood. Blocks away from the tourist center, the curbs were nevertheless packed bumper-to-bumper with cars. Some people refused to pay a dollar an hour for parking. The rest couldn't find a slot downtown if they offered a fortune. Either way, Lake Geneva was the ideal place to get your daily steps in.

That's exactly what a pair of officers from the SMART team were doing—walking door-to-door, knocking, asking residents to leave until further notice. Those who refused would be advised to shelter in place, such as in their basements. I noticed a trickle of homeowners getting into vehicles, backing out of driveways, finding a better place to be.

I pulled up beside a black patrol unit with a red swish across its doors—Walworth County Sheriff. Its lights flashing, it was parked in the middle of the intersection to prevent incoming traffic. Lehman rolled down his window and a short but stocky woman in tan pants and a dark brown shirt approached, hands on her duty belt.

"Beautiful day," Lehman said.

"Yep," Bryn Mccaffrey replied. Her dark brown hair was pulled back in a bun, black clips pinning down stragglers above her ears.

"Which house is it?" I asked.

She pointed down the street. "Next block down, right-hand side. White two-story. See it?"

The trees were thick on that block, but I glimpsed white between the greenery. "Any activity?"

"Nope."

"Knock on the door yet?"

"Nope. Huber and Duffy are just about done clearing the neighborhood."

I nodded.

"Well." Lehman settled back into his seat and lifted a soda can to his mouth. "How 'bout them Brewers?" He sipped noisily.

He and Bryn talked sports while I watched Huber and Duffy approach one more door. After a short talk with the residents, the deputies headed toward us. The homeowners got into their car moments later, packing a cooler. No sense letting a Fourth of July dinner go to waste.

"All cleared?" I asked the deputies.

"All cleared," Huber replied. At six foot seven, he towered over Bryn Mccaffrey.

I sat up and gave the steering wheel a smack. "Let's do this. You guys good to tag along?"

"Your wish is our command," Zack Duffy replied. Middling height and round, his looks were deceiving. His co-workers had nicknamed him the Duff Bunny, but I'd taken a self-defense training course with him and knew first-hand he could take you down faster than felling a tree. My right hip had never fully forgotten it.

Lehman and I got out of the SUV, grabbed our tac vests from the back, and strapped them on.

"No cell phones, no radios," I reminded my companions. The bomb gurus said it was unusual these days to find bombs that were activated by radio or cell signals; the air was too full of traffic in this day and age. But better to play it safe.

We all turned off our devices. Disconnected from my fellow officers, I felt naked. We were going old school. Really old school. Back to the days when a patrolman beat the sidewalk with his nightstick if he needed help. Only we weren't going to be beating any sidewalks, either. Not with explosives around.

Together, we headed down the street.

I focused on the plain white two-story. The historic home, 1920s or so, could have been cute with a little paint and a lot of new lumber. But that was the wanna-be house flipper in me. The front porch sagged, as did the roof. The lawn looked as if it hadn't been mowed all summer and an unruly willow tree draped half-way into the street, brushing the roofs of the parked cars. Lake Geneva didn't have a "poor side of town," just a smattering of random houses where the occupants couldn't keep up with the look of the neighborhood. This was clearly one of those low-income microcosms of the city.

Lehman clicked his tongue. "Ritzy."

We turned up the cracked driveway.

"We'll take the back," Huber said.

He and Duffy split left and right and waded through the grass toward the rear of the house. Lehman and I gingerly climbed the front steps, dried paint and half-rotted boards crackling beneath our shoes. We drew our guns, pointing them down, and pressed our shoulders to the wall on either side of the door.

It was open, a box fan hugging the screen and running full-blast, pumping warm summer air into the house. A desperate attempt at air conditioning. Through the screen, I could make out a living room with a worn wooden floor and a dingy 80s-style sofa, orange and boxy. Beyond that was a dining room, the table stacked with dirty dishes and a random assortment of junk.

Lehman rapped on the rickety wooden screen. "Police! Occupants of the house, come out now."

Silence, except the hum of the fan.

Lehman knocked again and repeated the order.

A heavy female voice yelled from the bowels of the house. "Sam! Someone at the door!"

"I'm on the phone!" a younger tone shouted back.

"I don't care!" The first voice mimicked the whine of the second.

Lehman and I glanced at each other, eyebrows lifted.

A moment later, creaking floorboards announced someone's approach. Sam turned out to be a young lady maybe high school or college age with blond hair pulled up in a messy bun. She wore short shorts and a loose red tee shirt sporting a blinged-out silver heart. A cell phone was pressed to her ear.

"Did you *see* the shoes she was wearing? My God, she looks like such an idiot. I wish she'd stop embarrassing

252

herself." The girl stopped with her hand on the screen and continued talking into her phone as if she hadn't seen me and my partner or the guns we pointed at the floor. She giggled. "OMG, yes, that haircut has to go, too."

"Sam," Lehman said, picking up on her name, "we need you to exit the house now."

Her eyes flashed upwards and she scowled as if put off. "Hey, Whitney, I gotta go. Cops are here." She crinkled her nose at whatever her friend said in reply. "I don't know what they want. I'll tell you when I find out.... All righty, see you tonight." She smooched into the phone and hung up.

The girl pushed forward on the handle. The entire screen door groaned then shuddered, the top hinge straining against the single nail that held it in place. With a bang, the door collapsed at Lehman's and my feet. The three of us stared down at it.

The girl shrugged. "It was ready to go anyway." She stepped over it onto the porch.

"Who else is in the house?" Lehman asked.

"Just my mom." She leaned on the door frame and called down a set of stairs off the entryway. "Mom! Cops are here!"

"The hell do they want?" the mother's voice yelled up from the basement.

The girl frowned back at us. "The hell *do* you want?"

"Is Jimmy here?" I asked.

"Nope. He's at work. Geneva Bar and Grill." She shouted down the stairs again. "Never mind, mom! They're here for Jimmy."

I was about to repeat that we needed them both to leave the house regardless, but the woman's voice rumbled from below.

"Oh, Christ's sake, what did he do now?" The stairs groaned ominously as she made her way up.

"Jimmy's not at the bar," I told the girl. "He left."

She shrugged, pulling a blasé frown and rounding her eyebrows. "Oh. Well, maybe he *is* here."

Her mother topped the stairs. A chunky woman in a loose-fitting tank top, she panted as she looked us up and down. She didn't even glance at the broken door. "You're cops?"

"Yes, ma'am," I said. "We need you and your daughter to step away from the house with us." I opened an arm, inviting them to walk down the driveway. At the same time, I holstered my weapon but kept a hand on the grip in case Jimmy was around.

The woman didn't move. "You arresting Jimmy?" she asked.

Yes, we were here to arrest Jimmy. A bomb threat was a Class I felony in the state of Wisconsin. In all likelihood, Jimmy would be tried as an adult, in which case he was looking at up to $10,000 and three and a half years in prison. But his mom didn't need to know that yet.

At the same time, it irked me she would jump so easily to the conclusion we were here to arrest him. It didn't say promising things about their relationship.

"We need to talk to him," I merely said. "If you'll come with us—"

"What'd he do?" she asked.

I tried not to sigh out loud, the expression "herding cats" coming to mind. Maybe being blunt would jolt them into action. "He made threats to detonate a bomb at work today."

The woman rolled her head and clapped her hand over her eyes. "Oh, my Jesus loving Christ. That boy will be the death of me."

"We need to find him and make sure he doesn't have any explosives here at home." I pointed down the street toward Bryn Mccaffrey's patrol car. "For your safety, we need you and your daughter to relocate."

"Safety, my ass," the woman grumbled. She jabbed a thumb over her shoulder. "Have you seen this place? It's a disaster waiting to happen." She laughed grittily and stepped over the broken screen door onto the porch. "Jimmy takes after his father, you know. That drunken piece of horse shit hasn't put in an honest day's work in five years..."

I walked her and her daughter down the driveway, leaving Lehman to guard the door. Mrs. Beacon talked my ear off all the way down the street, her complaints moving from her son and her husband to her poor thyroid and the stress this event would put on it. I nodded and made appropriate grunts. Back at my SUV, I pulled a hard-sided file folder from the compartment in the door and found a Consent to Search form. I began to fill out the lines that indicated where exactly we wanted to look.

"Is Jimmy home?" I asked, not lifting my head and not waiting for a polite moment to cut into her pity party.

"He comes and goes like this place was a goddamn motel. I never know where he is." Mrs. Beacon waived a hand toward her house. "Go ahead. Check the house and the garden shed."

I raised an eyebrow. "The garden shed?"

"He's turned it into some sort of doomsday bunker. That kid's got a screw loose. Always has. I never knew what to do with him. You find him, you can have him." She flapped her hand.

My jaw tightened, but I bit back the cutting remarks that sprang to my lips. No wonder this boy wanted to set off a bomb. No mother should give up on her child like that.

Like I had. Guilt roiled through my gut, the ghost of my daughter flitting at the edges of my mind. I put a lid on the twisted, black feelings creeping up from my belly. This was neither the place nor the time. I added the garden shed to the lines on the form.

"Do you consider Jimmy capable of making a bomb?" I asked.

Mrs. Beacon folded her arms. "If that boy's capable of anything, it's news to me."

Another tendril of hatred smoked up my throat like fire from a dragon's mouth. This woman didn't deserve to have kids.

I flipped my clipboard around so she could see the form. "We'll be applying for a search warrant to let us bring in our bomb technicians," I informed her. "In the meantime, will you sign a Consent to Search?" I showed her the paper.

She held it at arm's length and squinted at the writing. "You wanna look through the house?"

"Yes."

"And the shed?"

"Yes." I offered a pen.

"For Jimmy?"

I bit back a sigh. "Yes." I said it through my teeth.

She scribbled her name across the bottom, then laughed. "I warn you, I haven't cleaned in three years."

I merely took the paper and pen from her, stashed them in the box, and locked it shut. "Thank you. If you need anything, Deputy Mccaffrey can help." I motioned to Bryn, standing beside her car.

Bryn nodded politely at Jimmy's mother and sister but flashed me a silent glare. In the thirty seconds she'd observed the two family members, she already knew she was going to hate babysitting. Well, so long as she let Mrs. Beacon talk about her thyroid and Sam tap away on her phone, they'd be fine. Me? I was getting a lucky escape. All I had to do was walk into a house potentially full of bombs. It was a fair trade.

Moments later, I rejoined Lehman on the front porch. Instinctively, I reached for my radio to check in with our team—but remembered I'd shut my unit off. God, old school sucked. But if Huber and Duffy had found anyone, we would have heard shouts and police orders. And if we'd entered the house and found anything, they would have heard the same. We'd have to rely on common sense for this mission.

Lehman rapped on the vacant door frame. "Police! Jimmy Beacon, come out now!"

There was no response. Lehman shouted one more warning, then we nodded to each other.

"I got left," Lehman said.

"I got right," I confirmed.

"Move."

"Move."

Lehman, acting as point man, entered first, stepping over the broken door and around the box fan, letting his gun lead the way. He swept the left side of the room. A split second behind him, I slipped in too, clearing right and circling around the opening to the basement.

"Clear," Lehman said.

"Clear," I confirmed on my side.

We flowed into the kitchen, then moved into the hall toward what must have been the bathroom and bedrooms. At every door, we kept our profiles invisible behind solid walls, our eyes and our sights pointed in opposite directions. Each room was empty. No Jimmy. No bombs. As per Sergeant Burns' instructions, we didn't dig. Doors remained closed, objects unmoved. We didn't need to set off any booby traps.

At the end of the hall, we slipped into what looked like Jimmy's room. A bed with a slouching mattress sat in one corner, covered in a galaxy-patterned comforter. The walls were decorated with the kind of posters I remembered from my high school physics classroom. Apparently Jimmy Beacon was into science.

But the room was empty.

"Basement next," Lehman said.

"One minute." I cast my eye in a circle, soaking up information on Jimmy. The desk was scattered with paperwork, the sheet on top titled *The Master Plan of J. A. Beacon: A Pre-Autobiography.* I scanned the paper, but it didn't look like a manifesto. More like an outline of his academic and career plans. The names of some prominent high schools and colleges popped out, including the Harvard physics program. So this kid had dreams of attending one of the top schools in the nation? But instead he was detonating a bomb. All his potential, thrown away.

"Monica, check this out," Lehman said.

I turned away from the *Master Plan,* tensing, expecting him to point out a bomb. Instead, he was studying one of the black-and-white portraits that adorned the walls. A man with a thin face and a serious expression stared back at us. "Who's this?" I asked.

"J. Robert Oppenheimer."

The name vaguely rang a bell. It had been a long time since my last history class. "Refresh my memory."

"Designed the first atomic bomb," Lehman explained. "You know, Hiroshima. Nagasaki." He made a comical explosion noise with his mouth and blew up his hands.

Well, this was telling. Alongside pictures of Einstein and Edison, Jimmy kept a picture of a man who'd built a bomb. *The* bomb.

Lehman pointed to the bottom corner of the poster. I leaned in and read a messy scrawl. *I am become death, the destroyer of worlds.*

Lehman looked at me and popped his eyebrows significantly.

"What's that from?" I asked. "It sounds like a quote."

He shrugged. "Beats me. Sounds healthy and well-balanced, though, doesn't it?" He motioned toward the door. "Move on?"

I nodded.

We searched the basement. The second floor. Both were empty. Before stepping out the back door, we shouted to Huber and Duffy that we were coming. They met us in the yard, the four of us standing in grass up to our knees.

"Now we try the shed?" Duffy suggested.

I held up a hand, stopping them. "No." I eyed the small building, dressed in worn white boards that matched the house. "Mrs. Beacon called that his 'doomsday bunker.' I say we keep it under surveillance and leave it for the bomb techs."

"Doomsday bunker?" Lehman rocked on his heels. "That sounds exciting."

Lehman, Huber, and Duffy kept an eye on the house while I jogged back to Mccaffrey's car to meet the bomb squad. Mccaffrey, eyes glazed as Mrs. Beacon jabbered in her ear, was relieved to see me, as if welcoming her salvation. But I shot into the driver's seat of my SUV and grabbed a laptop as if I had things to do. Jimmy's mother made me want to eat cyanide.

Thirty minutes later, a huge black truck rumbled down the street, looking like something from a war zone. Lettering on its side announced the Milwaukee County Bomb Squad. Interdepartmental relations were a boon.

Two men in black uniforms leapt from the doors. I got out of my car and introduced myself to a man in sergeant's stripes, Tyrone Houston, then explained what we knew. From the corner of my eye, I watched Mccaffrey help the other man open the back doors of the truck and lower a ramp. The bomb tech stepped in. Moments later, a caterpillar-wheeled robot emerged alone, as if by its own will. One arm, upright, bore a camera. Another jabbed forward with a set of pincers on the end. "The wheelbarrow," as these robots were referred to in the trade. Apparently that was how the original bomb bot got around.

With the vital info passed along to Sergeant Houston, I made one more trip to the house.

"The bot's here," I told Lehman at his post just down the street from Jimmy's house.

"Sweet," he said and pumped a fist. He whistled sharply to Huber and Duffy.

Soon afterwards, we were congregated inside the Bomb Squad truck, an office and garage on wheels. Shelves carried boxes of carefully-organized accessories: spare parts, grip attachments with every conceivable tool—even an x-ray machine that could be mounted to the robot's arm and used to see inside suspicious packages.

At the desk in back sat the second crew member, the robot's technician, a forty-something African-American man who introduced himself as Rex Conroy. This, then, was the ghost in the machine. Before him sat a plastic box, hinged open. The control console. One half was a screen, currently showing a diagram of the very robot that sat in the street. The other half of the box was full of knobs and buttons.

Lehman leaned over Conroy's shoulder to study the device. "How long's it take to learn one of these?" His eyes glittered like a kid with a new toy.

Conroy turned in his chair and grinned a big, white smile. "It's like playing the violin, man." He waved his fingers over the console. "These are my strings."

Sergeant Houston gave Conroy the rundown on the situation. "These officers have already performed a basic search of the house. We start with the shed."

Conroy's fingers danced over the controls. The screen flipped to a live video feed showing Jimmy Beacon's street. The grip from the front of the robot was visible in the center of the field of view. Conroy touched a joystick and the machine rolled forward.

"This is great," said Lehman, rubbing his hands together.

I peeked out the back of the truck into daylight and swore I'd stepped into a sci-fi movie. The street was barren, post-apocalyptic, with the one-eyed, one-armed robot rolling down the road as if surveilling its domain. At Jimmy's house, it turned. Crawled up the driveway. Turned again and churned through the grass. Then it disappeared through the side yard.

I stepped back into the truck and watched the technician's screen. The robot approached the door of the shed.

"Looks like it's got a padlock," Conroy said.

"Can the robot break down the door?" Lehman asked.

"She can tow a car, man," Conroy said as if offended that Lehman would question his cool toy. "Easier to cut the lock, though."

"You can do that?"

Conroy waved over his shoulder. "Sure!" he said in a high-pitched voice, still dismissing little insults to his machine. "I got stuff for that." Back at the controls, he stuck the robot's eye right up by the handle of the shed. "And I don't get to use any of it. Door's open." The camera showed that the padlock was open, but its bar was hooked through both halves of the latch.

I squinted at the screen. "Why would Jimmy leave the door to his bomb lab unlocked?"

Sergeant Houston humphed, his arms crossed over his chest. "'Cause he *wants* us to go in." He jabbed a finger at the control console. "That's why we've got robots for this."

Conroy's fingers flew to a new section of controls. The robotic arm reached forward. Its pincer took hold of the padlock as gently as a human hand, twisted, and slid it free of the door.

"Wow," Lehman said.

"That ain't nothing," said Conroy, grinning to himself. "I could make origami with this thing."

The robot grabbed the door handle and pushed. The interior of Jimmy's lab came into view.

One wall was plastered to the ceiling with large sheets of drafting paper, their surfaces covered in what looked like blueprints for various machines. The back wall was built up with shelves and drawers, each bearing a label. In a corner sat a computer on a flower pot stand. On the last wall, a large work area stretched under a dusty window, and on it sat a small chemistry set. This place was nothing compared to the three state crime labs in Wisconsin, but not bad for a former garden shed remodeled by a high school student.

"Well," Lehman said with a heavy sigh, "we're at least getting him on a permits violation." He pointed to the computer on the flower pot stand. "What do you want to bet he didn't get the proper paperwork to run electricity to the shed?"

I rolled my eyes at him.

The robot rolled into the shed. "And now we search," said Conroy.

With brilliant precision, he maneuvered the camera and the grip into every conceivable angle, peering behind furniture, pulling open drawers, lifting objects that blocked the robot's view. No corner went untouched.

While the robot was poking around Jimmy's drafting table, Lehman lifted a hand to interrupt. "Can you just... can you focus on those drawings above the table?"

Conroy angled the camera upwards. A sketch of a bomb came into view. A big bomb. Shaped like a giant football, it had a box tail fin for aerial deployment. This was no IED.

Lehman whistled. "Well, if he built this, the whole state of Wisconsin's in trouble."

"That's military-grade," I said.

"*That's* Tsar Bomba," Lehman replied. "There's a label in the corner, see? Biggest A-bomb ever built. The Russians just about blew themselves off the map testing it."

I frowned and squinted more closely at the screen. "It looks detailed."

Conroy obligingly zoomed in. Measurements and lists of materials popped into focus.

"*Creepy* detailed," Lehman agreed. "The North Koreans might want this kid's number." He looked at us significantly. "Obviously, he ain't getting his hands on the parts to build Tsar Bomba, but if he knows how to build this, he knows how to build your kitchen-variety bomb."

Sergeant Houston nodded. "Hence the robot," he said again.

The robot kept going, pulling out drawers and boxes from the shelves on the back wall. On one shelf sat an organizer with small plastic bins labeled *screws, nails,* et cetera. The grip turned the box away from the wall to look behind it but didn't bother with the tiny drawers.

"Can you open those drawers?" I asked.

"Sure. But ain't no bomb gonna fit in there, unless you want to blow up mice."

"Open them," I said. I pointed toward the screen. "That one. *Nails.*"

Conroy dexterously caught the lip of the drawer with the edge of his claw and pulled it open. He angled the camera to look inside.

"It's empty," he said.

I pointed to another. "That one—*bolts.*"

He opened it. There were none. Catching on, Conroy opened a couple more—*screws, nuts, ball bearings, batteries.* They were empty, except the drawer for batteries. Several lined the bottom, but there was room for more.

"He built a terrorist bomb," I said. "The shrapnel's all gone." My heart beat a little faster. This was going to be like the Boston Marathon bombing. My stomach turned as I remembered the images on the news, just last summer. I thought about that happening here, in Lake Geneva. *Hell, no,* I thought. *Not on my watch.*

Conroy turned the robot's attention to the floor under the shelves. Cardboard boxes held lengths of steel pipe in various diameters. Coils of electrical wire.

"He has everything he needs," I said. "Everything but the actual explosives and the detonators."

Conroy tweaked his knobs. "We'll find 'em," he said.

He continued to pull drawers and boxes. There was little need to dig through anything. Each container was carefully labeled and organized. The only box that contained a random assortment of items was clearly labeled *Miscellaneous*.

The robot pulled out one last drawer. If the evidence was anywhere, it was here.

The eye peeked in. Plastic tubing, rolled up and tied neatly. No explosives. No detonators.

Conroy leaned back and spread his hands. "That was gonna be the big reveal an' all." He joked, but the disappointment was evident on his face.

We stared at each other.

Lehman shrugged. "Maybe he keeps them off site."

"We haven't searched the house yet," Houston pointed out.

A rap sounded on the back door of the truck. We turned and found Bryn Mccaffrey in the opening. "K-9's here."

Conroy looked up at his sergeant. "I say deploy the puppy-dog. There's gotta be explosives in there somewhere."

Houston nodded. "Deputy, take me to the K-9 team." He stepped out of the truck and followed Mccaffrey.

Conroy backed the robot out of the shed but kept the camera rolling so we could watch what was happening. Ten minutes later, a dog with a pointy nose and ears came into view. A Belgian Malinois, similar to a German Shepherd but smaller. Those in the know said they were more intense.

Leaning back in his chair, Conroy smiled at his screen. "That'd be Xena," he said. "Only been with us six months, but she ain't made a wrong call once."

Her nose glued to the ground, she trotted left and right, then glanced over her shoulder and gave a huge doggy grin. Her tail began to whip back and forth. A man in uniform entered the screen, picking up the slack in a long lead line between him and his dog. He pointed toward the shed and Xena dashed inside.

"And that's Jared Kemp, her two-legged partner. True fact: He's completely nose blind."

The K-9 zipped about the shed so fast, I couldn't imagine she focused on anything. The shelves, the tables, the walls—she checked them all with dizzying speed. What had taken us precious minutes of excruciating search, she did in seconds. She kept returning to the middle of the floor to sniff again. Finally, she sat down square in the center of the room and stared intensely at her partner.

"That's the signal!" Conroy said, sitting up. "There's something under the floor." Hunched over his dashboard, he tweaked the camera control, trying to zoom in even though the robot was parked at a distance.

Jared Kemp grabbed a tug toy from his duty belt. Xena flew from the shed and grabbed it while still airborne. Kemp played with her, then let her have her reward.

I shook my head. "She does all that for a ten-dollar toy."

"That's ten dollars well spent," Conroy said. As Kemp and Xena left the scene, he rolled the robot forward, craned the camera ahead, and zoomed in on the floor. "What'd we miss down here?" he mumbled. "Maybe he nailed something under the floorboards." He began to poke at them with his grip.

I pointed toward the screen. "Wait, look at that."

Conroy paused, hands off the controls, eyes darting. "What're we looking at?"

"What's that? The stain on the floor?"

Lehman squinted at it. "Oil stain or something. What about it?"

"There's another stain on top of it," I said. "See? That orange color—whatever it is. But look how it ends."

The orange stain ended abruptly at a sharp edge. Conroy zoomed in on the pattern of the floorboards. Most of them were staggered—except here. There was a seam. The orange stain had run down into it.

Sometime after the oil spill and before the orange liquid, someone had cut an opening.

"Woowee, we have a door here!" Conroy said. For a moment, he looked like a gamer who'd found treasure on the map of his digital world. He panned his camera all around the crack. "Okay, where there's a door, there's a door handle. Where is it?"

He searched fully five minutes but nothing turned up on the screen. No handle, no latch. Lehman frowned and Conroy muttered under his breath.

I put my fingers to my temples and thought. Wait, this kid was an engineer. A designer. An electrician.

"Look for a switch," I said.

"A switch?" Conroy repeated.

I smiled. "Every secret hatch needs a secret switch."

Conroy grinned. "Oo, I'm beginning to like this kid."

I laughed. Perhaps under different circumstances, Jimmy Beacon and Rex Conroy would have had much in common.

Conroy swiveled the camera around, pointing it in different directions, at different angles, at different heights.

"Go back!" I said, pointing. "Right there, beneath the workbench."

He lowered the eye again and pointed it upwards toward the underside of the bench.

"It's too dark," I said. "I can't make it out."

Conroy hit a button on his dashboard and suddenly the space was illuminated by lights from the bot. Mounted to

266

the underside of the workbench within easy reach of the trap door was a switch with a knob on the end.

The robot technician laced his fingers together and stretched them. "All right, people. This may be the day I blow up a two hundred thousand dollar robot."

He wiggled his fingers, then touched his controls and inched the grip toward the tiny switch. The claw bumped the knob, flipping it to the opposite position. We braced. The robot didn't rock or roll or fly camera over caterpillars. We heard no explosions. Felt no tremors in the ground. Conroy turned the robot's eye toward the floor.

A trap door crept open.

"Yes!" Lehman and Conroy exchanged high fives. When Lehman held his palm up to me, I simply shifted an eyebrow at him, arms folded, and let him stand there. Lehman opened and closed his fist a few times, looking awkward, before dropping his hand to his side.

"All right, all right, all right, what do we got?" asked Conroy. "Do we got stairs?" He poked the camera into the hole. "No, we do not. We got a ladder. Stairs I can handle. Ladders, not so much. She don't do well throwing herself over cliffs." He brightened the lights and swiveled the camera in all directions, poking it further into the hole.

My spine tensed. I half expected the form of a teenage boy to spring from a corner. But there was no boy. Just shelves. Boxes. Gallon jugs. The room had been dug out, perhaps six feet square and six feet deep. The camera strained to peer inside the boxes on the shelves. More pipes. Digital timers. Cannisters of gunpowder. No less than three containers labeled "detonators." The gallon jugs bore labels with the names of various chemicals I knew— chemicals that were perfectly legal to buy but perfectly deadly to combine.

"Holy shit," I breathed.

Shoes clanged up the ramp in the back of the truck. "How's it going?" Sergeant Houston asked.

MAILBOAT III

Rex Conroy swiveled around in his chair. "Sarge, this kid could blow up the city," he announced.

CHAPTER FORTY-SIX
BAILEY

Sitting on the edge of the fountain in front of the Riviera, I swung my feet and wondered when I'd hear anything from Ryan. It had been a while now since we talked, and I wondered if he was actually following up on my call or if he'd forgotten all about it. That would be lame if he forgot to tell me it was okay to go to work. I couldn't keep my mind from drifting to Bud and his leather belts. They were the extra thick and heavy kind.

So, you know that thing where you're thinking about someone and suddenly they call you? Or they just sort of show up? Well, it was like that. Only it wasn't Ryan. It was Bud, striding purposefully down the street. I crouched and pulled my knees in a little tighter. Crap, he was coming for me. He looked mad. I couldn't tell if he was wearing a leather belt. But apparently Jimmy hadn't blown up a bomb. There probably had never been a bomb in the first place. Jimmy was a pain in the butt, not a mass murderer. And now Bud was out to get me.

I closed my eyes and sighed. *Shi-i-it...*

But when I opened them again, Bud was still walking. He didn't even look at me. Just turned up Broad Street and kept going.

Sooo… he wasn't after me? But then what on earth could have taken him away from his restaurant on a day like today? He had to be filling beers and serving plates and pulling in the cash hand over fist.

But as my eyes followed Bud's retreating back, something caught my eye in the little park across the street kitty corner from me. You know, where you rent jet skis. On the bank above the riverside marina, I saw a skinny kid drop out of a tree. At least I thought I did. Whatever it was disappeared into the crowd. I strained my eyes and finally picked out a boy with a backpack ducking between the tourists. His dirty black hair was plastered to his head and he was wearing a tee shirt three sizes too big for him. It was Jimmy. He was traveling the same direction as Bud but keeping low.

He was stalking him.

Oh, this did not look good. Did Ryan know they were here? Maybe not.

Heart skipping, I picked up my phone and tapped the picture of the German Shepherd in sunglasses.

CHAPTER FORTY-SEVEN
RYAN

As a boy, I'd been absolutely convinced the state park was named "Big Foot" because it was a breeding ground for yeti. On family camping trips, I could barely sleep at night, waiting for the shadows on the tent walls to turn into a hairy hand creeping toward the door. I didn't dare imagine what would happen next. Finally noticing my distress and learning the cause, my parents had explained that Big Foot was the name of a famed Potawatomi chief who had lived on these shores many years ago.

I remember telling them that it was a terrible thing for anyone to name their kid and that he must have been bullied a lot at school.

Long gone were the camping trips of yore—the good times before my dad had lost his fight with depression. And instead of a hairy monster, I was now peeking in RV windows and pulling open doors, looking for a boy with a bomb. Mike Schultz decided a twenty-three foot travel trailer would be about right for his family. I pointed out he had nothing to haul it with. He asked if he could borrow my bike.

A sound like an oversized humming bird flew overhead, and being cops with a terrible sense of humor, we smiled and gave the middle finger to whoever was running the drone.

So far, no one had caught sight of Jimmy or Bud. The park had been emptied of vacationers, the drone had scanned every square foot with both a camera and heat sensors, and the dog from Walworth County Sheriff was sniffing the outbuildings. But we had nothing.

Schultz bounced up from the ground after looking under the hundredth RV. "How many pop-outs should I have?"

"Oh, twenty at least," I said.

My phone rang in my pocket. I reached in and pulled it out. The ID said it was Bailey. No doubt she was wondering what was going on. Feeling a little guilty for not checking in on her, I picked up.

"Hey, Bailey, sorry I haven't called. We're looking for Jimmy and Bud."

"I just saw them," Bailey said.

My ears perked up. "Are you still at the Riv?"

"Yeah."

Well, didn't we look like a bunch of idiots, strolling through the woods? The prey had already escaped our net.

Bailey went on. "They're headed up Broad Street."

"You're sure it was them?"

"Yeah."

"Bud's still chasing Jimmy?"

"What?" She paused, taking a moment to process my question as if it were as idiotic as a bunch of cops searching a forest with nobody in it. "No, Jimmy's following Bud. I don't think Bud knew Jimmy was behind him."

Really? This was possibly the most ludicrous game of cat and mouse I'd ever played.

"What do you want me to do?" Bailey asked.

"Nothing. Just stay where you are. Don't follow them. If you see them, walk the other way. Don't go anywhere near them, okay? We'll be downtown in a minute."

"Okay. Um..." She paused again and I waited for her to come out with her thought. "You gonna be all right?" she finally asked.

Bailey's words soaked into my skin, touched my heart with a flash of warmth, and left me standing under an oak tree speechless. A gray squirrel chattered at me overhead. Maybe I was standing on his stash. It had been a long time since anyone other than a supervisor reminded me to keep my hide intact. And come to think of it... this was possibly the first time Bailey hadn't hated me.

"I'll be fine, Bailey," I assured her. "Don't you worry. Just stay alert and stay safe, okay?"

"Okay," she said.

"Call me if something happens. I'll come for you as soon as I can."

"Okay."

Okay? No kicking? No screaming? Well, that was worth noting on the calendar. Had I finally made a fissure in her outer shell? Was she actually trusting me? All of a sudden, I couldn't wait to clear this thing up and go find her at the Riv, riding in like a knight on a white stallion—or a cop on a bicycle.

CHAPTER FORTY-EIGHT
JIMMY

✦

Using the crowd for cover, Jimmy skulked down the street, catching glimpses of Bud Weber between the pedestrians. Weber was within range now, but if Jimmy crept in a little closer, he'd be inside the kill zone. And then Jimmy would set off the bomb.

The tourists didn't matter. Coming out of this situation alive didn't matter. The only thing that mattered was punishing Bud Weber. The last moments of Jimmy's life would be his happiest.

Without warning, Bud turned and scanned the crowd behind him. Jimmy's heart leapt into his mouth. Finding a door to his left, he ducked through and pressed his shoulder against a wall plastered in lake-themed art. He peered through the glass door into the street. Bud's eye went past him and probed into other nooks and crannies. That had been close. How did Bud always seem to sense people around him? Nevertheless, Jimmy felt certain he hadn't been seen.

An ear-piercing alarm tore through the air. Jimmy jumped. What in all the galaxy? He scanned the shop left and right. Phones were going off everywhere. Five or six of them. People stopped browsing racks of summery blouses and rotating displays of jewelry. They were glancing in confusion at each other. Pulling out their mobile devices.

Jimmy looked back into the street. People there were also stopping to check their phones.

He peered over the shoulder of a middle-aged man sitting on an Adirondack chair for sale. He had perhaps paused to rest there, bored by his wife's pursuit of gift shop pleasures. *Emergency Alert,* the man's screen said. *Madison Street to Sage Street and Wisconsin Street to Baker Street. Potential bomb threat. Residents are urged to shelter in place, such as in a basement. Visitors should evacuate the area in a calm and orderly manner. Person of interest: Jimmy Beacon. 16yo, 5 ft. 1 in, 100 lbs. Dark hair. If seen, dial 911. Do not approach.*

A grin spread across Jimmy's face—from ear to ear, as the saying went—and sensations of warmth filled his thoracic cavity. This—*this* was the ultimate moment of his life. *Bomb threat. Jimmy Beacon.* That was him! His name and his bomb, The Revenge, were being broadcast across the entire town.

He looked up smiling, his heart beating light and fast. He wasn't a nobody anymore. People knew his name. And they knew that he possessed absolute control over their lives. He dictated whether they lived or died. He closed his eyes and breathed deeply, soaking in the moment. The sense of power coursing through his veins. The God-ness of it all.

He opened his eyes and glanced around the shop. No one was taking the text message's advice and evacuating the area in a calm and orderly manner.

"Is this a spam message?" one lady asked, bumping her phone screen with her finger.

"No, it's on my phone, too," said a lady behind the jewelry counter. "It's like the Amber Alerts. You sign up for them."

"Oh, did I? I thought they were a scam, too. You know, someone hacking into my phone. There's so much scary stuff out there nowadays. Makes me want to throw this thing away."

Jimmy scowled at the two women in fury. Didn't they get it? *Bomb. Person of interest: Jimmy Beacon.* He wanted to wave The Revenge under their noses so they'd get the point. But he couldn't risk derailing the mission.

He looked into the street again. Bud was gone. Dammit! Jimmy had lost him. But now something new was appearing. Police officers. Lots of them. They were approaching via car, foot, and bike. One of them proceeded to the middle of the intersection and began to direct traffic, diverting cars away from downtown. One driver was apparently distressed by the situation, gesturing the direction he wanted to go with the use of a middle finger. But the officer firmly indicated this was non-negotiable.

A tall man appeared in the middle of the shop. "Ladies and gentlemen, your attention," he said. It crossed Jimmy's mind this individual could be the store manager. Heads turned to look at him. He clasped his hands together like the chairman of a board. "It appears we have an emergency situation on our hands, so we'll be closing the store temporarily. If you're in the middle of a transaction, we'll finish ringing you up as quickly as possible. Anyone in line, feel free to leave your purchases on the counter and we'll hold them for you. Other than that..." He bounced on the balls of his feet and donned a smile that appeared both gracious and awkward. Then he swept his hands toward the door like a butler announcing dinner. "If you'd please make towards the exits. Maybe steer clear of this area for a little while. I'm sure the police will let us know when we can resume normal business. If you need assistance with anything, let me or one of my staff know."

Jimmy pulled his chin into his neck and scowled. That was how this man reacted to a bomb? He sounded like he was introducing a night at the theater, not telling people to run for their lives. Jimmy was tempted once again to flash The Revenge under his nose. Why weren't these people panicking? Hyperventilating? Dropping dead of heart attacks?

Well, they would. Soon enough. He just had to find Bud first. He cursed himself for losing his target again. Where should he start looking now?

Jimmy peered into the street. His heart stuttered as he observed a police officer headed straight for the shop door. Rats! He couldn't risk being identified. He had to get away before the officer—or anyone standing here—could notice he matched the description in the alert.

CHAPTER FORTY-NINE
ROLAND

A screech shattered the peace and quiet of Roland's front garden. As he dropped his trowel in the freshly-turned dirt, his mind went first to the wearable button he could push for a medical emergency. Then he remembered he didn't own one.

He pulled off a glove and tinkered with the volume on his hearing aid, which didn't seem to help. Finally he recalled that his phone was in his cardigan pocket—the same pocket from which the noise, he now realized, was emanating. He sat back on his heels, pulled off his other glove, and reached for his phone.

Emergency Alert, the screen said. *Potential bomb threat...*

Roland slumped and sighed. "Oh, Jimmy..."

He shook his head and dropped a clump of ornamental grass into the hole he'd made, throwing the trowel down after it, too absorbed in thought to bother setting the plant properly. What was there to be done? Nothing, he realized. Jimmy was out of his hands now. No one so much as knew where he was. All that he and the boy had discussed about colleges, careers, the future—wasted. Jimmy had thrown it all aside in favor of vengeance.

Roland asked himself if he should be surprised. No. Pain bottled up too long would vent itself anyway it could—usually to the detriment of others, even innocent bystanders. Perhaps that was why someone—Bud Weber or whoever it was—had killed Amelia Beacon in the first place. Amelia's murderer had foisted his pain on Jimmy. And now Jimmy was foisting it on the world. There was no end to the cycle, unless someone consciously put a foot down and called a halt.

Roland doubted that was Jimmy's way. Perhaps he'd been a fool to hope that it could ever be. And now Lake Geneva would pay the price.

He folded his hands in his lap and bowed his head. He had a heavy feeling this was goodbye to Jimmy Beacon.

CHAPTER FIFTY
BAILEY

❄

I was kicking my heels against the side of the fountain, waiting to see if Ryan would call again, when the alarm blared. I jumped so bad, I nearly took a swim in the fountain. I looked around. People all over the courtyard were staring at their phones.

"Emergency alert," a guy with a wife and a little boy read out loud. Whatever he was reading, it said to evacuate the area and call the police if he saw Jimmy Beacon.

Heat scorched my face. God, I hoped this whole thing wasn't just Jimmy pulling a prank. The kids at school would never let me live it down. *Remember that time Bailey cleared out the whole city?*

Evacuate the area. Sooo... like now? People were talking to each other as if asking the same question. I suppose it was pretty obvious. Just do what the text message says.

Yep.

I pursed my lips and kicked my heels against the side of the fountain. So, why was I still sitting here?

'Cause Ryan had told me to wait for him. I'd kind of looked forward to him showing up, coming to get me, telling me everything was okay now. It was small and ridiculous, but it was something to look forward to after all this chaos.

Maybe that's why I perked a little bit when a black and white police car rolled to a stop in front of the Riviera. I sucked in my breath and watched the driver's door swing open. A man in a cop's uniform stepped out.

He was big and burly and had gray hair and a mustache. It wasn't Ryan.

Okay, now I felt stupid. Why had I hoped it would be Ryan, anyway?

The man grabbed the little radio mic inside his car and held it to his mouth. His voice boomed from a speaker somewhere on the car. "Ladies and gentlemen, this is the Lake Geneva Police Department. Please evacuate the area now..."

I had a feeling Ryan would want me to do what this cop said. I glanced down at my phone one more time—the little picture of the German Shepherd—and sighed. It didn't matter. I slid off the edge of the fountain. Pushing my phone into my backpack, I grabbed the bars of my bike, kicked up the stand, and started walking.

Well, where to now? Not downtown, I guess. May as well head for the restaurant. Jimmy wasn't there anymore, after all. And Bud would be delighted that I started my shift in spite of a bomb threat.

CHAPTER FIFTY-ONE
JIMMY

Using dress racks for cover, Jimmy edged around the room. A doorway in back led into yet another section of the store, tables and shelves stacked high with lakeside knick knacks. He backed up against a cabinet of distressed wood and peered through the doorway into the first room. The officer—dark-haired, middle-aged, dressed in shorts of all things—was herding people out of the shop with the assistance of the manager.

"Is there really a bomb, officer?" inquired the lady suspicious of scams and hackers.

"That's not been confirmed," the man replied. "We're just clearing the area for everyone's safety." He offered the woman a smile but quickly returned his attention to the entire room, apparently counting noses and eager to keep things moving. His behavior was reminiscent of a keyed-up sheep dog rounding up reluctant sheep.

The woman finally bustled out of the shop, but an old man with two kids was right behind her. The gentleman wore a black collar with a white insert. A cleric of some sort. At sight of this individual, the officer's face relaxed into a grin.

"Bill, what are you doing here?" he asked.

The religious leader tousled the kids' hair. "Well, I was just showing these two youngsters a day on the town. We were about to pick up some ice cream, but I guess that'll have to wait."

Jimmy grinned as he eavesdropped. Yes, this was more like it. Lives disrupted. Plans diverted. People reacting because he, Jimmy Beacon, had finally taken action. Even depriving a child of an ice cream cone was sweet revenge.

The old man clapped a hand over the officer's shoulder. "You stay safe, Ryan. Let me know if you need me. I'm just a phone call away."

The officer nodded and thumped his shoulder in return. "Thanks, man. Hopefully we won't need your services today."

The cleric lifted his phone. "I'll keep an eye out for the boy."

"Appreciate it, man."

Their brief conversation having thus ended, the man of the cloth herded the two kids out of the shop and into the increasingly crowded street, where the masses shuffled slowly like commuters waiting for a subway.

The store manager and his employees were now the only ones left.

The officer pointed deeper into the store—towards Jimmy. "This goes back a ways, right?"

"It does," the manager confirmed.

"You should all get moving," the officer said. "I'm just going to do a quick sweep of the other rooms."

"The door—?" the manager said, motioning toward the front entrance and the lock.

"Don't worry about it," the officer said. "We'll keep an eye on things. No one will break in while you're gone. The important thing right now is to clear out of the danger zone."

The manager appeared reluctant but didn't argue. He and his employees turned and filed out of the shop.

Jimmy and the officer were now alone in a store turned eerily silent. The officer walked deeper into the store. Closer to Jimmy.

Jimmy spun on his heel and skipped through the labyrinth of home decor. Yet another entry led into one more display area. But at the very back, he finally found an actual door—one with hinges and a latch. He pushed on the handle and hoped it wasn't locked.

It wasn't. He tumbled into a back room. Tables were stacked with boxes, some taped shut, some unpacked. To the right was a small kitchen. A door to a bathroom. On the floor sat an array of boxes, some flattened, others three-dimensional. One box was low and long and open on one end. The picture on the side showed a whitewashed, barn-style coffee table with silver boat cleats to open the sliding door in the middle. Small print noted that the resin model lighthouse (pictured) was not included.

Jimmy peeked through the open end of the box. It was empty. He dove in feet-first and folded the flaps down behind him. They wouldn't close completely, but perhaps this was strategically beneficial. He could peer through the crack, a mere quarter of an inch across. He stilled his breathing. He was enclosed now in warm, brown darkness that smelled of cardboard and glue and new furniture—a pleasant cocktail of aromas that had never graced his own home. The furniture there smelled of potato chip grease and mold.

The storeroom door swished open. Rubber-soled shoes tapped across the floor. In the middle of his tiny cardboard window appeared an ankle. The shoes, noted earlier, were completely black. Well-worn. A leaf and slivers of grass stuck to the breathable fabric inserts, as if the wearer had run through woods. Jimmy considered that his own shoes may well bear similar foliage; that this particular representative from the local law enforcement agency may well have been running through the same woods as he had.

The shoes paused. The ankle rotated, as if its owner were turning from the hips, scanning the room. Then the shoes walked forward. Inch by inch, the entire person appeared in Jimmy's narrow viewfinder. Black cargo shorts. Black shirt with short sleeves, the yoke and shoulders royal blue. Over it all, an olive drab ballistic vest. He looked half like an officer, half like an exercise enthusiast.

The officer rapped his knuckles on the bathroom door. "Hello? Anyone in here?" When there was no answer, he opened the door. Glanced inside.

Then he turned and left. Walked straight out the door again back into the front rooms of the shop.

Jimmy was alone. He hadn't been found. And the doors of the shop would remain unlocked. He could leave at his leisure. All in all, a relatively positive outcome.

Jimmy crawled out of his bunker and fingered his backpack to ensure the Revenge was still inside. The mission was still on. But he *had* to find Bud. Again. Jimmy had never imagined detonating his final bomb would be so complicated.

CHAPTER FIFTY-TWO
BUD

———— ✺ ————

Leaning against the brick wall of a recessed doorway, Bud lit up a cigarette and watched the entire town flow by. That sixth sense of his for trouble was still alive and kicking. Jimmy had snuck up behind him somehow. That could have been close. But Jimmy Beacon was in the gift shop on the corner now. Bud had seen him go in. He'd seen everyone come out—except the kid. He was trapped in there with that cop—Ryan what's-his-face. The same son of a bitch who was always shaking things up for him and Bailey. What Bud wouldn't do to eliminate the kid and the cop at the same time…

But he hadn't thought of a good way to do that. He didn't have a weapon. His guns were all at home or in the safe in his office. He didn't even have the Little Babe. Bud had never been whatchacall clever, but he had an idea… It was a finicky plan. The trick was to get out of the way before the blast from the kid's bomb went off. Maybe the good ol' sixth sense would keep him from roasting his hide. Get his timing perfect. All he needed was for the kid to come out of the store before the street was empty. Jimmy would die—and Bud would look like the innocent victim.

The door of the shop opened and the policeman walked out. Well, there went his shining opportunity to kill two birds with one stone, but there hadn't been a chance anyway, so long as they were both in the store.

Bud grimaced at Ryan from the shadows of his doorway. The cops would never find out that he had, in fact, killed that little girl seven years ago. Bud already knew his trail was wiped clean, aside from the little pink bow. So far as he knew, Jimmy still had it. He'd have to make sure his little memento from the day he killed the girl was destroyed in the blast. Jimmy better not have messed with any of the other stuff in the beer stein. The thought of that kid pawing through his special keepsakes boiled his blood.

How Jimmy had pieced together the killing was beyond his reckoning, though he had an uncomfortable notion— the kind that felt like a wedgie when the health department guys were over to recertify your restaurant. Geez, it was one thing to fire a man; it was a whole 'nother shit show to get him killed. But Bud couldn't blame The Man Upstairs for trying to do him in. Now that Bud wasn't a hired hit man, he was just a liability.

Bud sniffed and wiped his nose on his arm. Well, he'd show him. The Man Upstairs would regret messing with Bud Weber.

CHAPTER FIFTY-THREE
RYAN

I left the gift shop and shouldered my way through the impossible pedestrian traffic we'd created by emptying the stores. In the middle of the intersection, Mike Schultz directed traffic, keeping the cars flowing north, away from the lake and downtown. Everything seemed to be moving along. I turned up the street to clear another shop.

A face I knew materialized from the chaos—Monica, coming toward me. She was wearing a bullet-proof vest over her polo shirt and looked like she was headed toward the shop I'd just finished.

I jabbed a thumb over my shoulder. "That one's done."

"Good work," she said, but her mouth was snarking beneath the black sunglasses. She pointed behind her in the opposite direction. "I cleared the whole rest of the block."

So much for the meaningful look I thought we'd exchanged at the middle school. Monica's jab was obvious: I sucked at meeting her expectations. It didn't matter how far she lowered the bar for me; I'd always manage to miss it. I thought again about my applications to other departments...

Tucking my thumbs into the arm holes of my ballistic vest, I toed the sidewalk. "It was a big store."

"You poor dear. You must be exhausted."

I tried to remember everything Bill Gallagher and I had talked about the other night at his house, but with Monica frowning down at me, his words rushed away like water through a strainer. Something about my not having the whole story... About hearing her out... But there was no time for a heart-to-heart. Maybe when this was all over...

"Monica, look." I stared into her sunglasses and tried to ignore my own reflection staring back. "I'd really like it if we talked sometime. You know, just got everything out on the table. Out in the open." I spread my hands as if smoothing a tablecloth.

I breathed, trying to steady my racing heart. Unable to read her expression, her eyes, I was walking blind. Maybe she was just waiting for me to finish making an idiot of myself and then she'd faceplant me into the sidewalk. Maybe I'm just a pansy, but the fear of rejection was on a par with an old man gunning for me in the street.

But since I was an idiot, I swallowed and kept going. "I have a feeling I don't even know everything I did wrong. But I'd like to know someday. I'd like to hear your side. Even if you just stab me in the throat afterwards. But I owe it to you to at least hear you out."

Monica stared at me, her eyes a black void of tinted plastic. I would have given anything to see past them. To see just how low she thought of me. But she said nothing. Her lips parted as if words had been sucked away from her. Maybe she thought I was an idiot for even bringing this up during a bomb threat.

Of course, she'd be right. She didn't even need to say it.

CHAPTER FIFTY-FOUR
MONICA

Townspeople and tourists brushing past, all I could do was stare at Ryan Brandt, jaw slack. A black emptiness crept up from my belly. Like a claw, it hooked and twisted. Reminded me of the void. The loneliness. The angel I'd let go. The angel I'd let die before even giving her a chance. Before even having a chance to look into her face.

And then I remembered Ryan's part in all of it. If he hadn't cheated on me, our child would still be here.

My jaw clamped shut like a vice. *You want to know the full story, Ryan Brandt?* I challenged him silently. *You don't know the half of it, you piece of shit.*

CHAPTER FIFTY-FIVE
JIMMY

———— ✪ ————

Jimmy stood outside his cardboard bunker and scanned the storage room at the back of the gift shop. How fortuitous! Opposite the kitchen stood a door which appeared to lead directly into the street. He pushed it open a crack and sighted down a short alley. Beyond, the sidewalk flowed with people. Vehicles in the street crawled forward at an estimated two point one miles per hour.

Jimmy slipped through the door and down the narrow corridor between the buildings. On the sidewalk, he joined the flow of foot traffic, keeping his head low. He would turn at the street corner and head for the place where he had last seen Bud Weber. The next time he sighted his target, he would not wait. He held the detonator in his hand.

CHAPTER FIFTY-SIX
BUD

Bud took a drag from his cigarette. Watched the street from his doorway. Waited. He felt like one of them funnel spiders, just waiting for his prey to wander by. And then he'd spring. And the boy would know Bud had been in charge all along.

He always was.

CHAPTER FIFTY-SEVEN
MIKE

———— ✾ ————

Standing in the middle of his assigned intersection, Mike Schultz kept the cars moving while a nice hot sun beat down on his uniform. With the shops evacuated, the foot traffic was a sight to behold—perhaps the most crowded he'd ever seen Lake Geneva. Granted, that made them vulnerable if the bomber was nearby.

But the light was at the end of the tunnel. In a few minutes, the street would be empty and the townspeople and tourists safe. Meanwhile, the heavy police presence would dissuade the bomber from setting off his device. From where he stood, he could see Monica and Ryan on one side of the street, Franklin and Lehman on the other, and more of his fellow cops at each of the adjoining intersections. They had this.

Mike grinned and nodded at a driver who had been kind enough to wave.

Of course, this wasn't how he'd hoped to spend his Fourth of July. Leaving Nicole and the kids at the beach had been a sad moment. Jackson had recently figured out what "Dad got called out" meant. Today, he'd hit the waterworks before Mike could even kiss him goodbye. Nicole took everything in stride, though, crying toddler and all, and Aiden making that face that promised a surprise package in his diaper. But Nicole was an expert as both a mom and a cop's wife, moving with the flow, changing plans on the fly. God, he was lucky.

He'd kissed her goodbye, then jogged to the station to throw on a uniform, a vest, and a duty belt. Running on foot had literally been the fastest way to get there past all the tourists.

And now, one hike in the state park later, here he was directing traffic—and considering that a twenty-three foot trailer might not be big enough...

The bomb squad was on call. The shops were evacuated. The whole town was keeping an eye out for Jimmy Beacon. Soon they'd find him and neutralize his bomb.

And then everything would go back to normal. Mike would head home and get the steaks on the grill while the detectives had fun sorting out the rest. He stole a glance at Monica and Stan Lehman, poor suckers. While they worked their asses off late into the night, he'd be watching the fireworks with his kids. From their backyard, they had a great view of the light show at the Grand Geneva Resort.

Mike couldn't wait. Jackson loved fireworks.

CHAPTER FIFTY-EIGHT
JIMMY

Jimmy moved with the crowd, keeping his eyes sharp. The trick was to spot Bud before Bud spotted him. He rounded the corner of the building and searched the street where he'd last seen his target.

Come to me, Bud Weber, he thought. *Justice awaits.*

CHAPTER FIFTY-NINE
BUD

———— ⚓ ————

Bingo. Two o'clock. Jimmy the dishwasher. The kid wore a deadly expression but never spotted Bud tucked in the doorway. Of course not. Bud was keeping a low profile, barely letting his nose poke out.

He looked away from Jimmy to study the cars in the street. There's what he needed—a big-ass pickup, right next to the intersection, waiting for its turn to go. That weren't no city slicker from Chicago behind the wheel. That was a farmer's truck, a nice layer of dirt on the fenders. Hell, he had a load of corn cobs in the back, all stacked up in cute wooden crates. Maybe he was headed for the festival at the Grand Geneva. Traffic musta forced him into a bad turn, sweeping him into the chaos of downtown. Tough luck for him. But it was exactly what Bud needed. Now it was just a matter of timing this whole thing. Letting his sixth sense kick into gear at just the right moment.

He pressed his shoulder against the bricks, waiting for Jimmy to get closer.

When the boy was only six feet away—when the little half-wit couldn't possibly miss him—Bud stepped out of the doorway, all casual-like, and paraded across the sidewalk, transecting the foot traffic like a big, fat slicing knife. The kind you use on veggies. But as he cut in front of the pedestrians, all of them grumbling and cussing at him, he made sure to glance at the dishwasher.

Jimmy saw him. The boy's eyes blazed like hellfire.

Like a steak grilled to perfection, it was a beautiful thing. *Moo-y bwayno,* as the Mexicans said.

CHAPTER SIXTY
JIMMY

Target acquired! Target acquired! The man himself—that slimy, primordial life form—had stepped in front of Jimmy as casually as one might step from their own front door. How much of an idiot did Weber have to be?

Jimmy shouldered a gaggle of teenage girls out of his way, but they were soon replaced by a clutch of middle-aged women. He tripped on the leash of a dog. Staggered as he collided with a three-foot-high child. Blast these tourists; he wasn't getting anywhere.

Jimmy observed a wooden bench on the side of the street. He jumped on top of it, alighting on the backrest so he was head and shoulders above the crowd. He grasped a tree limb for balance.

"Weber!" he yelled. His voice cracked through the air with authority. With vengeance. Like the voice of God.

Bud Weber glanced back. His big, fat face morphed into an expression of panic. He shouldered his way into the street where there were no pedestrians, and there he broke into the run.

Jimmy leapt from his bench and pursued. At last. Bud Weber was his.

CHAPTER SIXTY-ONE
BUD

—————— ⚙ ——————

Bud resisted dancing like a child. Ha! This was going to work! He stretched his hands in front of him and flailed them a bit, like a dumb actor running from the zombie apocalypse in a B movie. He made straight for the intersection. The pickup. The cop directing traffic.

"Hey, police!" he yelled. "Police! Help me! Help me!"

CHAPTER SIXTY-TWO
MONICA

The sound of someone shouting Bud Weber's name drew our attention—and gave me an excuse to break eye contact with Ryan. We looked toward the street. Saw a kid perched on top of a park bench. Bud Weber running toward the intersection, yelling for help. His panicked gestures would have been hilarious, if it hadn't been for the sight of a backpack on Jimmy's shoulders, a wire running through the opening and into his hand.

Jimmy leapt from the bench and chased after Weber.

My heart rose into my throat. There were people everywhere. Heads were only beginning to turn. Interest barely being drawn toward the disruption in the street. Understanding would dawn for these people all too slowly. Meanwhile, Bud, Jimmy, and the bomb were headed straight for Mike Schultz.

Ryan and I drew our sidearms. Jumped up on another park bench to get above the crowd.

"Get down! Get down!" Ryan yelled at passers-by.

Those nearest us stared in confusion, then dropped to the ground as they saw Ryan and me assume a shooting stance, weapons in hand.

I narrowed my eyes and stared through the sites. Aimed center mass. Pulled the trigger. Again, again, again. I vaguely registered shell casings from Ryan's gun pelting my arm and leg. I didn't hear his weapon fire, or mine. Tunnel vision. I saw and heard nothing I didn't need to see or hear—just Jimmy Beacon and his backpack.

I knew full well my bullets could hit a bystander. Could kill someone. I knew I could hit the bomb instead of Jimmy, killing us all.

But to shoot was better than to stand by and watch. I'd answer to my conscience later—and probably to a court of law, to the media, to the world. But right now, I had to do my job, to the best of my ability. And that meant stopping Jimmy with the only tools I had.

But the boy kept running. He reached out and grabbed for the back of Bud Weber's shirt.

CHAPTER SIXTY-THREE
JIMMY

Something hot and hard sank into Jimmy's back. Like the time he'd poked marbles into a wheel of cheese—one of his earliest experiments, when he was approximately three. His mother had scolded him. He hadn't had the vocabulary then to explain that he was studying the resistance of the cheese versus its willingness to yield.

In some far reach of his brain, he realized the objects pelting him in the back were not marbles, nor was he a wheel of cheese. And he didn't care. Adrenaline—that useful hormone in one percent of situations, of which the asking out of girls shouldn't be one—was performing it's biologically intended function, lending strength and determination he logically shouldn't have had. He wouldn't stop. Not now, when he was so close. He grabbed for Bud Weber's black tee shirt. He felt the fine cotton weave between the fingers of one hand, the button of the detonator under the thumb of the other.

CHAPTER SIXTY-FOUR
BUD

The good ol' sixth sense told Bud that Jimmy was close long before the tug on his shirt did. He put on an extra burst of speed and felt his shirt slip out of Jimmy's hand.

The cop in the middle of the intersection had finally pulled his gun and dropped into a crouch but hadn't raised his weapon and wasn't pulling the trigger. With Bud blocking the way, the sucker had nothing to shoot at. It didn't matter. Bud didn't need the stinking cop.

A whisper in the back of his brain, like that still, small voice his mama used to read about in the Bible, told him Jimmy was raising the detonator, getting ready to blast. Where was that, anyway? Book of Ely-gee-astese, or something.

Bud leapt for the pickup. He rolled over the hood, catching a glimpse of the driver's face as he went by. The farmer was forty-something. Stubbled jaw. Feed cap and grungy plaid shirt. His expression was covered in o's and semi-circles—his mouth, his eyes, his brows. He couldn't possibly have meant to drive into downtown Lake Geneva today. Get stuck in this hell of a traffic mess. The poor clod-digger was probably about to die.

Didn't matter. So long as Jimmy died and Bud didn't look responsible. This here wasn't a murder. It was an assisted suicide. Another feather Bud could add to his cap.

He dropped behind the truck on the other side, putting the engine block between him and Jimmy. Between him and the bomb. The still, small voice told him Jimmy was squeezing the detonator.

CHAPTER SIXTY-FIVE
RYAN

❖

Through the sights of my weapon, I saw Jimmy raise the detonator. Bud veered off at the last second and disappeared behind a pickup. I braced for the sound of an explosion.

And then, someone materialized from the crowd and ran at Jimmy like a linebacker bent on tackling the quarterback. Sacking him in the pocket. Preventing him from ever shooting that football across the field.

It was Bill Gallagher.

He wrapped Jimmy Beacon in one of his famous bear hugs—hugs that had embraced old friends, frightened children, beloved parishioners, cops trying not to be hugged, prisoners broken and at their wit's end. Bill wrapped Jimmy in one of those hugs and took him straight to the ground.

Moments before the flash.

The fireball.

The pressure wave.

I wrote in the report afterwards exactly what I saw. What happened when that bomb went off, sandwiched between Bill Gallagher and Jimmy Beacon.

I'm not going to write it again.

Except to say that I saw shrapnel flying in all directions. Expanding like a starburst. Like a sun exploding.

Without stopping to think, I hooked my arm around Monica's shoulders and dropped her to the ground where I held her tight, my body over hers.

CHAPTER SIXTY-SIX
MONICA

Ryan's body hit me like a truck. As I fell, something told me to get my finger off the damn trigger so I wouldn't shoot him or a citizen by accident. I hit the sidewalk, Ryan on top of me, his weight pressing me down, squeezing the air out of my lungs. He clutched me so tightly, there was no chance of getting out from under him.

The street filled with screams.

CHAPTER SIXTY-SEVEN
BAILEY

I was walking my bike along the lake near Flat Iron Park when it happened. A big bang, as if a firework had exploded right on the ground. You know, one of the really big ones that you can feel in your chest when it goes off. Normally those are lots of fun, but this time I flinched when I heard it. Everyone around me jumped and gasped.

I stopped where I was. That's when I realized the kids at school weren't going to make fun of me. That's when I realized leaving downtown was a really smart idea. That's when I realized that people in Lake Geneva had died just now.

And that I was never going to see Jimmy Beacon again.

All of a sudden, I felt really bad for avoiding him at the restaurant all the time. Would it have been so bad to drink a soda with him on break?

Everyone had stopped moving. People stared at each other. The entire town went silent. No voices. No traffic. Nothing. I could hear the people breathing on the opposite side of the street.

"Where's Allison?" one woman asked a friend, her voice the first thing to shatter the spell. She pulled out her phone and started dialing, her hands shaking.

"C'mon, let's go," a man said to his wife. They herded their three kids down the street as if shooing ducklings.

Everyone started moving again. Moving away from the sound of the giant firework. The only one who ran towards it was a cop. He dashed up the middle of the street like a streak of lightning, hand on his gun to keep it from bouncing.

I stood in the middle of it all beside my bicycle. People flowed past me like a river.

I really hoped Ryan was okay.

CHAPTER SIXTY-EIGHT
MONICA

———— ✦ ————

My cheek pressed to the cement, I watched a half-inch lug nut roll end-over-end across the sidewalk, impossibly fast. It skipped over a crack in the pavement as if it were a ski jump, but landed poorly on its edge. It began to run in ever-tightening circles, smaller and smaller, until it finally spun to a stop, landing on its side.

It left a spiral of blood on the sidewalk.

Ryan still pinned me to the ground. I felt his breath in my ear. Sensed his lips move. He was speaking. I heard nothing but bells. My eardrums were on fire.

His cheek was pressed into the back of my neck. It was warm. Familiar. The way he used to hold me. The way he used to rock me when I came home from work crying. Crying because another child was reported missing or dead. Crying because our own nursery was empty and always would be.

He was probably asking me if I was okay.

No, I wanted to say. *Stay with me. Don't let me go.*

I knew Jimmy Beacon was dead. Dead because he'd detonated his bomb. My heart was being shoved through a shredder. I wanted to pound the sidewalk and scream.

But I couldn't. I needed to be all right, and I needed to stay all right for as long as my town needed me. A citizen can turn to the cops for help anytime. A cop has no one to turn to but herself. I reached inside until I found my inner bitch. She, too, was crying in a corner. I slapped her in the face and propped her up in a corner.

"Get off me," I said. "I can't breathe."

As if afraid he'd hurt me, Ryan made a fast push up and rolled to the side. When he did, spots of blood hit the cement. I slid to my knees and looked at him. The left side of his face was pouring blood.

"Shit," I said, "you're bleeding."

He waved his hand. "Damn head wounds. You know they bleed like a fire hose." He leaned back against the park bench and gingerly touched his injury.

I slapped his fingers away. "Let me see." I grabbed a pair of nitrile gloves out of a pocket on my ballistic vest, snapped them on, and examined the wound, a cut just shy of his hairline. He was right. It wasn't deep. "I guess you'll live," I said.

"Well, damn. What a shame." He quirked a grin.

My gaze dropped to his eyes. They were smiling. He was playing to my jibes. The attacks I buffeted on him day and night. Acting like they didn't hurt, when I knew they did. What kind of a heel was I? This made twice now he could have been killed—twice since he'd come back home to Lake Geneva. Both times had made me sick to my stomach.

"Just shut up and sit still," I said, grabbing a medical kit out of my vest pocket. But Ryan pulled my hand away.

"I got this." He tapped his own pocket, the contents of which were identical to mine. "Go help," he said.

I bit my lip, fighting my need to fix everything myself. But he was right. It was triage time. Others closer to the blast would be wounded worse than he was.

I stood up and scanned the street, searching for
casualties. People still hugged the ground, trembling.
Husbands clutched their wives. Parents shielded their kids.
Friends held each other's hand. No one spoke above a
whisper. "Are you all right?" they asked. "You okay?" By and
large, the answer seemed to be yes. And I knew why. My
heart pounded. I knew. I knew, but I didn't want to see. I
forced the inner bitch to drive my footsteps forward. Into
the blast zone. I picked my way past stunned pedestrians
and pale-faced drivers. I looked toward the intersection.

Stan Lehman and Ted Franklin were already there.
Bending down. Feeling pulses. Mike Schultz was sprawled
on the ground where he had been directing traffic moments
ago. I knew without a closer look that he didn't need our
help. His eyes stared fixedly at the sky. Near him lay two
more bodies, Jimmy Beacon and Bill Gallagher. Or rather,
what was left of them. Stan touched their carotids anyway. I
guess you can live with less than a full body. But Stan didn't
initiate any life-saving measures. There were none to be
initiated.

I glanced at the pickup. The windshield was a spray of
cracks, but it had held. The driver sat behind it, white-
knuckled, jaw hanging. The stories he would tell his wife
tonight. The hugs he would give to his children. He knew
exactly how lucky he was, and tomorrow he'd probably sit
down and start that side hustle he'd always talked about.

From behind the pickup, Bud Weber slowly peeked
over the hood at the bodies in the street. A streak of blood
ran down his left arm. Other than that, he looked to be in
one piece. Ryan would be pissed.

I stared at the bodies again. Mike. Bill. These were
people I had known and respected. And then there was
Jimmy. A boy I'd never met in person and only known for
an hour. A boy who'd voluntarily cut his life short on the
edge of adulthood, taking the lives of others with him.

Anger burned in my chest, first a low smolder, then a crackling flame, then an inferno. Is this what his mother had wanted? Was she happy now? She was finally rid of the son she didn't want. I clamped my jaw tight so I wouldn't scream.

A hand squeezed my shoulder. A voice whispered in my ear. "You got this." It was Ryan.

Oh, did I? I had the world in both hands, and I was ready to rip it in two.

Sitting on the curb near the intersection, a man leaned over a woman. She clutched her leg and rocked back and forth, her face twisted. The man waved at us. "Police! Police! We need help!"

I took in the crowd more closely and picked out three more victims with injuries. A slashed leg. A broken arm. A bleeding shoulder. There should have been more. But Bill had voluntarily absorbed the brunt of the blast. I closed my eyes and balled my fists. *Why would you do that, Bill?*

I opened my eyes again. I needed to snap out of this. Get my butt to work.

But our brother and sister cops were pouring in from other streets and Ryan squeezed my arms. "Call the medics," he said. "Clear a way for the ambulance." He moved toward the woman with the wounded leg.

I nodded. "You okay?" I asked, glancing at the tidy bandage he'd wrapped around his head.

He pulled off the gloves he'd worn while treating himself. "Still vertical," he said with a shrug and a watery smile, then turned and ran toward the injured woman.

Still vertical. Good enough. We'd lived to see another day. Maybe I'd even have the chance to tell him the whole story, like he'd asked. Lay the cards out on the table.

He could have died today without knowing he had almost been a father. Was that what I wanted?

I closed my eyes. Hauled in a deep breath. Rallied. Then I unclipped a radio from my belt and asked Steph to get us

313

the medics. When she had confirmed the route the ambulance would take, I returned the radio to my belt and moved toward the intersection, ready to get these cars out of the way.

My phone rang. Thinking it might be the chief, the lieutenant, the sergeant—someone like that—I swiped without even looking at the screen.

"Yes?" I said.

"Monica Steele..."

The voice was low. Hoarse. Rasping. It sounded like something straight from the grave.

I stopped and frowned. "Who is this?" I demanded.

"Have you figured it out yet?" the voice asked, barely above a whisper. "Have you figured out what's going on around here? Have you realized yet that it's all connected?"

Chills ran up my spine. I glanced at Lehman in case he was playing a sick joke, but he was bandaging the woman with the bleeding leg. "What are you talking about?" I asked.

"The murders. The shooting. The bomb. Have you realized that it's all connected? It's a game, Monica. A game you *must* play."

I slid my phone away from my ear. Read the caller ID. It only said *Unknown*. Next, I calmly pulled up the app that let me record phone conversations. I needed evidence of this. I needed to trace the call, too, but I didn't have an app for that.

I was talking to the killer. The accomplice, maybe. The man behind it all.

I eased the phone next to my ear again. "What kind of game are you talking about?" I asked.

"A game of knowing, Monica. You see, I know everything. I know everything about this town and the people in it. I know your strengths. I know your weaknesses. I know how to exploit them. I even know how to exploit your children. Yes, Monica—*your* children."

Terror jolted through my stomach. My hand snaked over my belly. What was he saying? How was this even possible? *No one knew.* Suddenly, I was standing in the middle of a black room, naked, a light shining down on me.

"Who are you?" I demanded again.

Seconds lingered with no answer.

And then, with a simple air, he replied, "I'm The Man Upstairs."

The line went dead.

JOIN THE CREW

Ahoy, Shipmate!

If you feel like you're perched on a lighthouse, scanning the horizon for Danielle Lincoln Hanna's next book—good news! You can subscribe to her email newsletter and read a regular ship's log of her writing progress. Better yet, dive deep into the life of the author, hear the scuttlebutt from her personal adventures, spy on her writing process, and catch a rare glimpse of dangerous sea monsters—better known as her pets, Fergus the cat and Angel the German Shepherd.

It's like a message in a bottle washed ashore. All you have to do is open it...

DanielleLincolnHanna.com/newsletter

BOOKS BY DANIELLE LINCOLN HANNA

The Mailboat Suspense Series

Mailboat I: The End of the Pier
Mailboat II: The Silver Helm
Mailboat III: The Captain's Tale
Mailboat IV - *coming summer 2020*

DanielleLincolnHanna.com/shopnow

Pre-order available for Mailboat IV:
DanielleLincolnHanna.com/preorder-mb4

ACKNOWLEDGMENTS

It's been less than a year since I released *Mailboat II: The Silver Helm,* and the adventure only gets better. In many ways, my writing process has settled into a comfortable routine. In other ways, Bailey and the crew surprise and amaze me, pushing me to new limits. Best of all, I'm constantly surrounded by the friends and fans who have embraced both this series and me, the little writer behind it. It's for you, my dear readers, that I keep writing. Thank you.

As always, so many thanks to the Lake Geneva Cruise Line, operators of the real-life Lake Geneva Mailboat. What a treasure you have. Thanks for letting me share it. Gratitude specifically to *General Managers Harold Friestad (ret.)* and *Jack Lothian,* to *the Mailboat Captain Neill Frame,* and to *Office Manager Ellen Burling.* Smooth sailing to you all.

Research for *Mailboat III* took me outside my comfort zone to A Big City—Milwaukee. The one time I didn't get lost on the Interstate exchanges, I got lost in the parking lot of Froedtert Hospital, where I'd already been many times. So, massive thanks to *Annette Bertelson,* BSN, RN, CPHQ; Manager of the Trauma Program at Froedtert Hospital. She did the impossible and made me feel at home in a medical facility the size of several football fields. I asked for a rundown of the trauma center, and she gave me literally the best tour of my life. After I explained the storyline to her, she walked me through the hospital, department by department, showing me exactly where my characters would be and what was happening to them, both Tommy and his friends and family. In each department, she introduced me to staff members who worked there, explained the scenario to them, and asked them to show me what would happen to my characters in their part of the hospital. Two years after that tour, I am still speechless. Annette, you blew it out of the water.

On that tour, I met and spoke with the following staff members of Froedtert Hospital: *Inderjit Drew Pooni,* MSN, RN, ACNS-BC; Clinical Nurse Specialist, Surgical Intensive Care Unit. Thank you for the tour of one of your rooms in Surgical ICU. *Amanda Kelly,* RN; Charge Nurse, 2NT/Trauma & Acute Care Surgery. Thank you for showing me "the floor," your general hospital rooms for patients who have progressed from Surgical ICU. *Jack Patterson,* MSW; Social Worker, Social Services Department. We spoke briefly in the hall, but you talked to me about your job and how social workers like you are on hand to provide psychological evaluation to patients. *Josh Hunt,* PhD; Assistant Professor, Department of Surgery, Division of Trauma/Critical Care, Medical College of Wisconsin (Froedtert). Thank you for inviting me into your office to talk about the psychology program and the psychological evaluations and services offered to trauma patients.

I came away from Froedtert massively impressed with the level of medical, psychological, and personal care you offer your patients. Also, thank you for the care you provided to the daughter of *Telecommunicator Rita Moore* of the Lake Geneva Police Department, a personal friend and research assistant for this series. Finley wouldn't be here without you. Thank you, Rita, for the words, "a sprawling land of healing and terror." You spoke from the heart, and I can't think of a better way to describe how Bailey felt as she first saw Froedtert Hospital.

I would be lost without the in-depth help of my expert advisers and the flurry of emails that fly between us. *Lieutenant Edward Gritzner* and *Sergeant Jason Hall* of the Lake Geneva Police Department, I don't know how you haven't arrested me by now, what with me emailing you about bombs going off in your city. Instead, you welcome every storyline like a free training scenario. (You're welcome.) Ed even called me back two minutes after we hung up. "On second thought, let's put Incident Command at the Lake Geneva Middle School. The parking lot at the state park is too close to the potential blast zone." I admire how seriously you take your work. Even in a fictitious scenario, you are evaluating yourselves and optimizing your performance. Lake Geneva is in good hands.

Many thanks to the rest of my expert advisers. *Sam Petitto* (retired police officer, Durango, CO), shoddy policework will never make it past your sharp eye. Thanks for keeping Ryan and Monica on their toes—and alive. *Dr. Terry Jones,* a.k.a., Dr. Evil, thanks for going through medical school so I didn't have to. *David Congdon* (Threat Assessment and Countermeasures Specialist), thanks for providing psychological insights into the stories I simply write from experiences, observations, and the heart.

To my writer's club, *We Write Good,* thanks for keeping me sharp. Special thanks to *Elaine Montgomery* for explaining how neighborhood baseball really works, *Charles William Maclay* for applying science and nerd knowledge to Jimmy, and *Adrian Ashwah* for playing his mandolin in the coffee shop while I was outlining an unruly climax. I still say you provided the inspiration that jogged the final plot twist into play.

My amazing Early Reader Team read *Mailboat III* prior to publication and provided their comments, critiques, and corrections: *Susan Beatty, Stephanie Brancati, Loranda Daniels Buoy, Kathy Collins, David Congdon, Brenda Dahlfors, Beth Dancy, Nancy Diestler, Lynda Fergus, Amy Gessler, Lt. Edward Gritzner, Sgt. Jason Hall, Lynn Hirshman, Michelle Bie Love, Steve Maresso, Lisa McCann, Elaine Montgomery, Rebecca Paciorek, Linda Pautz, Sam Petitto, Sanda Putnam, Melissa Reuss, JoAnn Schwartz Schutte, Kathy Skorstad, Judy Tucker, Kimberly Wade, Carol Westover,* and *Mary-Jane Woodward.* Many thanks for your sharp eyes!

Thanks to *Matt Mason Photography* (www.MattMasonPhotography.com) for the photo of the Mailboat that became the front cover, *W. J. Goes* for escorting my photography crew around the lake in his Boston whaler, and *Maryna Zhukova* of MaryDes (www.MaryDes.eu) for the cover design.

Rebecca Paciorek, Susan Beatty, and *JoAnn Schwartz Schutte* of Blue Dot Marketing, you are the best promotions team an author could ask for.

A big thanks to *my readers* for keeping me company online over the past year while I wrote this book, for snapping up my writing, and for spreading my books to your friends, families, reading clubs, libraries, etc. This year, I became a full-time author. Thanks for making my dreams come true.

Thanks to *Fergus* my black cat for keeping it real and my reflexes sharp. Thanks to *Angel* the German Shepherd puppy for being irresistibly cute and doing your business outside most of the time. Thank you *Molly* for being my canine soul mate and first love. Your paw prints will always be in my heart. And thanks to my boyfriend *Charles William Maclay* for being my companion, my rock, my love.

ABOUT THE AUTHOR

Danielle Lincoln Hanna writes Hearth & Homicide Suspense. Equal parts touching and heart-stopping, her writing has been referred to as "cozy thriller." While Danielle now lives in the Rocky Mountains of Montana, her first love is still the Great Plains of North Dakota where she was born. When she's not writing, you can find her hiking with her boyfriend Charles, adventuring with her new puppy Angel, and avoiding surprise attacks from her cat Fergus.